COMING HOME

A WINDSOR FALLS NOVEL

Kimberley O'Malley

Carolina Blue
PUBLISHING

WHERE ROMANCE IS TRUE BLUE & RED HOT!

Published by Carolina Blue Publishing, LLC

ISBN: 1-946682-00-4

To my Mom, Joan Ann Stanton, for always telling me that I could do anything I put my mind to, be anything I wanted to be. I miss her every day, even though she is still with us. Dementia is a cruel and heart-breaking disease.

Chapter One

Waking to the ring of her cell phone at 5 A.M. was no big deal. After all, she had signed on for that when she became an emergency physician. The problem was that she wasn't on duty. Elizabeth squinted at the phone. The number wasn't familiar. But the area code was. North Carolina. Not a good sign.

"Hello?" Acid swirled in her stomach. There just wasn't a good reason for someone to call at this hour.

A calm, male voice answered. "My name is Dr. Eric Chamberlain, and I'm calling from Windsor Falls Regional Medical Center. I'm trying to reach Elizabeth Fitzgerald."

Elizabeth was fully awake now. She sat on the edge of her bed and placed her feet on the cool hardwood floors to brace herself. Even so, her stomach rolled. "This is Dr. Fitzgerald. You're calling about my mother." Her tone was flat.

"Yes, Dr. Fitzgerald, unfortunately I am. Diane is in my emergency department right now. She was brought in last evening with heart failure." Dr. Chamberlain cleared his throat. A chill snaked down Elizabeth's spine. There was more bad news coming. She'd been a doctor long enough to know this. "I'm afraid she's critical right now."

Elizabeth squeezed her eyes shut to the shaft of pain that pierced her chest. "I see." she said in a small, tremulous voice. But she didn't see at all.

She had no idea her mom was sick. How could she be critically ill without Elizabeth knowing? But that's what happened when you moved across the country and never came back. Silent tears ran down the sides of her face.

"Dr. Fitzgerald are you still there?"

Elizabeth sniffed back the tears. "Yes, Dr. Chamberlain, I am. Sorry about that. Please call me Elizabeth. I'm an ER doctor as well. Just tell me the facts."

"Okay Elizabeth. I'm Eric. Your mother was found unresponsive in her home. Luckily, she has one of those medical alert systems. The outcome might have been much different."

Elizabeth hadn't known about that either. Why was her mother keeping secrets from her? Her shoulders slumped under the weight of her guilt.

"Her heart has been severely compromised. She was barely breathing when she arrived. I had to intubate her. I've started her on medications to stabilize her and take some of the work off her already overburdened heart. She's on her way to the critical care unit as we speak."

Elizabeth sucked in a harsh breath and dropped her head into her hands. Hearing that her mother was not breathing on her own was just another blow. She had been worried about her mother's health for a while now, but Diane Abbott was a proud and stubborn woman. A potentially lethal combination.

"Thank you for being honest, Eric. I had no idea my mom was so sick. I'll be on the first flight I can get."

"That's a good idea, Elizabeth. I'll be honest. Your mom is very ill. The next 24-36 hours are crucial."

Elizabeth liked that he didn't sugar coat things, as some doctors were apt to do. She preferred the truth, even though it was bleak. Elizabeth sent a silent plea into the universe that her mother would still be alive when she got there.

"Eric, this is my mobile number. Please have someone call me with any updates until I can get there."

"Absolutely. Try not to worry. Your mom is stable at the moment, and we have excellent cardiologists on staff. Dr. Reynolds, whose care your mom is under, is one of our best. Your mom is in very capable hands. I'll let you go. I know you have arrangements to make."

"Thank you. I'm glad she didn't have to be sent out anywhere. I'll be there as soon as I possibly can." Elizabeth clicked off her phone and placed it on her nightstand. Her hands were shaking too violently to hold it. The knot of unshed tears in her throat made it hard to swallow. She took a deep, cleansing breath. There would be time for those later. Once she was back in North Carolina. Once she was home. Funny how after being away for ten years, North Carolina was still 'home.'

Chapter Two

The sun was just beginning to set over the majestic Blue Ridge Mountains as Elizabeth turned off the highway and drove into Windsor Falls. She had not been here in over ten years, and changes were evident everywhere. What had once been a hardware store owned by her friend's family was now a cute dress boutique. New, brightly striped awnings graced the store fronts on Evergreen Way, the main street of downtown Windsor Falls. Most of the streets in the center of town were named after trees or flowers. And yet, so much was familiar. In the town square, the gazebo that boasted summer band concerts still graced the lawn.

Elizabeth was grateful for this as she drove through town and out to the medical center. So much had changed in her life in the past ten years. Her hometown looking familiar and welcoming was a blessing.

In another fifteen minutes, Elizabeth pulled into the parking lot of Windsor Falls Regional Medical Center. Turning off the car, she leaned back and closed her eyes briefly. Rolling her shoulders and neck, she winced as the knotted muscles ached in protest.

More than twelve hours had passed since Elizabeth had received that alarming phone call. She had been in motion ever since, with little rest and less food. But now that she was finally here, Elizabeth was almost reluctant to go into the building. Afraid might be a better description. Dr. Chamberlain had texted her over an hour ago, to let her know that her mother was holding her own in the ICU. He was working night shift again tonight and had kindly invited her to check in with him when she arrived.

Knowing she couldn't delay any further, Elizabeth opened her door. She was instantly enveloped in the steamy evening air. Living in California had almost made her forget what North Carolina humidity felt like. In the few moments it took her to walk across the parking lot, her shirt was already stuck to her back. This would take some getting used to again. Craning her neck to take in the whole building, she was amazed at the changes. Her former community hospital was gone. In its place stood a large, sprawling medical center.

Elizabeth entered through the emergency department doors and approached the triage desk. A young woman with a name badge that read 'Becky' was seated there. She looked up as Elizabeth came to a halt in front of her.

"Good Evening, ma'am, may I help you?"

"Yes, my name is Elizabeth Fitzgerald. I'm here to see Dr. Chamberlain." She wondered how much she would need to explain about why she was here to see the ED Director.

Becky looked down at her desk and then smiled. "Oh yes, ma'am. I have a note that he's expecting you. If you'll just take a seat, I'll let him know you're here." She picked up the phone, and Elizabeth turned to find a seat.

She caught a blur of white coat as a man slammed into her. Strong hands caught her and prevented her from falling. A hastily muttered 'sorry' was all he said before he dashed away. Elizabeth got an impression of dark hair and height over six feet but that was all. She watched with curiosity as he sprinted across the mostly empty waiting room and disappeared through a stairwell door.

No doubt, whoever he was, the person who had almost knocked her to the ground was in a hurry. That usually wasn't a good sign in a hospital.

Elizabeth immediately thought of her mother, lying in the ICU, somewhere in this very building. She hadn't received another text update, so hopefully that meant Diane was stable. At least for this moment. She looked at the bank of elevators. Maybe she should just head up to make sure. But she heard her name being called.

Elizabeth turned toward the sound as a man in navy blue scrubs approached her. He appeared to be in his fifties with a trim build and dark hair that was more salt than pepper.

"Elizabeth? I'm Eric Chamberlain. Pleased to meet you. How was your flight?"

Elizabeth shook his outstretched hand. "Fine I guess. More of a blur than anything. I feel like I haven't stopped moving since we spoke early this morning."

"I can only imagine. Your mom is hanging in there. I just checked in with her nurse. She's resting comfortably. Let me show you to the ICU." Eric walked towards a bank of elevators.

Elizabeth looked all around her as they walked, taking in the new facility. "Wow! This place has really grown since I was here last."

"I've only been here about two years, and I can tell you even in that time there has been huge growth. I can only imagine the changes in a decade."

"Ten years ago, this was a small but excellent community hospital with under two hundred beds."

Eric laughed. "And now it's a level two trauma and regional medical center. So, I can see why you're so surprised. People got tired of having to travel to Charlotte or Raleigh for decent health care. Windsor Falls, along with the other, small towns around here decided to do something about that."

Elizabeth nodded in agreement. "They didn't mess around. This place is gorgeous." She admired the wall of glass that allowed a gorgeous view of the surrounding mountains.

"And state of the art. When you've had a chance to see your mother and settle in a bit, I'll give you the tour. I think you'll be impressed."

"I already am."

Eric tilted his head as if to sum her up. "Enough to stay? We're always looking for good doctors to join our facility."

Elizabeth's stomach tightened at Eric's question. Being back home, even for the few minutes she had been already, was a whirlwind of emotions for her. She had missed her hometown and the beautiful mountains that surrounded it. But she had a good reason for leaving. That hadn't changed.

"I have a life in Los Angeles, Eric. A good one. I have a job I love." She didn't know what else to add, which was telling. She did love her job and had friends, but Elizabeth also knew she had never made connections like she had here. Los Angeles had never felt like *home*.

Eric placed a kind hand on her shoulder. "I'm just putting it out there, Elizabeth. We happen to be down a full timer right now."

"You don't even know me."

"Oh, I asked around. I know enough to try you out as a per diem doctor if you're interested."

"Who did you ask about me? I haven't been back here since I left over ten years ago. I was an OB/GYN nurse then."

"Dan Williams."

"Dr. Daniel Williams? My residency director?"

Eric nodded. "Dan and I went to medical school together about a million years ago. He's a good judge of character. He vouched for you. That's enough for me."

"Wow! What a small world. I thought that was a Boston accent I heard. I'm glad Dr. Williams said nice things about me, but I'm not interested in coming back permanently." Was she? Elizabeth missed her hometown and her mother, but she had never given serious thought to returning.

"That's okay. I don't need an answer now. And you have enough on your plate. Go see your mother. If you need anything, anything at all, please don't hesitate to contact me." He handed her his card. "I wrote my cell on the back. I need to head back down into the ED. Dr. Reynolds, the cardiologist taking care of your mom, should be on the unit. He was paged up here just before you arrived for another of his patients who was crashing. He can catch you up on your mom's condition."

Elizabeth thought of the tall, dark haired man who had almost run her down in his haste. That was probably the man in question. She could cut him a break since she was just as dedicated. Elizabeth was known for going to extraordinary measures for her patients. And their families.

Elizabeth pushed the button for the elevator, and the doors opened. "Thank you so much, Eric. I appreciate your kindness. "

"You're more than welcome, Elizabeth. You want the sixth floor for critical care." He turned and strode back towards the ED.

Elizabeth got on the elevator and pushed six as instructed. Her stomach tightening once again had nothing to do with the movement of the elevator. Elizabeth clenched and released her hands nervously as she thought about was awaiting her. She wasn't sure how she would handle seeing her mom so ill.

At the sixth floor, the doors opened to the hushed atmosphere of the critical care unit. The silence always struck her after the din and chaos of the emergency department. Looking at her watch, she was shocked to see it was almost nine o'clock. At this hour, only essential personnel were about. The normally crowded waiting rooms would be empty except for the family members of those patients who were the most critical; those who might not survive the night. Peeking in a window, she was happy to see that the room was empty.

Wiping her sweaty palms on her capris, Elizabeth pushed the call button to the unit. She inhaled deeply and tried to calm her nerves. Within seconds, the door was buzzed open from inside. She was not fooled by the peaceful scene that greeted her as she stepped into the unit. Although it was quiet with dimmed lights, Elizabeth knew how busy critical care units could be.

She walked quickly down the hall to the nursing station, taking in the design of the unit as she went. Similar to that in her facility in Los Angeles, there was a large oval shaped desk with several computer stations. Patient rooms surrounded the station, allowing for close monitoring of their critical patients.

Elizabeth approached the desk, stopping in front of a monitor. A nurse was busily typing away behind it, her head bent. She looked up as Elizabeth approach. Just when she thought she had endured all she could tonight, she discovered yet another troubling surprise. The nurse was Katie Fitzgerald, younger sister of her deceased husband, Connor. Elizabeth and Katie had gone to nursing school together, and with Katie only being a year younger, they had shared many classes. The two had been very close. But that had been a long time ago.

When Katie looked up and met her eyes, Elizabeth felt the temperature in the ICU drop by twenty degrees. The younger woman's normally sparkling green eyes were flat. Weary in a way she hadn't felt since residency, she addressed her former sister-in-law, bracing herself mentally.

"Good evening, Katie. It's been a long time."

"Ten years. But who's counting?" came the acerbic reply.

Elizabeth bit back a sigh. This wasn't going to be easy. "I know you're angry with me. You have every right to be. But that's another issue for another day. My mother is all I care about right now. I'm glad that she has someone familiar caring for her but only if you can keep your feelings for me separate from your treatment of her. Now what can you tell me about her condition?"

Katie's face was impassive when she spoke. "I've only been on the unit since seven. I was just charting my initial assessment. She is sedated and intubated as I'm sure you're aware. Her vitals are stable, but her blood pressure has been low throughout the day. Dr. Reynolds has her on an IV drip for that. Everything considered, she seems to be holding her own. As for the rest of it, you're right. This is neither the time nor the place."

"Fine. I'm glad that we understand each other. Now, I'd like to see my mom."

"Certainly. She's in room six. Let me know if you need anything further." Katie resumed typing without another glance at Elizabeth.

The chill in Katie's voice wrapped itself around Elizabeth's heart and squeezed. The two women had been good friends, as well as sisters-in-law, once upon a time. Elizabeth was beginning to see the extent of the damage she had done by leaving so abruptly. She had her work cut out for her to repair relationships here. And not just with Connor's family.

An image of Sam Bishop flashed through her mind. Just over six feet tall and lean, Sam had literally been the boy next door; the first person she had met in Windsor Falls. He and Connor had been best friends when Elizabeth arrived as the new kid in town, a lonely seven-year-old whose parents were divorcing. Her chest tightened as it always did when she thought of Sam. She hadn't spoken to him since fleeing Windsor Falls all those years ago.

Elizabeth walked away from the desk and mentally prepared herself for what she would see when she entered her mother's room. Although she had treated hundreds of patients on ventilators, most of whom she had intubated herself, none of them had been her mother.

Diane had always joked about being from tough, German stock, but Elizabeth knew it went beyond that. She had taken on complete responsibility for raising Elizabeth long before her father was officially gone from their lives. Diane had worked long hours, yet always had time to help her daughter with her homework or other projects. Now those roles were switched. It was time for Elizabeth to take care of her mother. This was so much harder than dealing with her patients. She cared for them and about them, but they passed through her life quickly. This was different. This was her mother. She lacked the objectivity that had carried Elizabeth through even her toughest cases.

Was she ready for this, Elizabeth wondered as she stood in the doorway of her mother's room and surveyed the scene in front of her. Tears gathered in her eyes, but she ignored them. She approached the bed. While there was an alarming number of machines and wires attached to her body, Elizabeth took comfort in knowing the exact purpose of each. She felt better once she had reviewed all the settings. Taking a chair from the corner, Elizabeth sat next to her mother and held her hand. Being careful to not disturb the tube that was protruding from her mother's throat, she leaned in and gently brushed away a strand of hair from her face. Then she began to speak softly to her mother.

"Oh, Mom, why did you keep me in the dark? I could have helped you. I could have been here when you needed me. Why couldn't you tell me that you were so sick? Why couldn't you, just this once, ask for help?" She paused to wipe the tears from her face. "Well, I'm here now, and I'm not going anywhere. You're stuck with me. But I can't help you right now. This part is all you. You have to fight, Mom. You have to come back to me."

She paused as she felt the faintest pressure from her mother's hand. Although Diane was heavily sedated, Elizabeth felt sure she could hear her. Some physicians didn't believe it was possible, but she'd seen enough in her years to know better. And if that helped Diane in any way to recover, then that's just what she would do. It would have to be enough for now.

Elizabeth sat there for two hours, taking comfort in the sounds of the machines and that of her mother breathing. She stood up and stretched out cramped muscles as a wave of exhaustion hit her. Leaning over her mother's too still form, she whispered in her ear. "You've got this, Mom. I'm right here with you." With a last glance over her shoulder, she left the room and headed back to the nursing station.

Katie Fitzgerald was in the same position but on the phone. Elizabeth waited until she hung up before approaching. "You were right, Katie. She looks as good as possible for the situation. I'm going to try to catch a few hours of sleep in the family waiting room. Could you please get me if something happens?"

"Of course, Elizabeth. I'll keep a close eye on her, just as I would with any of my patients."

"I know you will, Katie, and I appreciate that." She smiled weakly as she walked away. She had been on her feet, so to speak, since five in the morning, and now she was spent. Elizabeth yawned hugely and headed for the lounge.

Chapter Three

"Dr. Fitzgerald, may I speak with you for a moment, please?"

Startled, Elizabeth turned to see a man in wrinkled, navy scrubs standing in front of her. She had been so exhausted, that she hadn't even heard him approach. "Please call me Elizabeth."

"I'm Flynn Reynolds, and I'm the Cardiologist in charge of your mother's care. Before we discuss your mother's case, please allow me to apologize for my earlier behavior." He stopped and held out his right hand towards Elizabeth. She shook it briefly. "In my defense, I didn't see you standing there. I get very focused while I'm here in the hospital; sometimes to the exclusion of all else. If it helps, I can assure you that you weren't the first person who's almost ended up under my feet. You probably won't be the last either." He smiled broadly to lessen the harshness of his words.

"Please don't worry about that. I'm an emergency physician and have probably run over many people in my haste to help a patient. Dr. Chamberlain told me about you briefly and mentioned that you were rushing up here for a patient who was crashing."

A brief shadow passed over his cobalt blue eyes, darkening their depths to almost black. "Unfortunately, that didn't end well." Flynn looked at the floor then, seemingly collecting himself.

It dawned on Elizabeth that the other doctor may have been here all last night while his patient had been so unstable. That would explain the thick, black stubble on his chin and the dark shadows under his eyes.

There were many people who thought doctors were arrogant and heartless, either with God complexes or only interested in making money. Elizabeth could understand how it might look that way from the outside, but she knew the truth. Most were compassionate, hard-working people with a tough job. In some ways, she mused, you had to be arrogant to do what they did, day after day. Sometimes, you had to believe, even when the patient themselves had given up. That could easily be mistaken for arrogance.

Flynn looked up and shook off his momentary lapse. "Sorry about that, Dr. Fitzgerald. Why don't we go sit in the lounge and discuss your mother's prognosis?" He took her elbow and led her down the hall.

The employee lounge looked more or less like every one Elizabeth had ever seen. There were several days of newspapers strewn across a beat-up couch. Dog-eared medical and nursing journals sat in a haphazard pile on a low table in the corner. None of the furniture looked very comfortable. But that never mattered, because none of the personnel ever spent enough time there to care. But there was a rather large coffee maker in a place of honor on the counter. Some things never changed.

"Please, call me Elizabeth. Let me guess, you take yours black, right?" She moved to get a couple of mugs from a shelf over the sink. She didn't really want coffee at this hour, but more than anything, she needed to keep her hands busy.

"Actually, no thank you. As tempting as that is right now, I'll never sleep at all tonight if I have anymore. As it is, I'm pretty much running on caffeine and fumes. Going on more than 40 hours with a catnap here and there, I really need to get whatever sleep I can tonight. Fortunately, my partner, Dr. Walker, is back from vacation tomorrow. I just have to make it through morning rounds."

He stifled a yawn. "You have your own sleep deprivation horror stories, so I won't bore you with mine. Let's talk about Diane and my plans for her. Let me preface this by telling you that I tend to be brutally honest with my patients and their families. I don't believe in sugar coating the truth. As a physician, I hope you can appreciate that."

Elizabeth immediately felt at ease with Flynn. She needed the truth more than anything right now. Deciding against coffee, she joined him at the table. "I would certainly appreciate candor Flynn. I'm not sure if Dr. Chamberlain told you, but I live in Los Angeles and haven't seen my mother in more than a year. This has all come as a big shock to me."

"Your mother has heart failure. How long she's been ill is anyone's guess. We'll have to wait to hear it from her directly. This didn't develop overnight. She's stable and responding to the medications well. The odds are in her favor right now, but of course I can't guarantee that. The next day or so is crucial."

"Her heart is very weak, so we're taking as much of the work off it as we can. I've started her on IV medications to reduce the fluids that have built up since her heart has not been pumping efficiently. She's also been intubated to improve her oxygenation and to allow her body to rest. Rest is the key to her being able to fight back right now. I'm also ordering some diagnostics, as she can tolerate them, to see exactly what we're looking at here. I'll have a better idea once we get more information. Given the fact that she's not been under a doctor's care, I'm surprised this crisis took so long to happen." Elizabeth's eyes widened at his frankness, but she nodded in agreement.

"Right now, we've done everything that we can. The rest is up to her. With proper diagnosis and treatment, she could return to a productive life. I would suggest that you go home and get some rest yourself, Elizabeth. This is a marathon, not a sprint."

"I certainly won't be doing that," Elizabeth protested. "I just arrived. I have to be here, at least for tonight, in case something happens." A shudder rippled through her slender body at the thought of the worst happening. It would be so very cruel to lose her mother just as she came back.

"Of course." Flynn nodded his dark head. "That's just the standard doctor line I feel compelled to say to family members. Make yourself as comfortable as you can. I'm going to check on her once more and then at least *try* to get a little sleep. Don't worry. I'm just down the hall if anything changes."

He held open the door to the lounge, and they both exited. Giving her shoulder an encouraging squeeze, Flynn turned and walked to her mother's room. Elizabeth felt better after talking with Flynn. Dr. Chamberlain had been right. If anyone could save her Mom, this man could.

*****

Katie glared at Flynn's back as he walked into Mrs. Abbott's room. She had watched as the overly slick doctor spoke with Elizabeth. Flynn Reynolds might be the best cardiologist they had on staff, but Katie found him just a bit too smooth. Of course, she also thought he was drop dead gorgeous, which might have been part of the problem.

She glanced around the critical care unit. There were four other nurses working tonight, but Katie had ensured that she would be the one to care for Mrs. Abbott. Being the charge nurse helped in times like this. Despite her hostility towards Elizabeth, she would ensure that Mrs. Abbott got the very best care.

Katie wrestled with her conscience for a moment before picking up the phone. Elizabeth would not thank her for this, but she shouldn't be alone in this moment. She needed someone to lean on, even if she would never admit it. Katie dialed the number from memory and waited. After a few rings, there was a mumbled hello on the other end. She spoke softly into the phone for a few moments before replacing the receiver and resumed her charting.

*****

Sam Bishop stood in the hallway just outside of the darkened waiting room wrestling with himself. Shock had ripped through him when Katie called him. Elizabeth was home. After 10 long years, she had finally come back. Sadly, it had taken her mother's life-threatening illness to do so. He had waited for this moment for so long. But now that it was here, he couldn't bring himself to open the door. He stood with his hand on the handle, hesitating. His heart pounded. He wanted so badly to see her. To hold her in his arms. Disgusted with himself, he opened the door silently and walked into the waiting area.

Light from the hall dimly illuminated Elizabeth's face where she slept fitfully. Clearly not designed for someone over four feet tall, the couch didn't look all that comfortable. She lay on her left side with her knees drawn up to fit. Although barely 5'3", Elizabeth was obviously too tall.

Sam stood there for a long moment, watching her sleep. Ten years melted away. Despite a long and difficult day, she was beautiful. If she had been wearing any makeup, it was long gone. Elizabeth had always had the kind of natural beauty that would still be evident when she was an old woman. The kind that was timeless and came from within. But even in sleep she looked troubled. She moved restlessly on the couch. An ache spread in his chest as he took in the dark smudges under her eyes; proof of the responsibility she carried alone. He longed to hold her hand and whisper reassurances to her. But he had given up that right years ago.

Elizabeth had likely traveled most of the day to get here. What she needed now was rest. Sam lowered himself silently into the not so comfortable chair adjacent to her and settled in as best as he could. The couch was positioned under a bank of windows, and with the blinds partially opened, she was bathed in enough moonlight for Sam to be able to see her clearly.

It was going to be a long night. He leaned his head back so that he could rest but still see her. She would not like him standing guard over her sleeping form. But he quickly brushed aside that thought. He needed this time with her to try and figure out some things. She needed the support, even if she'd be the last person to admit it.

Not for the first time, he thought back to when things had been so easy between them. He, Connor, and Elizabeth had really been inseparable, as only children can be. Elizabeth had been a tough little girl, not given to wearing dresses or playing with dolls. Of course, having boys for her two best friends would have made that difficult.

They had been three very different children with diverse personalities and backgrounds. Yet that never seemed to matter. Connor had been the happy go lucky one. Sam was the quieter, introspective one. Elizabeth had been the daring one. They had complemented each other nicely.

But change was inevitable. In the summer before their junior year of high school, Sam fell in love with Elizabeth. She no longer felt like just his friend. But things had only changed for him, and reluctant to wreck their friendship, Sam had never told her about his feelings.

Sam looked at Elizabeth to see the changes that had occurred in ten years. Most notably was that she had cut her hair. She had always worn her curly, black hair long, and when it wasn't pulled into a pony tail, the curls would tumble half way down her back. Now, her hair ended just below her chin. The same wild curls were there. Sam liked the way the shorter length framed her face.

His heart contracted painfully. He had never really been sure when, or if, he would see Elizabeth again. And though the circumstances were not great, he would take them. Elizabeth, his Elizabeth, was back.

He slumped down into the chair and tried to get comfortable. He must have slept, as a small noise pierced the stillness of the room. Sam straightened up, his muscles protesting. He couldn't believe he had been able to fall asleep in that chair. It was still mostly dark outside the windows. His cell phone read just after 5am.

Hearing the noise again, he looked over at Elizabeth. Her eyes were squeezed tightly as though trying to escape from a nightmare. A very soft, yet distressed noise escaped from her full, red lips. Leaning in, he noticed tears on her lashes. That was Sam's undoing. He had loved her for more than half his life and could never stand to see her in pain. Her distress cut through his gut like a hot knife. She looked so young and vulnerable, lying there, curled in a fetal position with her hands clasped under her chin.

Sam softly called her name as he placed his hand on her shoulder. Instantly, he felt a jolt of electricity where his fingers touched the bare skin of her upper arm. Even after being in the hospital for hours, she still had a trace of that scent that was uniquely hers. Her hair smelled faintly of coconut. She mumbled and thrashed on the couch. Sam hated to wake her but wanted to stop whatever was bothering her.

"Elizabeth, wake up." She didn't stir. Sam leaned in and spoke her name a little more loudly. It may have been the sensation of his warmed breath on her ear more than his voice that finally did the trick.

"Connor?" she asked in a confused, sleep roughened voice. Elizabeth blinked several times. She was on her feet before Sam could even tell her he was there.

All the air left his body. It was as though someone had punched him hard in the stomach. Connor had been dead for more than a decade, and yet his name was still on her lips. Sam shook his head in disgust. He had been a fool to ever think otherwise.

Elizabeth stared at Sam for a moment. She seemed to have trouble believing what she was seeing. "Sam?" A smile creased her face. Without warning, she launched herself into his arms. Sam stood very still, arms hanging at his sides, resting his chin on the top of her head. He closed his eyes, wishing the moment could last forever. But she stirred and took a step back to peer up into his face.

"How long have you been here?" Panic swept across her face. "Is my mom okay?"

Before she could run off to check, Sam caught her gently by the arm. "She's fine, Elizabeth. Katie promised me she would get us if anything changed. I've been here since around midnight." He scrubbed a weary hand down his face. "You were fast asleep, although how you could be on that tiny, uncomfortable couch is beyond me. I didn't have the heart to wake you."

"Oh, so that's why my legs feel like rubber", she joked. "Sam, it's so good to see you." Without warning she buried her face in his chest and sobbed.

Bewildered by the sudden outpouring of emotion, he lowered them both gently to the couch and held her as she cried. Having her in his arms was even better than he remembered. He stroked a hand over her short curls and whispered to her as he had ached to do earlier. He knew this moment wouldn't last, but for now he was content.

After a few minutes, Elizabeth straightened up and dashed away the tears from her eyes. She moved to her left a bit, putting space between them. "Why are you here, Sam?" Nervous laughter escaped her as she pushed her hair behind her ears. "Sorry. What I meant to say ask was how did you know."

"Katie called me."

She was silent a moment as if digesting that fact. "I don't understand why Katie didn't call her mother. Maggie would have come."

"Maybe she thought Maggie needed the sleep more than I did. Or maybe she knew I would come. After all, we used to be best friends."

Elizabeth raised her head to face him at the pain in his voice. "I'm sorry, Sam. I didn't mean it like that. I just don't have the right to ask you for anything after what I did."

Sam took her cold hands in his and rubbed them for warmth. "You did what you had to do, Elizabeth. I've always understood that. Your mom is very ill, and having a friend or two to help you wouldn't be the worst thing in the world."

Tears once again gathered in her clear blue eyes. "I've missed you, Sam."

Sam felt the first hint of thaw in the ice that had surrounded his heart for more than a decade. While he didn't hold out hope for being able to return to their former closeness, it was enough just to be with her. Because he had been in love with her for as long as he could remember, he would take any scraps she threw him. He'd never had much pride where Elizabeth was concerned.

"Why don't you get cleaned up and go check on your Mom? I'll wait here." Elizabeth nodded and silently left the waiting room.

Sam let out a long breath he'd been holding since Elizabeth had awoken. His lungs burned with the effort. He had missed her so much. And for so long. But being back with her was much harder than he could have ever imagined. It was a sweet torture. A familiar ache was beginning to build in his chest. There was no doubt that he was in love with her. Still. Probably always. What he didn't know was what he was going to do about it.

As he often did, Sam thought about Connor. Losing his best friend so young and tragically had changed Sam. Not a day went by that he didn't think of Connor, wondering what his life would be like if he was still here. Since Elizabeth was inextricably linked with Connor in his mind, Sam's thoughts drifted to her. He wondered about her life in California. He had heard gossip about her over the years, but that didn't tell him what he wanted to know. Was she happy? Did she miss Windsor Falls? Had she missed him? Her time away obviously agreed with her. She was lightly tanned and looked healthy.

But it worried Sam that Elizabeth had murmured Connor's name in her sleep. His friend had been dead for ten years. Why had she not moved on? Sam grunted at the thought. He should talk. He had certainly not let himself off the hook for Connor's death, even after all these years.

Sam moved over to the window to gaze down into the valley. The vantage point of the sixth floor gave him a view that was breathtaking. In the first streaks of dawn, the majestic Blue Ridge Mountains stretched in every direction. Except for his years at the University of Virginia, Sam had never lived anywhere else. Had never really wanted to. He loved to travel, and did so when his schedule allowed, but he loved to come home even more. He had never found another place that called to him. There was a lot to be said for small towns. Knowing the people who came into his store. Seeing familiar faces on Evergreen Way.

Of course, that held certain pitfalls as well. For months after the accident, Sam had felt as though everyone in town was silently accusing him of killing Connor. Judging him. It took him a long time to understand that they had just been concerned about him. Because he was one of them. But belonging had never come easily for Sam.

Chapter Four

Elizabeth entered her mother's room and carefully approached her bed. She was happy to see more color in her face. Checking her hands and feet, relief floated through her to see that the swelling had decreased. The medicine was working. All good signs.

Loathe to disturb her mother when she was resting so peacefully, Elizabeth left the room quietly in search of a bathroom. She ducked into the nearest restroom. After using the facilities, she washed her hands, glancing in the mirror reluctantly. The sight that greeted her was not a pleasant one. Her curly dark hair was flattened on one side where she had slept on it. There were dark smudges under her eyes from fatigue. Elizabeth shrugged her shoulders. Not much she could do about it. Yesterday had been the longest day ever. She could hardly be surprised when it showed on her face. She splashed water on her face and ran her wet hands through her hair in a failed attempt to tame it.

Pausing outside the door when she heard voices, Elizabeth saw that Sam was talking softly with someone. His head was bent down close to a woman's, and they whispered to each other for several moments. She was surprised that the woman who had her hand wrapped possessively around Sam's arm was Katie Fitzgerald. Something about their stance looked intimate, and she wondered if they were together.

Trying to respect their privacy, Elizabeth retreated into the family lounge. A moment later, Sam entered the room alone. He moved to the corner and switched on a table lamp, avoiding the harsh realities of the overhead lights.

"Hey, there you are. I was beginning to wonder if you'd gotten lost. Or gone home. How's your Mom? Did you get a chance to see her?"

"She's holding her own Sam. In fact, I might even go so far as to say she's doing a little bit better this morning. As for going home, I haven't even been to my mom's house yet. I drove straight here from the airport in Charlotte."

Sam smiled that lopsided smile of his that had always warmed her heart. He had been the quietest of the three of them, and many outside their tight circle found him unapproachable. But not she and Connor. Elizabeth had liked to think that grin that he was flashing her now was only meant for them. "I could still be your knight in shining armor and drive you to your mother's house if you're too tired."

"That's okay, Sam. I'm going to be here for a while. I want to talk with her doctor again before I feel comfortable leaving. You don't have to wait for me. I'm sure you have more important things to do today." Memories of him bent so closely towards Katie flashed through her mind. She knew the other woman would be off shift soon. For some strange reason, that wasn't a pleasant thought.

"If you look out the window, you'll see it's just about daylight already. I don't mind waiting. We could have breakfast before you go to your mother's house. I'm sure you haven't eaten much."

Elizabeth didn't answer right away. Instead, she shoved her hands into the front pockets of her capris. She always had to do something with her hands when she was nervous. Why she would be nervous about having breakfast with Sam was beyond her. They had eaten countless meals together in the past.

"Look, Elizabeth, if you want me to leave, I will. I was just trying to help."

Elizabeth shook her head, her curls bouncing wildly. "I'm sorry, Sam. I can't seem to make even the smallest decision right now. You're right though. Yesterday was a very long day, and I can't remember the last thing I ate." Her stomach grumbled loudly, and she laughed. "No point trying to hide the fact that I'm starving. So, if you really don't mind waiting, I'd be pleased to take you up on that offer."

By silent agreement, they both retook their earlier seats and watched as the sun made its appearance over the Blue Ridge Mountains. Elizabeth unconsciously leaned forward in anticipation of the view to come. Los Angeles was where she lived and worked. But Windsor Falls was home.

"I only had time to drive through town before coming here last evening. I was floored at the changes to the hospital. Tell me, Sam, is Windsor Falls much different as well?"

"Not as much as the hospital for sure, Elizabeth, but there are new businesses, and the downtown section has been spruced up a bit in the past few years. The powers that be are really trying to market Windsor Falls as a destination spot for tourists."

She arched an eyebrow in surprise. "And how do the locals feel about that?"

Sam laughed at her expression. "Maggie always said you should never play poker. I see that hasn't changed." He was rewarded with a pretty blush that spread across her cheekbones. "Naturally there are a few old curmudgeons who complain about the increased traffic, but mostly people are happy. The changes have breathed new life into the town and brought in a lot of tourist dollars."

"I saw the new town sign on my way in last night. 'Windsor Falls, a Place for All Seasons.' I like it. I noticed the population, 11,400, hasn't really changed much."

"There was a contest to come up with that slogan. I believe one of the high school teachers won. It fits really, with the outdoor activities around here. It's too bad you won't be here in the winter. There's a new ski resort just outside of town. "

Elizabeth stared at Sam before he burst out laughing. "Do you not remember my one ill-fated attempt at skiing?" Connor and Sam had whizzed down hills, graceful as ever. She, however, spent the day with her foot propped up and ice on it. After one attempt at the bunny hill.

"Oh, I remember, Elizabeth." He looked deeply into her clear blue eyes. "I remember everything."

Uncomfortable with the intensity of Sam's gaze, Elizabeth steered the conversation back to neutral topics. They talked about his life here and hers in California.

When the sun was fully in the sky, Elizabeth jumped up. "I'm going to find my mom's cardiologist. I'll be back in a little bit." She hurried from the room in search of Flynn.

*****

Elizabeth came back in looking tired but happier. "She woke up, Sam. It was brief, but she was awake. I think she knew who I was. She's as good as she can be for now, and they've just given her another dose of sedation. I feel like I can go get that breakfast with you then head home and get a shower and maybe some sleep. If I can just get a few, uninterrupted hours, then I can come back this afternoon and spend some time with her. If she continues to improve, they're going to think about removing her from the ventilator; maybe even as soon as this evening. We'll just have to see, but I need to be here for that."

Sam stepped away from the window and watched Elizabeth straighten up the small room. He realized that other than briefly holding her while she cried, he hadn't really touched her. In the many years that they had known each other, he must have touched her thousands of times. Sam had never considered himself a demonstrative person, yet from the moment he heard she was coming home, all he could think about was touching her. A lot. Of course, he also thought about kissing her and so much more…

Flynn Reynolds walked around the corner, just as Sam and Elizabeth were leaving the waiting room. "Hey, you're still here." he called out to Elizabeth.

She turned to Sam and held up one finger. "I'll just be another moment, I promise." She turned towards the handsome cardiologist, but not before Sam saw the first genuine smile of the day spreading across her face. He was amazed, as always, how one smile from her could light up the entire room.

Sam continued to watch as the other man ever so casually guided her to a computer monitor. He stood very close to Elizabeth in a way that was more familiar than Sam cared for. The sight of another man touching her was more than he could take. He'd better leave before he planted his fist in the middle of the doctor's handsome face.

"You never did get over her, Sam, did you?" He swung around to see Katie Fitzgerald leaning against the wall, smiling none too innocently. She was a dangerous woman.

Trying to maintain his composure, Sam struggled to keep his face as neutral as possible. "Wow, Katie! They should really put a bell on you, sneaking up on people like that." He laughed, but even to him it sounded stilted and uncomfortable. "I always knew you had a vivid imagination, but that one takes the cake. Elizabeth and I are just friends. At least we used to be friends." The very thought that someone else might know about his feelings for Elizabeth left him cold inside.

Katie straightened away from the wall and approached a wary Sam. "So, you want to punch Dr. Reynolds in the face more than anything in the world because you and Elizabeth are 'just friends'? Do I have that right?" A stunned Sam could only stare at her. "Because I'm trying to control similar impulses towards her, and it's not because I have friendly feelings towards Flynn. Don't worry Sam. Your secret's safe with me."

Katie glared at the other two, standing so closely together, just as Elizabeth's laugh drifted down the short hallway. "Oh yeah, nothing to worry about there." She muttered with an edge to her voice.

Sam did not like the way this was going. He nodded curtly towards Katie and walked away. As he passed Elizabeth and her mother's doctor, he spoke coolly over his shoulder, "I'll be in the parking lot when you're ready to leave." He waited until the elevator doors closed before breathing again.

*****

Elizabeth watched until the elevator doors closed before turning back to her mother's doctor. Flynn raised one eyebrow and looked speculatively at Elizabeth. "So, is that my competition?"

Still trying to understand what had just happened, Elizabeth realized Flynn's meaning. "Competition? For what? Is that your backhanded way of asking me out on a date?"

Flynn looked down at her and smiled broadly. "Well now that you mention it, that's a great idea. When your mom is feeling better, why don't you have dinner with me?"

Elizabeth shook her head in exasperation. The last thing she needed was a man in her life. Especially one who oversaw keeping her mother alive. "Thank you, but no. That's not a good idea."

"Mind telling me why?"

Elizabeth stared back at Flynn. "Well, for one thing, you're my mother's doctor. And I'm only here temporarily."

"That's a cop out, and you know it. We're both adults, Elizabeth. Your mother is my patient, not you. As for your other weak argument, I wasn't asking for your hand in marriage. It's just dinner. It's not like there's an abundance of single people in their thirties in Windsor Falls. If you don't want to go out with me specifically, then just say so."

"OK, Flynn, I don't want to go out with you. To be honest, I don't really want to date anyone right now. My life is already overwhelming. Thanks again for everything you're doing for my mom. I'll be back this afternoon once I've had some sleep. Enjoy your time off." Elizabeth gave him a casual wave and made her escape without looking back.

*****

Katie watched Flynn as he flirted with Elizabeth. Disappointment stabbed through her. Just what she expected she thought in disgust. But that didn't stop the pain that settled in her chest.

"Don't think I won't ask again, Elizabeth. I always get what I want" Flynn said to Elizabeth's retreating back. He turned and signed onto the nearest computer. Without even looking in her direction, he said, "Katie, would you mind checking Mrs. Abbott's urine output? I want to make sure she's still doing well on this dosage of Lasix."

"Check it yourself, Dr. Reynolds! I'm sure they covered that in medical school." Cheeks flushed with anger, Katie stomped off. Turning blindly into the staff restroom, Katie quickly locked the door behind her. She turned on the cold water and splashed some in her face. She was not happy with what she saw in the mirror. Her cheeks were splotchy, either form anger or embarrassment, and her eyes were overly bright from unshed tears. "Damn that man!" she muttered angrily. "Enough is enough! Didn't you already learn that lesson, Katie" she asked her reflection. But the Katie in the mirror remained mute. With renewed resolve, she dried her hands and went out to begin giving report to the oncoming day shift nurses.

*****

Sam was just where he said he'd be, in the parking lot, leaning up against a large, red pick-up truck with Bishop's Home & Garden on the door. Elizabeth approached him slowly, suddenly wearier than she'd been in a long time. On top of everything else in the past 24 hours, her conversation with Flynn had left her exasperated. She smiled weakly as she approached Sam.

"Where to? I'm starving."

"You must be exhausted. Why don't we just go to Bob's?"

A huge smile lit up Elizabeth's face. "Bob's! I've dreamed of his pancakes for a long time." Thoughts of her long absence immediately dimmed the smile on her face.

Sam linked his arm through hers and pulled Elizabeth along with him. "And since it's right across the street, we don't even have to drive."

Elizabeth was thankful for his kindness. Being back in Windsor Falls after so long was more daunting than she could have even imagined. Every place her eyes roamed held a memory. She was drowning in memories as they made their way across the blacktop.

Sam held the door as Elizabeth entered the diner. Bob's had always been an institution with the staff at Memorial. Waves of nostalgia rolled over her as she looked around the interior. Modeled after a true 1950's diner, Bob's had a long counter with stools and many booths. The seats were all covered in red vinyl. The floor, a faded black and white checkerboard style, was the same one she remembered.

"Elizabeth Abbott Fitzgerald! As I live and breathe! Come over here for a hug."

Elizabeth turned at the booming voice that could only belong to the owner, Bob Nelson. A bear of a man, Bob stood well past six feet and probably topped the scaled at over three hundred pounds. He was larger than life, and not just because of his physical stature. Somewhere on the far side of sixty, Bob had been running this diner since Elizabeth could remember.

She walked into his opened arms and hugged the big man, her hands not even touching at his back. He pulled her off her feet and swung her a little. Elizabeth's laughter rang out loud. "Bob, it's so good to see you again!"

Bob set her back on her feet a small distance in front of him. "Let me take a good look at you." He smiled broadly, exposing his famous gold tooth. The other teeth were a brilliant white against his skin which was as black as a starless night. He still maintained a faint musical tone to his accent that was from somewhere in the Caribbean. No one had ever found out where exactly. Just part of the mystery that was Bob. "You sure are a sight for sore eyes. What brings you back after all this time?"

Some of the light faded from her eyes. "My mom is very sick, Bob. I've been at the hospital all night."

Bob's smile turned into a frown. "I'm so sorry to hear that. She'll be in my prayers. Well I may be sorry for the reason but not to see you again."

Elizabeth squeezed both of his large hands in hers. Her heart swelled at his words. Bob's had been a constant in her college days. She'd spent many hours studying for her nursing classes in this very diner. Ironically, many of those were spent with Katie Fitzgerald.

"Right back at you, Bob. You have no idea how much I missed you and this place. You just can't get a decent bowl of grits in Los Angeles."

Bob made a face that showed his feelings about that. "No wonder you're so skinny, girl. Living in La La land all these years." He took her by the hand and led her to the corner booth she'd practically lived in all those years ago. "Don't you worry, Miss Elizabeth. You've come to the right place."

Bob turned to Sam. "Sam, my friend, what can I get for you? The usual?"

"That works for me, Bob."

The big man nodded and strolled back to the kitchen, as Elizabeth turned to Sam with questions in her eyes. "I didn't know you came here. Back in the day, it was mostly hospital staff and students."

"It probably still is. Although as fabulous as his food is, that surprises me. But this is Katie's favorite place to eat. I met her here for breakfast once after her shift, and I've been coming ever since."

Elizabeth thought about that for a second. Another reference to their relationship. Were Sam and Katie dating? It didn't seem possible. Katie was as outgoing as Sam was reserved. But they did have their heads together this morning. Katie pushed aside the slight discomfort that image caused.

"Are you OK? You seemed to disappear for a second there, Elizabeth."

She glanced at Sam to find him staring at her with a funny expression on his face. "Sorry, I'm just a bit wooly headed this morning. I know I slept, but it sure doesn't feel like it."

"Understandable after the day you had yesterday."

"You have no idea, Sam. I got the call in the early hours of the morning and rushed to get here as quickly as I could. That torture device disguised as a couch certainly didn't help matters. I was so worried about my mom the whole time I was travelling. Not to mention…" She stopped talking, not sure how to even continue.

Sam reached across and covered her hands with his own. "Not to mention the fact that this is your first time home in years. Is that what you were trying to not say?"

Elizabeth lifted her head and stared into Sam's familiar, chocolate brown eyes. "Yes, Sam, that's it exactly." Gratitude warmed her insides. Aside from the anxiety of her mother's condition, Elizabeth spent the plane ride, and then the drive, worrying about how she would face people here again. Sam was near the top of that list.

She looked down at their joined hands. "I have missed you more than you could imagine, Sam."

"Oh, I think I have a pretty good idea, Elizabeth. Everyone here missed you as well. It's been a long ten years."

She noticed he didn't say specifically that he had missed her. Considering how she had treated him the last time she saw him, she wasn't surprised. Yet Elizabeth had to know. "What about you, Sam? Did you miss me too?"

His eyes searched hers. "I missed you, Elizabeth. I'm glad you're home; for however long." And that was Sam for you, she thought. He was never a game player.

"I'm so very sorry, Sam." Her voice was so soft that she was almost whispering to him. "I just couldn't stay."

Sam tightened the hold he had on her hands. "You did what you had to do. I understand that now."

Bob arrived at just that moment, carrying more food than the two could ever possibly finish. Elizabeth's eyes widened at the spread he laid out before them.

She opened her mouth to protest, but Bob beat her to it. Holding up one massive finger, he shook his head. "Now I know you haven't eaten well in ten years dear, so don't go protesting. Just eat. Besides my friend Sam here will help. He's got quite the appetite." With a wave of his hands, he lumbered off chuckling.

Elizabeth placed her napkin on her lap and picked up a fork. "You heard him, Sam. Dig in!"

Sam did just that. Grinning, he started in on a short stack of pancakes.

Elizabeth added honey to her grits. "I wasn't lying before. No one makes these like Bob does." She moaned in delight with the first taste. "This alone would be enough to make me consider moving back."

Sam's head snapped up from his plate. "Really? Are you thinking about moving home?"

"Uh, actually no. Not really. Maybe?" At the look of confusion on Sam's face, she started over. "I don't really know, Sam. It wasn't something I had been thinking about, but my Mom is very sick. If she gets better." Elizabeth stopped and cleared her throat noisily. "When she gets better, she's going to have a long road ahead of her. Staying here, at least for a while, makes the most sense."

Sam nodded in agreement as he swallowed. "She really is going to need some help I imagine. But what about your life in California? What about your job?"

"Oddly enough, Dr. Chamberlain, the Emergency Department director at Memorial just offered me a job last night."

Sam's left eyebrow reached his hairline. "Just like that? He doesn't even know you."

"That's what I said, but he knows my residency director well. And since I was offered a job at the hospital where I trained and have been there for a few years, he knows me very well. I guess he said some good things to Dr. Chamberlain."

"What did you tell him? When he offered you the job?"

She shrugged her shoulders and pushed her fork around the plate. "What could I tell him? I had just travelled across country. I was worried about my mom and exhausted. I told him that I was flattered but that I would have to think about it."

"Okay, but you never answered my question. What about your life in California?"

Elizabeth had just taken a large bite of one of Sam's pancakes. It was just what she would have done when they were younger. She thought about her answer as she chewed and swallowed. "California is great. I've been very happy with my job there. These past few years have been the best, now that I'm done with my medical training. I just don't know, Sam."

"When you talk about California, you only talk about your job, Elizabeth. What about your life?"

"My job is my life, Sam. I love what I do. I loved being an OB nurse when I lived here. But after." She stopped and cleared her throat. Her throat was suddenly raw, as though she had swallowed something sharp. "After everything that happened here, I knew I needed a change; not just of scenery but also profession. I wasn't the same person after I lost Connor and then our baby."

Elizabeth put down her fork and sat back in the booth. Weariness flooded over her again. She looked across the table at Sam. Really looked at him for the first time in ten years. He was the same yet different. Sam had always been handsome, even though Elizabeth had never thought of him that way. How could she when she had met the love of her life at sixteen? But Sam was older now. More mature. He had grown into his looks. His dark brown hair was thick and needed a trim. Nothing new there. His chocolate brown eyes were warm. He had certainly filled out. No wonder Katie had been leaning into him. Who could blame her?

But beyond the physical stuff, this was Sam. He, along with Connor, had been her world growing up. He had always been there for her. But that was a long time ago. Before she had hurt him so badly. She was on her own. She sighed. "I really have missed you, Sam."

He was quiet for so long, that Elizabeth wasn't sure if he had heard her. She grew restless under his intent gaze. "Have you, Elizabeth? It's been ten years without a single word from you, so I guess I'm a bit surprised to hear that."

Her heart clenched. "You're right, of course. You have every reason in the world to not believe me. But it's true. There wasn't a day that I didn't think about you." She smiled sadly at him. "Something would happen, and I'd want to tell you about it like I always had in the past. But I couldn't of course."

Sam put down his fork and leaned forward across the table. "That's just it, Elizabeth. You could have. All you needed to do was pick up the phone. Reach out. But you never did."

Her chest tightened at the sadness on Sam's face. That face that was so dear to her. She was responsible for that, and she had no idea how to fix it. "That goes both ways, Sam. You didn't reach out to me either." She hadn't meant to say that, but she was overwhelmed with guilt. Striking back was reflex.

Sam's brown eyes widened. "You made it pretty clear, Elizabeth, when you left without saying goodbye that you weren't interested in staying in touch."

"I never said that." Her pulse kicked up and her heart beat erratically as the conversation spun out of control, but Elizabeth had no idea how to stop it.

"You never said anything. That's my point." Sam stood abruptly and threw some bills down on the table.

"You have no idea what I was going through, Sam. I was just trying to survive" she said to his retreating back. The normally busy diner had fallen quiet at their raised voices.

Sam turned slowly to face her. "I lost him too, Elizabeth." With those simple words piercing her heart, Sam left the diner.

Tears pooled in her eyes as the full weight of his words struck her. Elizabeth fought for control, not wanting to give the nearby customers any more of a floor show. She gathered her purse and ran into the ladies' room.

Chapter Five

Sam stalked across the street and into the hospital parking lot. Jumping into his truck, he almost peeled out of the space before remembering where he was. He took a deep breath and blew it out slowly before driving carefully out of the lot. On the way to his store, Sam replayed the conversation with Elizabeth in his head. He had missed her for every single day of the last ten years. He had imagined a thousand different reunion scenarios. The reality sucked.

After pulling into his parking space behind the home and garden store he owned, Sam got out of his truck and entered through the employee entrance. Lesser chance of running into anyone that way. His mood was black and didn't lend itself to polite conversation. He didn't stop until he reached the sanctuary of his private office, stopping just short of slamming the door behind him. His staff knew not to bother him unless it was an emergency when the door was closed.

Sam crossed to his desk and sank wearily into the leather chair. Resting his elbows on the desk, he lowered his head into his hands. It was painful to remember what had just happened. Where had all that anger come from? He had dreamed for so long of seeing Elizabeth again. This was a disaster.

Leaning back in his chair, he lifted his boot covered feet to the corner of his desk. Unfortunately, that brought his gaze to the only decoration in the room; three picture frames on a shelf of his bookcase. All three photos had been taken that fateful spring day just over ten years ago. Sam closed his eyes as the painful memories washed over him.

It was late spring, a humid day that spoke of the blistering summer heat that was just weeks away. He, Connor, and Elizabeth were in the backyard of the couple's home. Sam had been at work when he received a call from an excited Elizabeth. She asked him if he could stop by the house. Sam had been up to his eyeballs in paperwork, but he dropped everything to come. He had never been able to deny her anything.

Connor and Elizabeth were on their deck when he arrived. As soon as he approached them, he could tell something was up. His two best friends were grinning at him. For some reason, that left Sam chilled. He couldn't shake the feeling that life was about to change once again.

"Hey, Sam!" Connor had approached him, holding out his hand which Sam dutifully shook. His friend looked back at Elizabeth, almost as if for permission. Sam swallowed hard as she shook her head yes.

"So, you're probably wondering what this is all about."

Unease clawed at Sam's stomach, causing it to twist. He looked at the two most important people in the world to him; his best friend and the woman that he loved. The fact that they were married to each other was ironic and painful. He covered his discomfort with a tentative smile. "Well, now that you mention it, this does seem a bit strange."

Connor laughed in that booming way of his. Reaching behind him to grab Elizabeth's hand, he addressed Sam. "Well, I have a question for you. Actually, we both do." Sam's gaze strayed to her, taking in the pure joy he saw on her face. She looked as though she had a secret.

"Elizabeth and I would like you to be the godfather of our baby. What do you say?"

The implication hit like a ton of bricks. Sam glanced at Elizabeth's still flat belly and the hand she held protectively there. The pain in his heart was breath taking. He had known this day was coming of course. After all, he had been the best man at their wedding last summer. His friends had been eager to start a family. Yet somehow, he wasn't prepared. But they didn't know how he felt about Elizabeth, and this wasn't about him.

"Wow! Of course, I will." He knew his voice sounded strained, so he pasted on the brightest smile he could summon. Sam threw his arms around them both in an awkward group hug. With his face averted, he took a moment to feel the full weight of his pain. He loved them both and truly wanted everything in the world for them. They deserved it. But he couldn't help the fact that his heart was breaking just a little more.

Elizabeth broke away first. "Okay, everything you hear about pregnant women is true. I'm starving. All the time!" She smiled at both men and then looked intently at her husband. "Connor, you know what I'm in the mood for?"

Connor smiled indulgently at his newly pregnant wife. "Let me guess. Pizza with pineapple on it." He made a face as if he found the combination repulsive.

"Exactly!" She leaned in and kissed her husband. Turning to Sam, she whispered in his ear. "You've made us so happy."

Sam gently extracted himself from her grasp. Her moist breath on the sensitive skin of his ear was almost his undoing. He tried to touch her as little as possible. It was too painful. "Of course, Elizabeth. Anything for you guys."

Connor slapped him on the back in an age old male expression of affection. He turned to his wife. "Why don't you go ahead and call it in. Sam and I will go pick it up. You rest."

"You're so good to me." Her love for him shone in her bright blue eyes. She turned and walked into their home.

"She gets tired a lot, and I guarantee you she'll be napping on the couch when we get back. Do you mind driving? My car's in the shop."

Sam dug his keys out of his pocket. "No worries. Let's go." They retraced Sam's path to his jeep. Hearing Connor as his friend talked about his wife's pregnancy was almost more than he could take. The pure joy that radiated from Connor's face twisted the knife a bit deeper in Sam's gut. How could he be so happy for them and yet so miserable at once? He needed to get some distance from Connor and Elizabeth. He thought that when they married last year, he would accept how things were and move on. But that still hadn't happened.

These thoughts were rolling through Sam's mind when a drunk driver blasted through the intersection. Sam had only a split second to realize what was happening. Connor, who was turned to face him, never saw the other car coming. Time slowed as Sam watched in horror. The dark blue pick-up truck barreled down on them, never even slowing. He tried to swerve, but there wasn't any time. Connor's name was on his lips as the truck smashed into the passenger door. There was only the dreadful screech of metal on metal and glass exploding inward before everything went black.

When Sam awoke, he was still in the driver's seat. Every muscle in his body hurt. His head pounded ferociously. Warm, sticky blood oozed down the side of his face. He could hear people shouting, possibly to him, but it was as though the voices were miles away. Turning his head to the right, Sam saw Connor's body slumped in the seat. His eyes were opened but unseeing. In that instant, Sam knew he had killed his best friend.

Sam pulled his feet off the desk as he ran a shaky hand through his hair. His pulse still galloped wildly, and he was covered with a fine sheen of sweat. That hadn't happened in a while, he thought ruefully. Usually the nightmares came when he was sleeping.

He stood up and paced the small office. For a long time after the accident, Sam had been consumed by his role in Connor's death. If only he had reacted sooner. If only he had taken a different road or even left thirty seconds later. But 'if onlys and good intentions could not change what had happened. Connor was still dead. Sam had eventually moved on with his life. Unfortunately, he had to do that without Elizabeth as well. Her leaving just days after the funeral had been almost as heavy a blow as Connor dying.

He cringed thinking about the exchange he had just had with Elizabeth. It was inexcusable. Elizabeth was home, even if temporarily, and he needed to make things right with her. Sam walked out of his office, through the store and outside to the garden center. Maria Adams, one of his favorite employees was watering a new shipment of perennials that had just arrived.

Sam waved to her. "Hey, Maria, I need some advice."

The older woman turned off the hose and smiled in return. "Anything for my favorite boss." It was a running joke between them, as he was obviously her *only* boss.

"So, I need something that says 'I'm sorry.' Something that tells her that I never meant to hurt her feelings."

"Wow! That's a lot to ask of a plant, Sam" Maria joked. "What did you do to Katie?"

Sam bit back a groan. He and Katie Fitzgerald were just friends, but no one in town chose to believe that. She was very special to him, but not in the way everyone assumed.

"How many times must I tell you, Maria? Katie and I are just friends."

Maria dried her hands on her store apron and placed one on his forearm. "Oh, I know, Sam. I was just kidding."

"Really? How come no one else in town knows? We get ribbed about our supposed relationship everywhere we go."

"Others just assume. But anyone who bothers to take a second to really watch you two knows you're not right for each other."

"In what way?" he founded himself asking. He was curious to hear what she thought.

Maria laughed. "Why in the most important way, Sam. Chemistry. You two don't have any." Her tone suggested she was talking to someone who wasn't very bright.

Maria was right. He and Katie were only meant to be friends. "Anyway, back to my problem. I need the right olive branch, so to speak."

Maria's normally cheerful face darkened slightly. "Oh. You're talking about Elizabeth."

Sam was shocked. He shouldn't have been of course. After all, Windsor Falls was a small town. Everyone either knew each other or of each other. Gossip was practically an Olympic sport here. But still, Elizabeth had only been back for under twenty-four hours.

"How did you know?"

"Quinn was on the engine that responded to the 9-1-1 call to Mrs. Abbott's home the other night. Sick as she is, I figured Elizabeth would be on her way." A look of concern had shadowed the older woman's eyes.

Quinn was Maria's son and a firefighter. He had also been on the engine that responded to the accident. Sam looked in Maria's face. And there it was. The inevitable pity that came along with any reference to Connor's death. Even though Maria hadn't worked for Sam back then, she knew that Elizabeth had been Connor's wife. Ten years later, and he could practically feel the sympathy oozing from Maria.

"Yes, Maria, she's back. I was at the hospital with her this morning, but it didn't end well."

"Hmmm. What did you do?"

Sam smiled at that. "Why do you think it was all my fault?"

"Well, for one, I don't see her in here looking for a gift. And secondly, you're a man. It tends to happen that way. Even my Michael, God rest his soul, could put his foot in it with the best of them." She stared at him, daring Sam to contradict her.

Since she was right, he didn't. Sam had the grace to appear sheepish. "You're right of course. It was me. I said something, or a couple of somethings, that I shouldn't have. Thus, the need for flowers."

Maria cocked her head. "And nothing says forgive me like a perennial? Shouldn't you be looking at fresh flowers? Roses maybe?"

"No, she was never a fan of roses. Too predictable." He looked around the outdoor section for something suitable.

"What's her favorite color?"

"Blue" Sam answered without any hesitation. He deliberately ignored Maria's raised eyebrow.

"Well okay then. How about Hydrangeas? They're already blooming, and you can plant them in her yard."

"Perfect!" Sam selected the best one and yelled his thanks over his shoulder as he carried it out to his truck. He drove home to collect a shovel and some potting soil before heading to Mrs. Abbott's house. Planting a bush may not be the most common way to apologize, he mused. But hopefully it would catch Elizabeth's eye.

*****

Elizabeth awoke to the sound of a car door slamming. Disoriented at first, she opened her eyes and stared at the wall of her childhood bedroom. A science fair ribbon, faded and dusty, hung next to an old poster of a boy band from the nineties. Yep, she was definitely in her old bedroom.

Remembering why, she rolled over and grabbed her phone off the bedside table. She had left the ringer on in case someone from the hospital called her. Relieved to see that she hadn't missed a call, she glanced at the time. Noon. She had managed to get in a decent nap. Elizabeth had learned to get by on little sleep after her years of medical training.

She got up and stretched, heading into the small adjoining bathroom for a shower. On the way, she checked in with the hospital to make sure her mother was still holding her own.

Feeling more like herself when she was finished, Elizabeth headed downstairs in search of coffee. Happy to see the Keurig she had given her mom for Christmas last year, Elizabeth set it into motion and then leaned against the counter waiting for her cup to brew.

That's when she noticed the pretty, blue flowers in her mother's backyard. Hydrangeas. She loved Hydrangeas. Elizabeth walked outside to take a closer look. The first thing she saw was freshly turned earth. Clearly these had just been planted. She wondered if her mother had a gardener. Probably not as she considered the rest of the neglected yard. Gardening had always been her mother's passion. The sight of her untended yard brought a hot lump to her throat. It was further proof of her mother's decline.

Elizabeth stared at the newly planted bushes. The smell of wet dirt reached her; not an unpleasant scent. She had missed this, living in her condo in Los Angeles. She worked long hours and had decided that buying a maintenance free condo made more sense. But now, with the crisp grass tickling her toes, she regretted that decision.

The slight breeze flapped a piece of paper tied to one of the branches. Elizabeth leaned in and pulled it off. In a bold, dark ink was written *'I didn't mean to hurt your feelings.'* No signature, but she knew immediately who the shrub was from. She cringed as she thought back to their conversation this morning. She was not proud of herself.

Giving the flowers one last glance, Elizabeth went back inside to drink her coffee. During the mad dash to get here yesterday, she had not been able to sleep. Instead, Elizabeth had spent most of the time thinking about what it would be like to be home. Dealing with her mother's illness was hard enough. Even though she didn't know how long she'd be here, she needed to start mending some fences.

Elizabeth finished her coffee and grabbed a banana before heading out to her rental car. First, she would go spend some time with her mother. Then she could figure out how to deal with everyone else.

Chapter Six

Elizabeth walked into the ICU and continued to her mother's room. She dragged a chair closer to the bed, sat, and picked up her mother's hand in her own. She was pleased to note the improved color in her face. She looked so much better than when Elizabeth had gotten here last night. Even better than this morning.

"Hey, Mom. I'm back. You're doing great, but you have to keep fighting. I'm going to help you with that."

"Pardon me" came a deep voice from the doorway.

Elizabeth whirled at the voice. "Oh, that's okay. I was just talking to my mom." She stood up and approached the stranger in the signature white doctor's coat.

"Then that makes you Dr. Fitzgerald." He moved in closer, extending his hand. "I'm Sebastian Walker, one of your mother's cardiologists. I believe you met my partner, Dr. Reynolds, last evening."

Elizabeth laughed. "I certainly did." She shook his hand, hers lost in the size of his. "I'm so happy to meet you. I'm Elizabeth Fitzgerald."

"Let me guess, Flynn made a questionable first impression." His laughter lightened the harshness of his words.

"Let's go with memorable. He almost squashed me in the main lobby on his way up here. It got better after that."

"Well that's good at least. Flynn tends to be very focused, usually to the exclusion of all else. Great for a doctor. Not so much for innocent bystanders." Elizabeth nodded in agreement. "So, I hear you're from here but living in Los Angeles. And you're an ED doc?"

Elizabeth laughed outright this time. "Wow, this place hasn't changed. Do you know my shoe size as well?"

Sebastian joined in her laughter. "No, I definitely didn't hear that. Anyway, let's talk about your mother, shall we?" He stepped closer to the bed and surveyed first his patient and then the various machines to which she was attached. Elizabeth watched as he listened to first her heart and then lungs.

"So, your mother has left-sided heart failure. How long she's been ill is anyone's guess. But this didn't happen overnight. She's made it through the first 24 hours; an excellent sign. I need to do some further testing, but not until she's a little stronger. She's over breathing the ventilator; another good thing. Hopefully we can take her off that very soon. Possibly this evening."

Elizabeth watched as her mother's chest rose and fell. As a doctor, she knew that this meant her mother could breathe on her own, above and beyond what the ventilator was set to do. This meant she may be able to be weaned off the machine altogether. Tears welled in her eyes, and she dashed them away quickly. "Sorry. It's been a crazy twenty-four hours for me."

He placed a comforting hand on her shoulder. "There's no reason to apologize, Elizabeth. I can only imagine what you've been through. As I said, if she remains stable through the afternoon, I'll think about taking her off the ventilator this evening. Of course, she still has a long way to go. That's just the very first step."

"Absolutely. But I would feel so much better if she was breathing on her own fully."

"This is a marathon, not a sprint. Your mom has a long road ahead of her. She'll need to be in the hospital and then probably a rehab for a while. How long are you here for?"

Elizabeth met his kind gaze. "That's a good question, Sebastian. I spoke with my boss on the way to the airport yesterday. I had no idea, however, what I would find when I got here. I do have a lot of vacation time saved up. Most likely, I'm going to take a leave. I'm certainly not going back anytime soon." She brushed a hand lovingly along her mother's hair. "I need to be here with her."

"Good. I believe that my patients recover better with a good support system." He took a card from his wallet and scribbled on the back before handing it to her. "Here are all of my numbers including my cell on the back. Please don't ever hesitate to call me. Anytime. For anything. Now I have to go check on another patient in the unit."

Elizabeth thanked him as he left the room. She slipped the card into her back pocket. Sebastian had given her a lot to think about. She needed to have a conversation with her boss that he wasn't going to like. But she knew he would understand.

She sat back down at her mother's side. "Well, Mom, it looks like you're stuck with me for a while." Elizabeth watched as her mother's eyes fluttered but didn't open. She was sure that her mother could hear her. "That's right, Mom. I'm not going anywhere until you are well on your way to recovery." She had only been back less than a day, but already the thought of returning to her life in Los Angeles held little appeal.

A young nurse entered the room. "Hi, Dr. Fitzgerald. I'm Sophie. I'm taking care of your mom today."

"Hi, Sophie. I'm happy to meet you, but please call me Elizabeth."

The younger woman nodded. "Your mother is looking better with every hour that passes. I have a good feeling about her."

"I do too." Elizabeth grimaced as her stomach growled.

Sophie laughed. "Our cafeteria is still open for lunch. It's not bad. Why don't you run down there? I'll be here."

Elizabeth glanced at her mom. "I'd say I wasn't hungry, but we both know that would be a lie. I think I will, thanks." She got up and headed for the door.

Sophie stopped her before she could leave. "I almost forgot to tell you. Dr. Chamberlain called for you. He asked if you could stop down sometime today to see him. His office is in the hallway just behind the ED."

"Okay. Thanks. I'll do that now before I grab something from the cafeteria."

Curious, Elizabeth headed for the stairs and ran lightly down to the first floor. Exiting the stairwell, she glanced around to get her bearings. After getting directions from a volunteer, she found herself before Eric's open door. His back was to her as he spoke into the phone. Not wanting to be rude, she tapped softly to alert him to her presence. Eric swiveled in his chair and smiled when he saw her. He motioned her in and held up a single finger.

"Yes, honey. I promise to be home on time for dinner. I love you. See you later." He hung up the office phone. "Sorry about that, Elizabeth."

"No worries, Eric. Sounds like someone has been working too much."

Eric laughed. "You have no idea. That's why I asked you to stop by. But first, how's your Mom?"

"Better thanks. I just met Dr. Walker, and we had a nice chat about her progress. It's a long road, but I'm beginning to feel a bit more optimistic."

"Great news. Well, with that in mind, let me ask you a question." He leaned forward and flexed his fingers as he stared at her. Elizabeth felt as though he was struggling with what he had to say.

"What is it, Eric? You're spooking me."

Eric broke eye contact and leaned back in his chair a bit. "Sorry. It's all good. I'm just wondering how best to say this."

"Just out with it works well for me."

"No hiding the fact that you're an emergency doctor. Ok then. Here's the thing. I was wondering how long you were planning to be here and whether you'd be interested in picking up some shifts in the ED." He laughed as her eyes widened in surprise. "Didn't expect to hear that, did you?"

"No, I certainly didn't. I pretty much thought you were joking last night. I, uh, am flattered, but I just don't think I can commit to anything right now."

Eric held up his hand. "Before you say no, let me explain. We're a bit short staffed. One of our full-time docs just had a baby and won't be back for at least another 6-8 weeks. Then, on top of that, Dr. Mallory's wife had a serious riding accident over the week-end. She survived but has a crushed pelvis. They have two small kids, and David is overwhelmed. He's taking leave for a few weeks until she's stable and he can find a nanny. As you can see, we're in a bit of a bind."

"Wow, you really are, Eric. I'm so sorry to hear that. It always seems like everything happens at the same time. I'm just not sure how I can help. You know my life is in California. I'm not even licensed here."

"And you know that we can get you emergency privileges. If you were interested."

It was Elizabeth's turn to stare at Eric. She had no idea how to answer that. Was she interested? In helping, maybe. In staying here permanently? This was the second time she'd been asked that in twenty-four hours. She hadn't given it serious thought, but her mother was going to have a long recuperation. And Elizabeth was already reluctant to leave her again after almost losing her.

"You don't have to answer right now."

"Yes." Elizabeth blurted out her answer.

"Really? I thought that would take more persuasion."

Elizabeth's heart was pounding. She felt a bit shell shocked. Had she really just agreed to this? "It's the right thing to do, Eric. You need help. I have some time. Just keep in mind that this is temporary. When my mom is better, I'll be going back to Los Angeles." At least that had been her plan.

Eric came around the desk and shook her hand. "I totally understand, Elizabeth. I promise to not try to convince you to stay. At least right now." He laughed and she joined in, her head still spinning.

"Thank you for the opportunity, Eric. I'm probably going to be here for longer than I had originally thought. Keeping busy while my mother recovers will be a good thing."

"I hate to rush you, but getting you privileged here may take up to a week. Can you stop by human resources before they leave today? I'll let Sally know you're coming."

Elizabeth agreed and left his office, continuing to human resources. She met with Sally, had her picture taken for her new badge and got the required paperwork started.

Elizabeth walked into the cafeteria, almost dizzy what had just happened. She was reaching for a tray when she noticed Flynn standing in front of her in line. She tapped him on the shoulder.

He turned and smiled at her in surprise. "Twice in one day. Miss me, did you?"

Elizabeth couldn't help but feel the weight of his charm. Luckily, she was immune to such things. "Or it could just be the fact that we're both back at the hospital where you work and my mother is a patient. Not to mention where I apparently now work as well."

"What? You're on staff now? How did that happen? What about California? This *is* my lucky day. I should probably ask you out to dinner right now."

She bit her lip to keep from laughing aloud. No point in encouraging him. "I'm working here temporarily; just picking up some shifts to help out until my mom is better. Eric Chamberlain was telling me about the staffing issues they've been having and asked me if I was interested. And I don't date."

"What do you mean you 'don't date'?"

"Naturally, that's the one thing you'd focus on. I'm just too busy for that whole thing, so I don't date."

"The whole thing?" Flynn raised an eyebrow. "Which whole thing exactly? Now I really am intrigued."

Elizabeth blew out a long breath to tamper her frustration. This wasn't going well. "Okay, I'm only going to say this once. Try to follow along. My work is everything to me. When I'm not working, I have a couple charitable organizations to which I donate my time. Dating requires time and effort. I really don't have either." She didn't have the desire to have her heart fractured into a thousand pieces again, but she wasn't going there. Flynn just might be the only person in Windsor Falls who didn't know her tragic history.

"What about sex?" Flynn's voice had risen with his incredulousness. Several people stopped talking and turned to stare at them.

"Lower your voice" she hissed at him. Elizabeth paid for her sandwich and walked towards a table in the corner; as far away as she could get from the curious onlookers.

Flynn followed and placed his tray across from hers. "I'm sorry" he stated insincerely.

"That might be more convincing if you weren't laughing at me."

"I was just surprised. You're beautiful, intelligent, funny. What's wrong with the men on the West Coast? Are they blind or just stupid?"

"We just met. I'd rather not discuss my sex life with you. Even if I was dating, you'd be last on the list."

Flynn dramatically laid a hand over his heart. "Direct hit! Now that one hurt. May I ask why? I'm not exactly repugnant. And I shower daily."

She fought to hold in her laughter. "This conversation is ridiculous, but I'll tell you just to shut you up. First, you're my mother's doctor. Second, we are about to be colleagues. Third, I'm only here for a short time. And last. You're just not my type. Are those enough reasons for you?"

He took a big bite of his hamburger and chewed thoughtfully for a moment while he continued to stare at her. Elizabeth deliberately went about eating her lunch.

After wiping his mouth on a napkin, Flynn tackled her objections. "We've already discussed the first. As for colleagues, that doesn't really count. If you were a cardiologist working in my practice, then I'd give you that one. Workplace romances can get tricky. And I know you're here temporarily. You've mentioned it several times already. But as I've mentioned, I wasn't asking you to marry me. Just have dinner. We could be 'friendly' temporarily. And last, I'm not sure what your 'type' is, but does it really matter? After all, this is 'just temporary.' I'm quite the catch; educated, witty, not bad looking. I could go on if you need to hear more of my attributes."

"It's a shame you're so lacking in self-confidence. Since you're obviously perfect, I'll just stick with no because my life is a mess right now. My mom is very ill, I'm about to start a new job here, and my real life is on hold. How's that?"

"That works. You're right. But that doesn't mean I'm going to give up. Consider yourself warned, Elizabeth. Now let's go see your mom."

He accompanied Elizabeth back to the ICU. She shifted her weight from one foot to the other and held her breath while he conducted a thorough examination. Flynn adjusted the settings on the vent, and Elizabeth held her breath.

Flynn shook his head. "I know what you were hoping for Elizabeth." Flynn waved a hand at the ventilator. "But, I've decided to wait until morning to remove your mother from the ventilator to give her the best possible chance at staying off it. She's doing great, but I want to be sure. I'll lighten her sedation tonight so that she's doing more of the work of breathing. If she remains stable, then tomorrow morning it is."

"That's fine, Flynn. I'd rather have her off now, but you're right to be cautious. Hopefully tonight goes well." Her voice quivered at the end.

Flynn stepped to her side and gave her a brief hug. "You'll see, Elizabeth. She's a fighter. It's only a few more hours. They know how to reach me. As do you." He squeezed her hand before leaving the room.

Elizabeth spent the rest of the day sitting by her mother's bedside and staying out of the way of staff who were caring for her. By eight o'clock, she was yawning uncontrollably. She left, confident that her mother was in much better shape than last night. Getting a full night sleep in her old room was a better idea than trying to sleep on that tiny, uncomfortable couch in the waiting room. Again.

Elizabeth gathered her purse and kissed her mom good night, promising to be back early the next morning. She headed to the nursing station to let them know she was leaving. Once again, Katie Fitzgerald was seated behind a monitor. Weary and resigned, Elizabeth approached her cautiously.

"Hi, Katie. I just wanted to let you know I'm going home for the night."

Katie looked up from what her typing to fix Elizabeth with a cool stare. "Thanks for letting me know. Let me make sure I have your number on file. Just in case." She rattled off Elizabeth's Los Angeles cell number.

Elizabeth tried to not flinch at the lack of any inflection in the other woman's voice. It was hard to imagine that they had once been such good friends. She kept her own voice neutral. "Yes, that's it. By the way, thank you for calling Sam last night. You didn't have to do that, but it was nice to have the support."

Katie searched her face before responding. "I hope that was the right thing to do. I know this isn't easy for you. But please don't hurt Sam. Again. He's very special to me." Another nurse called Katie's name, and she walked away. Elizabeth turned and left the ICU quickly. She was in the parking lot before she remembered to take a breath.

Elizabeth fumbled for her keys when she reached her rental car. Heat blasted her as soon as she opened the door. She quickly turned on the car and then air conditioning, opening the windows as she slid in. She made sure the vents were all opened and then leaned her forehead on the steering wheel.

Her head was throbbing, and the muscles in her neck felt as though they might snap at any moment. The stress of the past two days was taking its toll. Elizabeth replayed the conversation with Katie in her mind. She had thought that the younger woman and Sam had seemed cozy this morning. Katie was certainly protective of him. She wondered when that had developed. Her mom had not mentioned it, but then her mom never talked about Sam. Elizabeth never understood why her mom didn't like Sam, but that's the way it had been since they were teenagers.

Sam's face swam before her eyes. She had been serious when she told him how much she had missed him over the years. He hadn't seemed to believe her though. Elizabeth could hardly blame him. She had left without warning or even saying goodbye to him. She squeezed her eyes shut tightly as she thought about the last time she had seen him.

She was just into her second trimester when Connor died. After his funeral, the Fitzgeralds had thrown a proper Irish wake for Connor at their home. Seemingly, the whole town had come. Elizabeth was exhausted and grief stricken. She hadn't been in the frame of mind to entertain and had mostly hid in the kitchen or in the yard. Early that evening, she had terrible stomach cramps. The last thing she remembered was calling out for Maggie, Connor's mother, who had been seated beside her.

When she awoke, Elizabeth was admitted to the hospital, on the very Labor & Delivery unit for which she worked. She was rushed into the operating room when it was discovered that she had suffered an incomplete miscarriage. Complications from bleeding had kept her in the hospital for two days. She had not seen Sam in that time.

A few days after her discharge, Elizabeth was lying in bed, as she had done pretty much since Connor's death, when she heard a soft knock on her bedroom door. "Mom, I'm not hungry. I just need to sleep." Elizabeth squeezed her eyes tightly shut as if to will away her mother. Maybe if she wished hard enough, they would all go away and leave her alone. The only person she wished to see was the one she never would again.

"I'm not your mother, but I do think you should eat" came the reply in a deep, grief-roughened voice. Elizabeth stiffened at Sam's voice. Struggling to a sitting position, Elizabeth wrapped her arms around her stomach as though trying to protect the baby she had lost. She brushed the limp hair away from her face. Elizabeth looked at Sam, shocked at what she saw. His normally warm, brown eyes were dulled and red rimmed. There was a few days' growth of hair on his face. He looked haggard.

She hadn't spoken with Sam since that terrible night in the emergency department. She wasn't ready to speak with him now. She might never be. It was just too hard.

Thinking of Sam, and seeing him alive and well, reminded her too much of all she had lost. Sam and Connor were inextricably linked in her mind. Even though somewhere deep in her mind she knew that wasn't fair to Sam, she couldn't help how she felt.

"I've been so worried about you, Elizabeth. I've come by. I've called." He stopped and ran a hand through his hair. "I don't know what to do. I don't know how to help you."

Struggling to get past the burning lump in her throat, Elizabeth forced herself not to cry. "There's nothing you can do, Sam. There's nothing anyone can do." She smothered a sob. "I'm sorry, Sam. I just can't..." Her voice dropped off then, unable to finish the sentence. She pulled the covers up to her chin and rolled away from him. The only sound was the soft click of the door as Sam left without another word.

Elizabeth cringed as she remembered just how badly she had treated Sam in those horrible days. It hadn't been intentional, but she had hurt him just the same. She was filled with an overwhelming need to make things right. Or to at least start to repair the damage. She didn't even have Sam's phone number or know where he lived. Whipping out her phone, she Googled his store. Elizabeth loaded the address into her rental's GPS and headed in that direction.

The drive was short. He had moved the store his grandfather had started from the small, crowded space in town to a larger property on the outskirts. She glanced around as she pulled into the parking lot. There were a few other stores around his, but Sam's was the only home and garden store. She briefly admired the large outdoor section as she walked through the front door.

Glancing at her phone, she realized closing time had already passed. Elizabeth looked around, admiring the wide variety of merchandise available. She tentatively called out.

"Hello, Elizabeth." Sam rounded an aisle and approached her. Her pulse thrummed at the sight of him. This had seemed like a great idea, but now that she was here, in front of him, she wasn't so sure. What could she possibly say?

"Hey, Sam. I thought I'd come by and check out the new place." Really? That's all she could think of? UGH! This wouldn't be easy.

He took a tentative step closer to her. "Yep, this is it. I opened this site about five years ago. I always told my dad that we had to expand."

"Well, he would surely be proud of what you've accomplished, Sam. It's too bad he didn't live long enough to see this." Sam had lost both of his parents within months of each other the year before Connor died.

The expression on his face grew tight. "I'm not so sure about that. It was always the biggest bone of contention between us. He wanted to stay in that small space and just continue as his father had done before him. Even though the store was failing. He couldn't admit he was wrong. He struggled right up to the bitter end."

"Your dad was stubborn and old fashioned. Still, I think he would admit he was wrong now. Look what you've accomplished."

"Thanks. That means a lot to me. It's probably not true, but the sentiment is nice."

Growing up, Elizabeth was aware that Sam and his parents had always seemed distant with each other. They had Sam late in life, long after they had given up on having children. His father had worked long hours trying to keep the store afloat. Sam's mother had been a quiet, sad woman who did whatever her husband asked of her. It seemed to Elizabeth that Sam had spent more of his childhood in Connor's home than his own. But then, so had she.

"Well, for what it's worth, I'm proud of you. I know you're technically closed, but can I get a tour?" Elizabeth was delaying the inevitable, but just being with Sam again was wonderful. She wasn't ready to wreck that by bringing up the past.

"I'd be happy to. Let's start outside, and I can close up as we go." He led the way out a side door into the gardening section. Elizabeth was immediately overwhelmed by the vast array of flowers for sale. She hadn't done any gardening since moving to California, but she had loved helping her Mom as a child.

"Sam, this is fabulous!" She touched him on the arm to underscore her enthusiasm. His skin was warm and covered some impressive muscles. Her fingers tingled. "Look at the variety. I bet you know the names of every plant here." Elizabeth could feel Sam watching her, but she kept her face turned away from him under the guise of taking it all in.

"Well not all. But most I guess. I have a wonderful manager for this area. Maria helped me to pick the Hydrangeas for you."

She turned to face him. "Busted. That was one of my reasons for stopping by tonight. Thank you for the lovely gift. It wasn't necessary." Her breathing quickened and her palms grew sweaty under his intense gaze.

"What other reasons did you have, Elizabeth?"

Her pulse beat frantically like the wings of a Humming Bird. "Oh Sam." She wailed quietly. Elizabeth walked to a nearby bench and sat, tapping the seat next to her. "Please sit with me. I have so much to tell you."

Sam hesitated before joining her on the wooden bench. "I'm sorry for snapping at you this morning. I'm not sure where that all came from. It's all water under the bridge, Elizabeth."

She shook her head, not quite trusting herself to speak. Elizabeth placed one shaky hand on his knee. "No Sam, it's not okay. You were my best friend. I know that you lost Connor too. At least now I do. Back then, when everything was ripped away from me so quickly, I couldn't think about your pain. Maybe that was selfish of me, but I was lost Sam. For a long time."

"And what are you now, Elizabeth? Have you found yourself again in California?"

Sam's face was cast in shadows with the gathering night. His jaw was darkened by a day's growth of beard, so Elizabeth couldn't see his expression clearly. She could however hear the pain in his voice clearly. The pain she had caused.

"I don't know what I am, Sam. I have a life in California that works for me. I know who I am there. But coming back here, coming home, is difficult. I wasn't ready for this."

"The last thing I want is to make it harder for you, Elizabeth."

"You're not Sam. At least not in the way that you think. I was thinking today about the last time I saw you. I was so terrible to you, Sam, and I'm so sorry."

Tears formed on her lashes, spilling over and down her face. She made no move to brush them away.

Sam made an inarticulate sound deep in his throat before pulling her into his arms. "Please don't cry, Elizabeth. You know I could never stand to see you unhappy."

They stayed that way for some time, and Elizabeth enjoyed the way he softly stroked her back. She loved being an emergency physician, but it was emotionally draining at times. She didn't have anyone in California to comfort her like Sam was doing now. That was her own fault of course, never letting anyone close to her. She had her reasons, but right now she was regretting her choices.

"I've missed you more than you could ever know. Yes, that's the third time I have said it, but it's true, Sam. I don't have what you and Connor and I shared out there. I miss talking with you, just being with you. And, of course, I miss Connor too. Being back home makes that so real for me."

"I know, Elizabeth. I've missed you too. And I miss him. Every day. Living here makes it impossible not to be reminded of him."

She straightened up and pulled back from him. The night immediately felt a bit cooler without his body heat against her. For the first time, she looked directly into his eyes. The jumble of pain and regret she saw there made her ache. She had been so selfish.

"That's exactly it, Sam." She took his hands in hers. "I need to make you understand why I made the choice I did. Losing Connor, and then our baby, was more than I could stand. I was suffocating here. Every place I went reminded me of him. Everyone wanted to help and to make it better for me. But I needed to do this alone. On my own schedule. No one could make it better for me. So, I left. It may have been wrong or cowardly, but at the time it was the only thing that made sense."

Sam squeezed her hands. "I understand now, Elizabeth. But back then, not so much. We were all hurting. Your mom. Connor's whole family. Me. We all lost Connor. And then, just a little while later, we lost you as well. It had always been the three of us, Elizabeth. In the blink of an eye, I was the only one left. That hurt." Fresh tears flooded her eyes, and Sam gently wiped them away with his finger.

"I'm so very sorry, Sam. Hurting you was the last thing I ever intended. I was so blind to everything but my own pain. I was drowning, and leaving was my only way out."

"I do understand, Elizabeth. Let's put this behind us. What's important is that you're here now. Please don't cry anymore. I'll be up all night planting more Hydrangeas."

Elizabeth laughed through her tears. "I really missed that, Sam. You always could make me laugh, especially at myself." She wiped her eyes and brushed her hair from her face. "So, now that we're back in the same place again, tell me all about yourself."

Sam stood and pulled her up next to him. "Ten years is a lot to cover, but this is a good place to start." He held his arms wide, gesturing to the store. "Much like you, work has been the better part of my life. I don't know if that's good or bad. It just is."

"That I can understand. Once I decided to become a doctor, my life was no longer my own. All of my time and energy was wrapped up in my training."

"Exactly. This place really saved me, in a way. I didn't know how bad off the store was until after my dad died. Even though I was meant to one day take over, he was very guarded about it. Then I knew why. It sounds harsh, but if he hadn't died when he did, we would have lost everything."

Elizabeth winced at his words. "Wow, Sam. I had no idea. Why didn't you ever tell me?"

"You and Connor had just gotten married when my dad died. And then it was awhile before I learned the full extent of it. I was just trying to keep it all together and figure out how to turn things around when Connor died. And then you were gone." He held up a hand to strop what she might have said. "I'm just telling you how it was."

"I had no idea."

"No one did, Elizabeth. Not even my mother. Their marriage was very old fashioned that way. Anyway, after everything that happened, I was feeling lost too. But having to save the family business really gave me a purpose. It kept me going."

"Well you've done a wonderful job here. This place is huge and gorgeous. I'm so happy for you, Sam. But what about the rest of your life?"

"Oh? You think there's something else to my life?" Sam grinned as he said it.

Elizabeth lightly batted him on the arm. "Come one, Sam. Who do you think you're fooling? I know there must be a special someone in your life. I remember how much you dated in high school." She thought again about how he had acted around Katie. Maybe he would tell her about that now.

"If you remember, Elizabeth, I had a lot of *first* dates in high school."

"You're a successful business owner who isn't bad looking." She grinned cheekily at that understatement and looked him up and down. Sam had really filled out in the past ten years. While he had always been cute, he was now a grown man with the body and face to match. "I can't believe the women around here aren't lined up for you."

"You'd be surprised then, Elizabeth. Much to Maggie Fitzgerald's chagrin, and not for her lack of trying, I'm still single. Being a small business owner is time consuming. I don't really have a lot of free time for dating."

"Maybe you just haven't met the right person yet, Sam."

Something passed over his eyes so quickly that Elizabeth wasn't even sure she had really seen it. Regret? Sadness? She wasn't sure. But the fleeting emotion was gone as quickly as it had come.

"That must be it. At this point, I might have to move. Maggie has already tried to pair me with every single woman under forty in Windsor Falls."

He reached behind her to turn off the floodlights, and Elizabeth caught a whiff of Sam. It was a combination of woodsy outdoors and a light spice. But it was all male.

Slightly off kilter at the way her thoughts were going, Elizabeth tripped over a hose lying on the ground. She would have fallen if Sam had not reached out to grab her around the waist.

"Careful. Are you okay?" He kicked the offending garden hose to the side and glanced into her face.

Elizabeth was thankful for the darkness as a dull red crept up her face. "Well, as you can see, I may have grown up but I'm certainly not any more graceful."

They both laughed at the reference. "You were a lot of things, Elizabeth; funny, smart, kind. But graceful was never one of them. Nice to see you haven't changed."

They stood there, with his arms around her waist and her hands on his chest, for just another moment. Perhaps a moment too long. Elizabeth could feel the muscles of his chest where her hands touched him. His pecs were hard and well defined beneath his shirt. For one second more, she rejoiced in the luxury of leaning on another person. That was something she hadn't done in a very long time. Not since Connor died. Disturbed by these thoughts, Elizabeth pulled away from Sam quickly, putting some distance between them.

"You're right, Sam" she said nervously, "that certainly hasn't changed." Elizabeth walked into the brightly lit store, desperate to regain some composure. She tried to banish the memory of Sam's well developed chest from her mind. Yeah, good luck with that.

She turned to say goodnight, eager to escape to the safety of her car, and nearly crashed into Sam. "I see you haven't lost your ability to sneak up on me." There was as stillness to Sam that Connor had lacked. They had really been almost the exact opposite yet best friends.

Sam looked at her for so long that Elizabeth grew more nervous. Finally, he nodded at her. "What's going on in that head of yours, Elizabeth? I can see the wheels turning a thousand miles per hour."

"Nothing worth mentioning, Sam. I should get going. It's been a long couple of days." Elizabeth avoided looking at him. Her keys were making indentations in her hand where she clutched them nervously. She had never felt this way around

Sam, and she had no idea why she was now. She needed to get out of there. Before she did anything else clumsy or stupid.

"I understand. Let me walk you to your car." He grasped her elbow lightly and led Elizabeth outside. Theirs were the only two cars in the lot. "Rental, huh?" Sam asked as he pointed to her car.

"Yes. I picked it up in Charlotte when I landed. I'm going to drop it off tomorrow and use my mom's car while I'm here. She won't be driving it anytime soon." Sadness swept across her face at the thought.

Sam gently placed his hand under her chin and tilted up her face to look at him. "She's getting the best care possible, Elizabeth. You have to have hope." His soft words warmed her.

"I do, Sam. I think she's going to recover. But she has a long road ahead of her with many lifestyle changes. She's going to need help. And you know she's not likely to ask for it."

"Maybe being this sick will be enough to make her realize that."

Elizabeth's expression was pure skepticism. "Have you met my mother? Things need to change. A lot of things." She turned and opened her car with the electronic key fob. "Anyway, thanks again for the lovely Hydrangeas, Sam. You really didn't need to do that, but they sure brightened up the yard. I'll probably be back here for some more stuff. Her yard, and house for that matter, really needs a lot of work."

"Well, I'm your man. I'm happy to help you with anything you need Elizabeth."

"Unlike my Mom, I'm not too proud to ask. Have a good night." She got into the car and drove away.

*****

Sam stood there, watching until her taillights were no longer visible. He couldn't stop the grin that spread across his face. Elizabeth was back. They had a conversation that didn't lead to another fight. And he had held her in his arms. All in all, not a bad way to spend forty-five minutes.

He wandered back inside to lock up before heading home. Sam gave a long, low whistle, and two Australian Shepherds came running from the direction of his office. Lily and Cooper came to the store most days, hanging in his office and sometimes walking the store with him to greet customers. They were well known and made friends everywhere they went.

"Let's go home, shall we?" He opened the door to his truck and the agile dogs jumped into the back seat. Sam strapped them into harnesses before getting in the front. He smiled when he thought of home. He was in the middle of building a house right in the mountains. The location offered room and privacy and yet only a twenty-minute commute.

The house was finally close to being finished. He had sold his parent's home for the down payment and moved out of theirs at closing. At the time, the new house was only partially completed, and he spent the first week in a sleeping bag. On the floor. His thirty-five-year-old back had quickly let him know that wasn't a good idea. Sam had made his first furniture purchase ever. A king-sized bed.

The house was nearing completion now. Sam had done most of the interior work, learning as he went. Growing up in a hardware store had come in handy. He wondered what Elizabeth would think of it. He shook his head. Of course, he would think of her. Even in her absence, Sam had thought about her. Every day. Wondered about her life. Was she happy? Was she with anyone? He assumed she was over the years. After all, ten years was a long time.

Sam pulled into his driveway with more questions than answers. He let his dogs out and watched as they chased each other along the edge of the woods. Sam went inside and was greeted by high pitched happiness from the kitchen. Griffin, his third Aussie, jumped up to wash Sam's face with his tongue. Just over six months old, Griffin was still very much a puppy, full of exuberance and lacking in the discipline his older dogs had. For this reason, Sam clipped him to a long lead before taking him outside to do his business.

Lily and Cooper ran back towards the house, and the three dogs excitedly swarmed each other. Sam took a deep breath of clean, mountain air and tipped his head back to see the stars. This house was his dream. Growing up in Windsor Falls, Sam had always loved the mountains and wanted to live closer to them. And now he did. But the dream wasn't complete. It never would be. His dream included Elizabeth and maybe a few kids.

Sam whistled for the dogs and headed into the house. He fed the dogs and grabbed a beer for himself before heading out to the patio. It was large and offered an excellent view on all sides. There was enough room for a table that could seat eight and a kick ass grill. Because what man didn't want that? In the corner was a hot tub for six.

Sam turned on the jets and stripped off his clothes. No need for a suit without neighbors close enough to see. He took a long pull of his Blue Moon before setting the bottle on the edge. Sam sunk lower in the water and tilted his head back so he could see the stars. They were infinite, and that had always comforted him. Although Windsor Falls wasn't the big city, he still couldn't see the stars in town the way he could here.

Sam played back the time spent with Elizabeth in his mind. The ten years had been kind to her. Although there were faint lines around her mouth and eyes, she was still the freshly pretty woman he remembered. And been in love with all these years. If anything, she had matured into an even more beautiful woman.

Sam remembered the feel of her body against his when she had almost tripped. They lined up in all the right places. Just the thought of her full breasts against his chest was enough to make him hard now. He took another drink and sighed. Seeing her again was wonderful, but did he really want to torture himself all over again?

Frustrated, he got out of the hot tub and walked naked across the patio. The cool night breeze felt good on his wet body. He walked inside and straight into the first-floor master suite. The enclosed master bath held a huge shower stall with dual heads. He turned the water to as cool as he could tolerate and stood under the streaming water. Sam hoped this would erase the memory of Elizabeth in his arms.

When he was done, Sam dried off and went to bed. He reached over and plugged his cell phone in and placed it on the nightstand. Flipping over onto his back and staring at the ceiling, he watched as the fan blades circulated. He and Elizabeth were still on shaky ground. He needed to keep his ever-present feelings for her to himself. They had enough to deal with.

But there wasn't any peace to be found, not even in his sleep. In his dream, Elizabeth was lying on her stomach on one of his patio lounge chair. She was clad only in a very brief, electric blue bikini. As he approached her, he could see that the top was untied. She must have heard him approach, because she opened her eyes and smiled sleepily up at him, squinting in the bright summer sunshine.

"Hi, honey" she murmured to him. "Be a love and put some lotion on my back please. I don't want to burn." She closed her eyes again and lay her head back down on the towel. Sam lowered himself gently onto the edge of the chair and reached for the sunscreen. With somewhat shaky hands, he squeezed out a liberal amount into one hand and rubbed both together. The lotion was warm from the sun. He started, ever so slowly and carefully, to rub her back in a small, circular motion. Her skin was hot and soft and felt like pure sin. With increasing boldness, he moved his hands down to the small of her back. She was slender, and he could easily span the width of her waist with his hands.

She sighed aloud with pleasure; a purely feminine noise. Wanting to increase her pleasure, he ran the fingers of one hand under the edge of her bikini bottom, gently caressing the swells he found there. With the grace of a cat, she rolled over and sat up in one motion, her top falling away as she moved. Her small but firm breasts were in full view. Bracing himself with one hand on either side of her slender torso, he leaned in and lathed one dusky nipple with the tip of his tongue.

The shrill ringing of the phone awakened him. Sam groaned aloud in frustration. He was painfully hard thanks to that dream. He cursed himself for not remembering to shut off the ringer on his phone. Refusing to answer it, he headed for the shower. This one would be decidedly colder.

Chapter Seven

Elizabeth sat in her mother's kitchen and stared into the backyard. It really was a mess she thought with a sigh. Her mother's developing illness had prevented her from keeping up with things around the house. Elizabeth knew that would have been painful for her. Diane Abbott had always been proud of her immaculate home and lovely gardens. Now, as Elizabeth glanced around, she noted a layer of dust on surfaces that she had never seen before.

That was easily enough fixed. Getting up to put her breakfast dishes in the sink, Elizabeth thought about where she would start. Before starting, she called the rental car agency and arranged for them to pick up the car. She hurried to get ready. She wanted to be at the hospital first thing. Hopefully, Flynn would be taking her mother off the ventilator today. She crossed her fingers in a rare show of superstition.

Elizabeth left the rental keys under the front mat of the car and got into her mother's car. She wasn't sure the last time it had been driven, but the car started smoothly right away. Thankful for that, Elizabeth drove to the hospital.

She stifled a yawn as she sang along to a local country station. After the past forty-eight hours, she had been exhausted when her head hit the pillow last night. But although Elizabeth had fallen right to sleep, it had not been a restful one. Strange fragments of dreams throughout the night prevented her from feeling fully rested this morning. For the first time in a very long time, she had dreamt of

Connor. She was following him down a series of hallways. Each time she almost caught up with him, he would turn a corner and suddenly be further away again.

But that wasn't the most disturbing part. At the last corner, she turned, expecting to once again be far behind Connor. But she walked right into his outstretched arms. Only when she leaned into him and inhaled his scent, it wasn't Connor anymore. Sam held her in his arms, just like he had last night.

The dream had been so vivid. She could feel the corded muscles of Sam's arms. He was warm and solid, and she smelled the same cologne he had been wearing last night. She had felt so safe and secure, just like when he had stopped her from tripping over the garden hose.

But there was an element that was far more disturbing to her. Beyond security, she had felt a pull, low in her belly and parts further south. A physical, chemical pull. She'd been attracted to him. Even now, fully awake, Elizabeth felt a tingling from the memory of the dream.

Elizabeth tried to shake it off. But even as she had showered and eaten breakfast, she couldn't help remembering the dream. Sam had always been handsome, but Elizabeth only had eyes for Connor when they were growing up. The two had started dating in high school and were together until his death.

If she was being honest with herself, there had been *something* there when Sam had touched her last night. Something that left her flustered. Something that had never been there before. She shook her head, as much in bewilderment as denial. She didn't have time for thoughts of Sam. Giving herself a firm talking to, Elizabeth drove to the hospital.

Flynn was the first person she saw when she exited the elevator on the critical care floor. He was standing in her mom's doorway. Elizabeth paused for a moment to look at him. Flynn was wearing his usual navy blue scrubs, and she could appreciate his strongly muscled arms and shoulders. He was over six feet tall, and there didn't appear to be an ounce of fat on him. His hair was thick and as black as a raven's wing. It practically begged a woman to run her hands through it. Flynn was definitely the type to make women take a second look. And a third. But not her. Huh.

Her reverie was shattered by a smug, male chuckle. "You were just checking me out." Flynn continued to laugh, harder as her face burned with embarrassment. "Don't even try to deny it."

Always a brutally honest person, Elizabeth didn't. "You're right. I was 'checking you out.' But I'm sure you're used to that."

As she approached him, Flynn murmured more quietly to her. "Like what you saw?"

Elizabeth burst out laughing, covering her mouth quickly as the unit was its usual quiet. "You know very well of how pretty you are. You don't need me telling you that." Her voice was a bit more strident than she would have wished.

"Pretty?" he asked with an arched eyebrow.

"Handsome. Attractive. Whatever. You know what you look like. I'm sure women fall at your feet."

"Never the ones I want." It was spoken so seriously, that Elizabeth knew he was no longer joking. "Have you given any thought to my dinner invitation?"

"Actually, no. I gave you my reasons why that's not going to happen yesterday. Nothing has changed."

"That's okay. I have all the time in the world. I have great news. Your mom did very well last night. She's ready to come off the vent."

Delight flashed across Elizabeth's face. "That is good news. When?"

"Should be soon. I've been weaning her off the sedative for the past few hours. She's barely under at this point. Maybe another hour. Why don't you go sit with her while I see a few other patients? I'll be back." Flynn squeezed her shoulder as he passed by her.

Elizabeth turned to watch him go before entering her mother's room. Nothing. She felt absolutely nothing when he touched her. Flynn was hot. And wickedly funny. Not to mention brilliant. So why didn't she feel something? Why didn't she feel the spark she had felt at Sam's touch last night? Just another of life's great mysteries she mused.

She glanced at the monitors, pleased with their readings, before taking a seat next to her mother's bed. Carefully taking her hand in her own, she raised it to her lips and kissed it. "You look so much better, Mom. There's color in your face, and your vital signs are great. I can't wait to talk to you. For now, I'll do the talking." She rambled on about everything that had happened since coming home. Time passed quickly, and Elizabeth was startled to look up and see Flynn once more in the doorway. "How did rounds go?"

"Great, thanks. Both of my other patients are being downgraded and transferred off the unit. Always a good thing."

"Soon that will be my mom as well."

"Absolutely. Let's look, shall we?" Elizabeth watched as Flynn conducted a thorough assessment of her mother. She was impressed with his manner and skill and told him so.

"You're impressed with me but won't have dinner with me. Is that right?"

She laughed at his continued outrageousness. "That's exactly right."

"Hmm. My loss, but I haven't given up. Your mom looks good enough to try extubating. Let's do this. I'll be right back."

Elizabeth took her mother's hand again. "Okay, Mom. This is it. Dr. Reynolds is going to remove the tube from your throat. I need you to breathe."

Diane's eyes fluttered open. Although they were still unfocused and she appeared confused, Elizabeth took this as a good sign. "Hi, Mom. I'm here with you."

"I see my patient is more than ready."

Flynn walked to the bedside and peered into Diane's eyes. "Hi there. I'm Dr. Reynolds. I'm a cardiologist and have been taking care of you for a couple of days. I'm going to take that tube out of your throat now. I need you to not panic as I do. It will be briefly uncomfortable. Try to cough as I'm pulling it out. That will help." Flynn turned to the nurse who had walked in with him. "Please have suction and a mask at twelve liters ready."

When she nodded, Flynn turned back to Diane. He carefully undid the tape that had secured the tube at her mouth. "On the count of three. One, two." At three Flynn gently removed the tube from her throat. Diane coughed weakly, and the nurse stepped in and suctioned saliva from her mouth before placing the mask over her face.

Elizabeth stepped forward and held her mother's hand. Tears gathered in her eyes. She leaned in close. "Welcome back. It's so good to see you breathing on your own." Diane tried to say something, but Elizabeth stopped her. "Don't try to talk yet. Just breathe in and out. I know your throat is sore. Give it a few minutes."

Flynn looked at the monitor. "Her blood pressure is still stable, and more importantly her oxygen level is good. These are all great signs. I'll leave you two alone for a bit. Elizabeth, call me if you need anything."

Elizabeth sat back down and held her mother's hand, watching Diane breathe. Just the smooth rise and fall of her mother's chest warmed Elizabeth's heart. The past two days had been rough, but now the tightness in her own chest was loosening. Hope bloomed with in her, and for the first time since that five AM call, Elizabeth felt at peace.

A while later, Diane tried to say something to her daughter, but her weak voice was muffled further by the oxygen mask. Elizabeth shook her head. " Mom, I'm right here. Save your strength." But her mother was determined. Elizabeth held the mask briefly off her mother's face. "What did you want to say, Mom?"

Diane cleared her throat and tried to speak once again. Her voice was hoarse and weak but audible this time. "I'm so glad. To see you. Elizabeth." Each small burst was followed by a rest and deep breath. Elizabeth felt like her own lungs were burning with effort just watching her mother struggle to speak. She replaced the mask on her mother's face.

"Try to relax now, Mom. You need to conserve your energy. I'm right here, and I'm not going anywhere." Her mother faintly squeezed Elizabeth's hand in response and closed her eyes. Within moments, Elizabeth could tell she had fallen asleep.

"Good, that's what she needs." Came a deep voice from the doorway. Without turning, Elizabeth knew it was Flynn. She nodded her head and dashed away the tears from her eyes.

Flynn came into the room further and pulled Elizabeth from the chair. He made soothing noises as he held her. "It's okay. She's doing so much better, and this is very promising."

Elizabeth shuddered against him as she thought about how close her mother had come to dying. Longing and regret rippled through her. Why had she stayed away so long?

Flynn gathered her more closely in his arms and ran a hand over her short curls. "You've had a rough few days, Elizabeth. Why don't you take a break? You're Mom needs to rest now. Go get some air and come back later."

"Oh, excuse me" came a male voice from the doorway. Elizabeth looked up just in time to see Sam turn away. She stepped away from Flynn and excused herself. Walking out of the unit, she was just in time to see the elevator doors closing. Impatiently she stabbed the button for another one and then decided to take the stairs.

Elizabeth reached the ground floor and sprinted across the lobby. She saw Sam walking through the exit doors and took off after him. By the time she caught up with him at his truck, she was breathing heavily.

"Sam, wait up." She was satisfied to note that he didn't get into his truck. He turned around slowly and looked at her. "Give me a moment." She leaned over, placing her hands on her knees and concentrated on slowing her breathing. "I'm really going to have to start hitting the gym again" she muttered to herself.

Elizabeth straightened and looked at Sam. His face was closed off. "Hey, Sam. What are you doing here?"

"I stopped by to see how Diane is doing. The better question is what were you doing, Elizabeth."

She didn't care for his tone nor his intimation. "What exactly are you asking me, Sam?"

"What's the deal with Dr. Smooth? Is he that friendly with all of his patient's families?"

Elizabeth was taken aback by the coldness of his tone. Sam had never spoken to her like that before. She fired back equally. "Not that it's any of your business, Sam, but Flynn happens to be the man who saved my mom's life the other night. He's also a colleague. Or at least he's about to be, once I officially start next week. What's it to you anyway? If I didn't know better, I'd say you were jealous." She knew of course that wasn't the case, especially after seeing him with Katie.

"Jealous? Is that what you think? I'm only thinking about you. You just got home, and I'd guess you have enough on your plate with flying half way across the country on a moment's notice, not to mention your mom's health. What you don't need is to be fighting off the unwanted advances of some hospital Romeo."

Elizabeth clenched her fists at her side and spoke through clenched jaws. "If you remember, Sam, I've always been perfectly capable of taking care of myself. Even when we were kids. That hasn't changed. Besides, if I did want to get involved with someone right now, I could certainly do worse than Flynn." There was no need to mention the fact that she didn't feel the slightest stirring when Flynn touched her.

Sam's eyes were blazing, but his voice was flat when he responded. "Fine. You seemed a bit unsteady last night, and I was just stopping by to check on you; and your mother. But you don't need anyone anymore, do you Elizabeth? I guess not hearing from you in ten years should have told me. Thanks for the reminder." Sam whirled angrily and got into his truck. He drove away without looking back, leaving Elizabeth wondering how it had all gone so wrong, so fast.

*****

Sam mentally cringed as he drove back to the store, reviewing the confrontation between them. What could he possibly have been thinking? He sounded like a jealous sixteen-year-old. But that was how he felt around her. He had such good intentions when he went to the hospital. But the last thing he expected to see was Elizabeth clinging to that way too confident doctor. Katie had told him about the new Cardiologist in town, but Sam hadn't met him until now.

He stopped through a fast food drive through to grab a late lunch before returning to work. Sam was supposed to be in his office right now, catching up on the always dreaded paperwork. He would have been better off staying there. Instead, he had just managed to make a complete ass of himself. Again.

This wasn't going well at all. He kept pissing her off. Open mouth, insert foot up to mid-thigh. He had to find a way to make it easier between them, like it used to be. The problem with that plan was that it hadn't really been easy between them since they were fifteen. At least not for him.

If they were going to be friends again, he would have to find a way to come to terms with his feelings for her. But that wasn't something he had managed to do when there had been an entire country between them. How was he supposed to do it now, with her back in the same small town? He still loved her, and he knew he always would.

Not for the first time, Sam wondered why he couldn't have met the 'perfect girl' for him, just like Maggie Fitzgerald wanted. It certainly wasn't for lack of trying. But he was fooling himself. He had just left the answer to that standing in the hospital parking lot, looking like she wanted to slug him. He had long ago met the perfect girl for him. She just didn't know it.

Chapter Eight

Elizabeth drummed her fingers nervously on the steering wheel of her mother's car. She was parked across the street from Connor's family home, listening to an old country ballad as she gathered her courage. Her stomach was in knots. The deep breathing exercises she had learned in her residency weren't working. She ended up almost hyperventilating instead.

All she needed to do was get out of the car and walk up to the door; something she had done a thousand times before and never with any anxiety. But this time was different. She hadn't seen Maggie, Connor's mother, since leaving town. What if she was angry? Even worse, what if she was disappointed?

Elizabeth placed her fingers on the door's handle, feeling the cool metal. Just open the door she told herself. With a final deep breath, she did so. Now all she had to do was walk across the street.

She put one foot in front of the other until she reached their driveway. A large black pickup with *Fitzgerald Construction* stenciled on the side came up the street and screeched to a halt next to her. Elizabeth yelped and jumped back in surprise. Without even bothering to turn off the engine, the driver jumped out, ran towards her and scooped up a startled Elizabeth in an exuberant but oddly gentle bear hug.

"Good God girl, it sure took you long enough to come to your senses." Donovan, the oldest of the Fitzgerald siblings grinned down at her from his considerable height. While his dark hair now held more than a touch of gray at the temples, he still sported a lean, hard body that he hadn't gotten in a gym.

A sigh of pure pleasure escaped her at his familiar face. The fact that her exile had been self-imposed did not make it any easier to bear. "Well if I had known I would receive this type of welcome, I might not have stayed away so long", she said somewhat jokingly to Donovan. She hugged the big man fiercely, whispering into his chest. "I know it was selfish on my part, but I didn't know how to do it any other way."

Donovan hugged her tighter. "Nobody can fault you Elizabeth. And it can't have been easy, being so far away from everyone plus the tremendous demands of medical school. We really did miss you though. Losing Connor and the baby was awful, but then…"

Hot tears threaten to overflow. She backed out of his embrace and placed her hand on his arm. "I know. I know that I made everything harder for y'all. But, at the time, I just couldn't see any other way. After a while, the wounds slowly began to heal, and I could think about home, and all of you, without breaking down. But by then, so much time had passed, and I wasn't sure if you would forgive me. Maybe it was cowardly, but I thought I would be doing everyone, including myself, a favor by staying away."

Donovan reached down and squeezed his former sister-in-law's shoulder. "Whatever the reasons or the amount of time that's passed, you are always welcome here. This is your home. You were already part of the family, Elizabeth, long before you married Connor. It's so good to have you back!" Donovan hugged her roughly again, his eyes suspiciously bright.

Elizabeth hugged him back as hard as she could, but her arms barely met around him. Striving for a lighter note, she smiled up at him. "So, do I need notes to keep up with all the changes around here?"

Donovan laughed and said, "I think you'll be fine. We haven't changed all that much in ten years. Just older and hopefully a little wiser."

"Well, I've already seen Katie at the hospital." Her grim expression told the story.

Donovan nodded, his mouth tight. "I can imagine. Katie always was a tough nut to crack. Probably comes from having all those older brothers."

At least I know you're still married to Nora. How long has it been now?"

Donovan's expression softened at the mention of his wife. A huge smile split his face, and love shown in his eyes. "Believe it or not, it'll be 20 years this summer. Can you believe she still puts up with me? And wait until you see the kids. They've grown so much. Kieran is 18 and will be starting college in the fall. Colleen is 16, going on 30, and her main job in life is giving her father gray hair." Ruefully he pointed to his temples. "You see what I mean. And of course, you never met Liam."

Elizabeth's eyes dimmed at that. Donovan and Nora had tried for years for a third child. She and Nora had been pregnant at the same time, due only months apart. Meeting Liam would be a challenge for her, not matter how she was happy for them.

Donovan took her hand in his. "I'm so sorry, Elizabeth. I know that's tough for you."

She shook her head. "It's all good, Donovan. It's been a long time, and I'm just sorry I haven't met Liam before now." She smiled in reassurance, but it never quite reached her eyes.

"Enough of memory lane" replied Donovan gruffly. "You need to go see Mom. She's been so excited once she heard you were back in town. How is your mother by the way?"

"She's doing much better, thanks. I was with her earlier when they took her off the ventilator. She's resting now. I should have stopped by sooner. I've missed you all so much." She stopped and looked at the front door. "But now that I'm here, going in seems overwhelming."

Donovan nodded in understanding. "I'm sure it's not easy being back, Elizabeth. But you just have to do it." He gently pushed towards the door. "Now's a good a time as any."

But before she could even reach for the door, it was flung open. Maggie Fitzgerald stood there wiping her hands on an apron. Donovan's mother, and her former mother-in-law, was a diminutive woman in a family of giants. While her sons had all passed six feet and her youngest daughter was five feet ten, she was a mere five feet tall in her bare feet. Only Katie shared her mother's small build. But what she lacked in stature, Maggie made up for in personality and strength of character. She was known for her ability to stop squabbles between her children with a mere glance.

Without saying a word, Maggie stepped over the threshold and opened her arms as widely as she could. Elizabeth rushed into them gratefully and buried her face in the older woman's shoulder. Tears now flowed freely from both women's' eyes.

"There, there" Maggie whispered soothingly. She gently untangled herself from Elizabeth's embrace and backed up a few paces. "Let me get a good look at you darling. All grown up and an important doctor. I always knew you would live up to your potential. It sure does my heart good to have you home again. Come in to the kitchen and let make you a cup of tea."

Elizabeth rewarded her with a watery smile as Donovan quietly left the porch. A cup of tea had always been the older woman's cure for everything; from a scraped knee to a broken heart. Entering the kitchen, Elizabeth paused to take it all in. The past came rushing to meet her. She glanced around the room before settling into a chair at the table.

The Fitzgerald home was rather large and sprawling. Rooms had been added onto the original house as more children blessed their family. But the kitchen remained the heart of this home. The room was large and open with several windows and a sliding door for natural lighting. The walls were painted a soft, sunny yellow and stenciled with flowers of every color. On the windowsills sat pots of various colors and size all bearing herbs that Maggie used in her cooking. Even now, something savory bubbled in a large cooper pot on the stove. Elizabeth inhaled deeply, enjoying the delicious scent.

The table was made of sturdy oak and bore the scars of many years and many small hands. Each told of a memory that could make you smile. Maggie bustled around the kitchen, making tea and putting out homemade muffins.

"You can't know what this room has meant to me." Elizabeth whispered as she tried to get past the gigantic lump in her throat. "I've thought of it so often. When I was getting through those horrible shifts in my residency, I would dream of sitting at this table." She absently traced her fingers along the scarred surface. "How many times did I do my homework here? How many meals and after school snacks did I eat here? How many hours must I have spent sitting here, with all of you, as though I were a part of the family?" She stopped then, unable to utter a single word.

"But that's exactly what you are dear, a part of this family; long before you married our Connor." Maggie reached across the table and gently patted her hand. "You officially became my daughter when you married my son. Nothing will ever change that."

Elizabeth gave her a watery but grateful smile. "You have no idea what that means to me, Maggie. Coming back has been so difficult. At least Mom's doing better. The rest of it, I'll have to deal with in time."

"Has my Katie given you a hard time? She mentioned seeing you at the hospital. I told her I won't have it." Maggie's normally serene expression grew stormy. "That one might just be the death of me yet. Hasn't had an easy day since she was born."

"No, she was fine." At Maggie's raised eyebrows she continued. "Well, there's definitely tension between us. And that's my doing, not hers. I haven't had a chance to speak with her away from the ICU." Truthfully, she was dreading it, but she wouldn't tell Maggie that.

"Tension, huh? I imagine it was worse than that. But you're right to handle it in your own way. I won't interfere."

"Actually, I've had a harder time with Sam." Her blue eyes darkened to navy at the mention of him. She really had no idea why he was acting the way he had. Or what she was going to do about it.

"From the look in your eyes, there's a story there. Tell me, Elizabeth. What's wrong?"

"I'm not really sure, Maggie. He's just. It's just. Different. I know that doesn't make any sense. Things between us are weird." She didn't mention the strange dream or the reaction she had felt at his touch last night. These things were so jumbled in her own head that she couldn't think of trying to talk about them with Maggie.

"Sam was always the hardest of you three to understand. Kept things to himself a lot, that one. The three of you were so close back then. Thick as thieves. You couldn't see one without the other two not far behind. 'The Three Musketeers' I always called you."

"I remember" Elizabeth said, nostalgia flitting across her face. "I've never had that kind of closeness since."

"I don't mean to hurt you, Elizabeth, when I say this. But Sam changed after you left. First, he lost Connor and then you. He was sad and withdrawn from everyone. Saving his father's business became his focus. An obsession really."

"I saw the new store last night. Sam certainly did a terrific job. It's beautiful, from the parts of it I saw."

"Yes, it is. There's a lot of his blood, sweat, and tears in that place. I think it really saved him after… Well, after everything." She hesitated. "Can I ask you something, Elizabeth?"

She dreaded what that might be but would never deny Maggie anything. With dismay pooling in her stomach, she nodded. "Of course."

"What happened with you two? After Connor died."

Elizabeth picked at an imaginary spot on her shorts. She paused before answering, unsure what to say. "Honestly, Maggie, I'm not sure. Those days were all a blur. Between losing Connor and then our baby…" Her voice cracked on the remembered pain. Elizabeth thought she had dealt with this loss long ago. But being back here, where it had all happened, ripped open old scars.

Taking a moment to compose herself, she drew in a deep breath. "Seeing Sam hurt too much. I know that's an awful thing to say, but it was true. He reminded me of what I had lost. But then, just being in Windsor Falls was too much for me. That's why I left."

Her slender frame shook with sobs. Maggie handed her a tissue and wrapped her arms around Elizabeth. "It's okay, dear. That was understandable. You had lost so much in such a short time. Anyone could understand why you needed to leave." She rubbed the younger woman's back soothingly.

After a few minutes, Elizabeth composed herself. "Coming home has been one big sob fest for me. I'm a wreck." Although she never wore much make-up, Elizabeth did have mascara on. She wiped under her eyes and then laughed at the black smudges on her fingers.

Maggie swiped at the tears on her own face. "So, dear, what's the plan? How long are you home for?"

"I'm not sure, Maggie. It's all up in the air right now. I guess it depends on how my Mom does. Oddly enough, I agreed to take some shifts in the ER while I'm here."

"Really?" Maggie exclaimed, her voice rising with surprise.

"I know, right? I come racing home to see my Mom, and I end up with a part time job." She explained to Maggie the circumstances that had led to her accepting.

"But eventually, you're going back to California, right?"

"Of course, Maggie. That's where I live." Something in her chest felt cold at the thought returning to Los Angeles.

Maggie placed a hand on Elizabeth's arm. "I know that's where you live, honey. But is it home?"

Elizabeth picked up her keys, nervously playing with them. "As long as I've been there, no it's never felt like home. But I'm happy there. My work is very satisfying." Even to her own ears that sounded flat. "I have to get back to the hospital. I just wanted to come by to see you."

Maggie got up and walked her out to her car. She hugged Elizabeth heartily. "Even if it's just temporarily, I'm so glad to have you back dear."

"Even though the circumstances aren't great, I'm so pleased to be here."

"Oh, I almost forgot! We're having a big party for Donovan's and Nora's twentieth anniversary next Saturday night. You'll come of course. If you're still here."

"I would love to come. I'll put it on my calendar." Elizabeth leaned in and kissed Maggie before walking to her car.

Chapter Nine

Diane continued to improve. A sure sign of this was the hard time she gave the hospital staff. Human Resources was almost done with her emergency credentials, and she was scheduled to pick up a shift on Monday. Elizabeth wandered around the ED, getting the lay of the land. She wanted to familiarize herself with everything prior to starting. The early morning staff meeting that she had just attended gave her the opportunity to meet some of her new co-workers. Everyone had been very welcoming, the other doctors especially. They were looking forward to a little relief in their schedule.

Since she had come in early for the meeting, scheduled between night and day shift to catch the most staff, Elizabeth had skipped breakfast. The growling of her stomach reminded her. As she entered the cafeteria, she saw Flynn huddled over his breakfast, alone at a corner table. After purchasing her meal, she approached him.

"Mind if I join you?"

Flynn lifted his head to reveal blood shot eyes. But his face brightened when he saw her. He waved to a chair. "Of course, Elizabeth. You don't need to ask."

She set her tray down. "Well, you were off in the corner by yourself, so I wasn't sure if you wanted company."

A wide smile revealed perfect, white teeth. "Company no. You absolutely. Have you missed me?"

Elizabeth made a face at him. "I see your ego hasn't shrunk. As I just saw you yesterday, no, I haven't 'missed you'."

"You wound me, Elizabeth." Flynn placed his hand dramatically over his heart.

"No, Flynn, I didn't. And not to burst your bubble, but you look like crap."

"Ouch!"

"Let me guess. Another all-nighter in the ICU."

"Yes, and not a pretty one either." At her alarmed expression, Flynn held up his hand. "Your Mom's fine. I have a new patient who tried to die on me last night. Several times. I just came down to get some sustenance before taking a nap in the on-call room. Sebastian is covering morning rounds for me. At least I can catch a few hours and shower before seeing patients this afternoon."

"That's one of the reasons I like emergency medicine so much. I do my part then ship them on to you. No calls in the middle of the night."

"I know. What was I thinking? But I love cardiology, even if the hours are brutal."

"It's good that you love what you do. I feel the same way." Elizabeth stopped talking as she watched Flynn's head tilt to the side. "Okay, what's up?"

"I'm just wondering why there's a guy staring a hole through you. He's sitting over there with Katie Fitzgerald." He motioned with his fork. "Now, I know why Katie's giving me a death glare. That's the norm for us, but the guy looks like he just might want to punch me."

Elizabeth knew it was Sam without looking, but she turned her head anyway. Her heart sped up when she spotted Sam sitting with Katie at a table for two. And although Flynn had a flair for the dramatic, he wasn't wrong this time. Sam was indeed staring at them. Or her. His lips were flattened. Probably not a good sign. Katie's bright green eyes were practically spitting fire. An even worse one.

She turned back to Flynn. "That's Sam Bishop. He was my best friend growing up."

"He doesn't look very friendly at the moment."

"I could say the same for Katie. Exactly what did you do to piss her off?"

"Probably just the fact that I'm breathing." He laughed at Elizabeth's raised eyebrows. "That's a long story for another day. I'm exhausted. I'm going to go catch some winks. Shall I walk you up to the floor?" Flynn didn't wait for her response before gathering up their empty dishes and taking them to the window.

"Wow, such nice manners." Elizabeth got up and walked with Flynn to the exit. Naturally, they had to pass by the table with Sam and Katie.

"I was raised right, Lizzie. You'd know that if you ever agreed to that dinner." His reply happened to occur as they reached the table where Katie and Sam sat. Elizabeth's smile grew falsely bright.

Sam stood as Elizabeth reached his chair. He might be smiling, but she knew him well. His rigid posture gave him away.

"I'm Dr. Flynn Reynolds. I don't think we've been properly introduced." Flynn extended his hand towards Sam.

Sam hesitated a moment, staring at Flynn's hand as though it was a serpent, before shaking it. "I'm Sam Bishop, Elizabeth's oldest friend." The words were uttered cordially enough, but the fierce smile gave him away.

Flynn tilted his head. "That's funny. Lizzy never mentioned you before, Sam." Flynn grinned cockily at Sam. "Well, no matter. We won't keep you any longer. Nice meeting you. See you later Nurse Fitzgerald." He turned and walked towards the exit, pulling Elizabeth with him. She didn't say a word to him until they reached the bank of elevators.

Flynn raised one eyebrow. Amusement danced across his face. "Tell me again how you two are 'just old friends'.

"Not that it's any of your business, but he is exactly who he said he is 'Sam Bishop, oldest friend'." Elizabeth frowned deeply. "At least he used to be. We didn't keep in touch when I left." That was certainly an understatement, but she kept the details to herself.

"Friend? Are you sure about that? It seemed like a bit more to me, at least in his mind. Sam looked at you like a starving man looks at a steak. You may think he's just your friend, but I wouldn't bet anything you're afraid to lose. If I were given to jealousy, I might be worried about him." He grinned broadly at her and winked saucily. "Luckily for you, I'm not." The elevator doors opened, and they got in. for once, they had the car to themselves. Flynn reached around Elizabeth and pushed the button for six.

"No, I guess not. You're far too arrogant to be jealous. But you're wrong about Sam. He and I grew up together. Actually, the three of us grew up together. He was the best man at our wedding. Nothing more. Nothing less. It's true that things have been a bit odd since my return, but that's to be expected. We didn't actually part on the best of terms." Her expressive eyes were suddenly shadowed.

Elizabeth paused and took a deep breath. Blowing it out swiftly, she looked directly at Flynn. "There's more to the story, Flynn. My husband, Connor, was killed in a car accident just before our first anniversary. A drunk driver hit them when they were on their way home with pizza."

"Them?"

She shook her head. "Yes, them. Sam was driving that day. The other car hit his Jeep on the passenger side. Connor was killed instantly." She said the words calmly yet her heart clenched at the memory. After all these years, the memory of that terrible day still haunted her. "Sam fared better with some lacerations and a concussion."

They reached their floor, and Flynn looked at her with concern. Guiding her with a hand in the small of her back, he pulled her into a small on call room, shutting the door for privacy. Taking her icy hands in his, Flynn gently rubbed them. "That's terrible, Elizabeth. I'm so very sorry. But I feel like there's something more to the story."

She raised her stricken eyes to him. Her voice was now barely a whisper. "There is, Flynn. I was pregnant at the time. Just over 12 weeks with our first child. We had just decided to start telling our families. In fact, we had just told Sam right before the accident. Asked him to be the godfather. Connor and I were planning to tell everyone else at a family picnic the next day." Her voice broke altogether on a sob that erupted from her throat. "After the funeral, I started to bleed heavily. Before I knew it, I had lost everything."

Flynn gathered a sobbing Elizabeth into his arms. She felt a tearing in her chest as if her heart was breaking all over again. Her whole body trembled, the weight of her grief almost too much to bare. Flynn led her to the bed and sat beside her, holding her as the sobs racked her body. He didn't say a word, but silently rubbed her back.

After what seemed an eternity, Elizabeth sniffed in the last of her tears. Embarrassed that she had cried all over Flynn, she couldn't make herself meet his eyes. "I don't know what's wrong with me" she mumbled into his chest. "It's been years since I've cried for them."

Flynn placed a finger under her chin and raised her face to his. "You have nothing to be ashamed of Elizabeth. What happened to you was a terrible tragedy. And I'm sure being home for the first time in a decade has brought all the feelings to the surface."

She stared into his blue eyes. She had been surprised at the depth of his compassion. Without giving herself a chance to back out, Elizabeth leaned in, closing the small distance between them, and placed her lips on his. She felt him stiffen, probably in surprise, before he kissed her back. She wrapped her arms around him and ran her fingers into his hair, trying to feel something other than the pain of grief.

After a moment, Flynn stopped and pulled away from her. Her arms dropped to her sides as a dull flush crept across her face. "Nothing, huh?"

Flynn sighed heavily. "Not a thing. Oh Elizabeth, if only it could be that easy."

"Should I apologize?"

His face lit up in a wolfish grin. "Never! A beautiful woman just tried to take advantage of me in an on-call room. We're practically an episode of *Grey's Anatomy*."

A huge bubble of laughter escaped her. She doubled over, clutching her sides and fighting for air. When she finally stopped, Elizabeth walked over to the sink and splashed cold water on her overheated face. Grabbing a paper towel, she turned to Flynn. "You're good for me, Flynn. I could use a friend right now. Coming back here has been so much harder than I ever thought."

He stood and bowed deeply, winking at her rakishly. "I'm happy to be of service, madam. For whatever you might need."

"I think we just proved we are completely lacking in chemistry, so you can cut the act." She cocked her head and eyed him speculatively. "What are you doing next Saturday?"

"Well", he drawled seductively, "if you're asking me out, then I'm free."

"I guess I am, in a manner of speaking. Donovan is Connor's oldest brother. He and his wife Nora are celebrating their 20th wedding anniversary. Connor's mom invited me if I'm still here, and it looks like I will be. I can't wait to see everyone again, but I would feel better if I didn't have to go alone. Will you be my plus one, Flynn?"

"I'd be honored. Besides, Katie will be there, and nothing gives me more pleasure than torturing her." His grin was pure devil.

"Oh, no you don't. Don't make me regret asking. You can only come if you promise to behave. After all, they're family to me. I can't have you making a scene."

Flynn sighed dramatically. "Oh, all right, if you insist. You're no fun."

"I'm okay with that, Flynn." Elizabeth gathered her purse from the bed. "Now, I really am going to see my mother. And you're going to take that nap you so desperately need." Flynn yawned hugely as if to underscore her point. "Thank you so much for listening, Flynn. You'll never know how much that meant to me."

"I'm glad I could be here for you. You don't have to do this alone, you know. You can always call me when things get tough."

"Good to know. I may just take you up on that. Enjoy your nap." She kissed his cheek and left the room.

*****

Sam picked up his now cold coffee and took a sip, curling his lip. He put the mug back on the table. "Lizzy?" Sam muttered aloud. No one had ever called Elizabeth that. Not him. Not Connor. Not anyone. Just who did this Flynn think he was? He'd known her less than a week, and he already had a nickname for her? The thought of the overly confident doctor coming on to his Elizabeth made him want to plant his fist right in Flynn's face.

"For someone who describes himself as Elizabeth's 'oldest friend', you seem pretty upset at Flynn's possessiveness towards her." Katie picked up her coffee mug and studied Sam over the rim. "Not sure green is your best color, Sam." Amusement and a less easily defined emotion flitted across her face.

"He's just her mother's doctor. And anyway, I thought we were here to talk about the anniversary party. Although I have no idea why. You know your mom has that planned to the tiniest detail."

Katie smirked at Sam. "Are you really that naïve, Sam? Of course, we aren't actually planning the party. We've been 'Maggied'. This is just another of my mother's infamous yet misguided attempts at matchmaking. She thinks we'd be perfect for each other."

The look of disbelief on Sam's face was priceless. "Are you kidding me, Katie? Us? Why?' Immediately horror replaced the disbelief and he smiled sheepishly. "What I meant to say is that you and I are friends. Nothing more. Nothing less."

"Don't sweat it, Sam. I know what you mean. I grew up with you. Kissing you would be like kissing one of my many brothers. Yuck."

Sam was not pleased with that analogy. He had grown up with Elizabeth, and he certainly didn't think of her as a sister. And he definitely wanted to kiss her. In fact, that was the least of what he wanted to do.

Katie snapped her fingers in front of Sam's face. "Hey. Where'd you go?"

Her knowing smile told Sam that she knew exactly where he had gone. But he wasn't going to admit it. "Oh nowhere in particular. Just 'wool gathering' as my Mom used to say.

"Well, thanks for breakfast. I'm exhausted, and I'm back in at seven. See you Sam."

Sam watched as Katie strode away, her curvy hips swaying under her forest green scrub pants. She really was a beautiful woman, he thought. Why couldn't he have fallen for her? The Fitzgerald family had been like his own for years. This would have been so convenient. But there was nothing convenient about love.

*****

Elizabeth found her mother in the midst of being transferred out of ICU. She almost laughed at the scene Diane was making. Diane thought she could walk to her new room. Elizabeth stepped in before it could get out of control.

"Now, Mom, you know there are rules about these things. You have to let them take you in a wheelchair." An obviously flustered tech gave Elizabeth a grateful smile.

"These people have rules about everything! Why take their side, Elizabeth?" She turned to the nurse who was busy switching her patient to a portable cardiac monitor. "My daughter's a doctor you know. In California." The harried nurse nodded in agreement on her way out of the room.

Elizabeth watched the younger woman make her escape and bit back a laugh." Mom no one cares that I'm a doctor."

"Well, I do. I tell everyone who will listen. And even the ones who won't." Diane laughed at her own joke, causing a coughing spell.

Elizabeth grabbed a handful of tissues and helped her mother regain her breath. "The point, Mom, is that you're getting better. Moving to a telemetry floor is a good sign. You're too healthy to tie up an ICU bed anymore."

"Well if I'm that healthy, then that cutie pie cardiologist can just send me home." Her eyes were lit with merriment and more than a little trouble, causing Elizabeth to sigh inwardly.

"I'm assuming you're referring to Dr. Reynolds?"

"Who else? Although his partner isn't bad either."

Elizabeth rubbed at the knots in the back of her neck. With more patience than she felt, she addressed her mother. "You can't go around calling a cardiologist 'cutie pie'. It's not professional."

"Well, of course not Elizabeth. I call him 'Dr. Cutie Pie'."

Elizabeth was saved from answering when a young man in black scrubs entered the room. "Hi. I'm Brent, and I'm from patient transport. Ready for your new room Mrs. Abbott?"

"More than ready." She turned to her exasperated daughter. "If I had known he was going to be this cute, I wouldn't have protested."

Elizabeth shook her head as Brent helped her mother transfer from the bed to the wheelchair. She gathered up her mother's belongings and followed along, listening in horror as her mother proceeded to tell Brent all about her daughter the doctor. Single doctor at that. The fact that Brent was at least ten years younger than Elizabeth didn't seem to slow her mother down one bit.

Once her mother was settled in her new room, Elizabeth stepped out to let the new nurse complete her assessment. Frankly, she needed a break. Her mother could be exhausting. About five years ago, Diane had decided that Elizabeth was ready to start dating again. Every time Elizabeth mentioned someone in her life in California, her mother asked if they were single. There was no telling her mother that Elizabeth was more than capable of finding a date. If she wanted one.

When Elizabeth reentered the room, Diane was sitting up in bed. Her face was very pale, almost devoid of color. She pulled over a chair and sat holding Diane's hand.

Diane gave her hand a squeeze before she leaned her head back against the pillows and closed her eyes. Her voice held none of its usual cheerfulness when she spoke. "That took more out of me than I imagined. I'm just going to close my eyes for a few moments, dear." She was asleep immediately.

Elizabeth's phone buzzed with a text from her boss in California looking for an update. She walked out into the hallway to deal with that as her mother rested.

Chapter Ten

Entering the final note in her patient's electronic chart, Elizabeth leaned back in her chair. Stretching lazily, she rubbed the tight muscles in the back of her neck absently. She could finally leave the busy ER. Her first day had been a busy shift, and Elizabeth was more than ready to go. She had already given report on her remaining patients to the oncoming doctor. With a last wave towards him, she headed for the stairs. She would check in with her mom before going home.

As she walked up several flights of stairs to the telemetry unit, she realized how good it felt to be back at work. Elizabeth loved being an emergency physician. Even though the years of training had been brutal, she was pleased that she had persevered. Being able to step into a person's life, when they most needed her, gave her purpose. Most times, she could make the situation better for her patients. But even when she couldn't, when the odds were against them, she knew that at least she had given them the best chance they had.

And when the worst happened, Elizabeth spoke to the family with quiet dignity and respect. Every time she had to tell someone that their family member had died, Elizabeth was reminded of that day long ago when she had been on the receiving end. The gently compassion of that physician had inspired her.

Shaking off the memory, Elizabeth exited the stairwell on the fourth floor and walked to her mother's room. Diane continued to improve daily, and Flynn was talking about discharging her to a rehabilitation center in the next few days.

Her mother's room was darkened, and Diane was asleep in her bed. Elizabeth entered quietly and sat in the chair at her bedside. She rested her head on the bedrail, exhaustion evident in her posture. Although she worked twelve hour shifts in Los Angeles, Eric Chamberlain had insisted on a shorter one today. Elizabeth had protested at the special treatment, but he had been right. Today's eight-hour shift had kicked her butt. She spent the first few hours learning the rhythm of the place and its employees as she saw a seemingly endless line of patients.

Elizabeth closed her eyes and drifted for a bit. She thought about Sam. She hadn't seen him since that morning in the hospital cafeteria. She needed to clear the air between them. The thought of conflict with him, something that had never happened in their past, caused her chest to tighten. Elizabeth desperately wanted to get back to where they had been ten years ago. She just wasn't sure it was possible.

Her mother shifted in the bed but didn't awaken. Hopefully she would sleep through the night. Elizabeth took this as a sign to go home and get some rest herself. She leaned in and brushed a kiss on her mother's cheek.

Still looking over her shoulder as she left the room, she never saw Flynn Reynolds standing in the open doorway and walked straight into him. Only his quick thinking kept her from falling. "Oh, I'm so sorry, Flynn. I didn't see you there. I really should be more careful. Are you OK?"

Flynn smiled broadly down at her. "I don't think you weigh enough to do any damage. How's your Mom?"

"You tell me, Flynn." Elizabeth smiled broadly up at him. "After all, you're the 'brilliant cardiologist who saved her life'. At least that's how she describes you. Of course, I should probably stop saying that. If you're not careful, your head won't fit through the doors soon."

"I'm pleased with both her condition and the compliment. At least up until your remark about the size of my head."

"Dr. Reynolds, your head is perfectly proportioned, as you know."

"Now I know you're mad at me if you're back to calling me Dr. Reynolds. Let me make it up to you. Come on, I'll buy you a hamburger at Bob's. I know what the ER was like today, so I imagine you haven't eaten."

Glancing at the clock on the wall, Elizabeth realized it was way past dinner time. "OK, Flynn, you're on. But it's only because the last thing I had to eat today was a diet soda and vending machine crackers. And that was a long time ago."

"Such faint praise. I may swoon…" he mocked jokingly. "Well even if you're only agreeing to avoid low blood sugar, I'll take whatever meager scraps of affection you're willing to toss my way. Just give me another ten minutes to finish up my charting, and I'll be ready to roll."

Elizabeth turned towards the employee rest room to freshen up but found herself face to face with Katie. She was surprised to see her former friend on a different nursing unit and said so.

"They're short staffed tonight, so I agreed to come in." The coldness of her tone told Elizabeth everything she needed to hear. Even so, it would have been very hard to miss the angry expression on the other woman's features. Elizabeth had never been so actively disliked.

"What exactly is your problem, Katie? I get that you're still angry with me, but this has got to stop. You've been nothing but rude and hateful towards me since I came back. We used to be friends." Elizabeth heard the strident note in her voice, but she didn't care. Enough was enough.

"You can actually remember back that far, Elizabeth? That comes as a shock! Well, that was then and this is now. Things change as they say." She stood there with her hands on her hips. Her face was flushed an incensed red.

"Fine! If that's how you want to play this, then so be it. But you will not continue to treat me in such an unprofessional manner. When we are at work, you will treat me with respect. Is that understood?"

Not waiting for an answer, she turned on her heel and stormed off the unit. A shudder ran through her as she remembered Katie's hurtful words. Elizabeth was very disappointed in the way things were going between them. She and Katie had been such good friends and even family at one time. Now the other woman couldn't stand to be in the same room with her.

Elizabeth inhaled deeply. Katie was just more collateral damage. Glancing up, she caught Flynn looking at her speculatively. He raised one eyebrow in a silent question.

"Sorry about that. Katie and I apparently have a personal issue to settle. The tricky part is that I don't even know where to start." She blew out a deep sigh. "It's a shame really, because we used to be such good friends."

"I agree that she's been very difficult to work with recently, always snapping at me." Flynn paused and put a supportive hand on her shoulder. "If you want, I can have a word with the nursing director."

Horror flashed across Elizabeth's face. "No. Please don't. That will only make things worse. Katie is, as you probably already know, very proud and very head strong. She and I go back a long way. We went through nursing school together. We'll work it out in our own way."

Flynn nodded his head in agreement. "OK, but only if you're sure."

"I'm sure. Now let's go get that hamburger you promised me." She placed her arm through his and walked to the stairway door. Sam was standing in front exiting it.

"Good evening, Elizabeth." She started and jumped away from Flynn, guiltily snatching her arm back. Though she wasn't sure why. Why should she care what Sam thought about her relationship with Flynn? Sam's eyes were dark and unfathomable. It was ridiculous really. Just thinking about this was giving her a headache.

"What are you doing here at this hour, Sam? Is everything OK?" Much to her chagrin and bewilderment, her heart went into overtime.

"Everything's great. I was stopping by to see Katie for a few minutes. It seems like all she does these days is sleep or work. I can't seem to ever catch her, so I thought I'd try her here." He held up a fast food restaurant bag. "I brought food as well. She never remembers to eat when she's working. I'm sure Maggie's told you about the big Fitzgerald bash coming up to celebrate Donovan's and Nora's

20th anniversary. Katie and I are helping Maggie to plan it. Which is code for Katie and I are doing what Maggie tells us to do." His grin softened his words.

Flynn turned to Elizabeth and grinned. "Is that the party you were telling me about, Lizzie? The one I'm accompanying you to?" His tone was pure innocence, but Elizabeth knew the devil was behind it. She would have kicked him in the shin if she could get away with it.

She nodded in agreement. "I thought that it would be good for Flynn to go and met some people from town. He's only recently moved here from Atlanta."

"Oh. How's your mom feeling?" asked Sam in a soft voice.

""She's doing much better, thanks. They moved her to this floor. I just stopped in after my shift, but she's sleeping. I'll come back tomorrow."

"Your shift?" Sam's eyes wandered up and down her frame causing Elizabeth to squirm. "That would explain the wardrobe choice."

Elizabeth tucked her hair behind her ears. "I guess I didn't have a chance to tell you the other night, Sam. The ED director asked me to consider picking up some shifts while I'm here. They're having a bit of a staffing crunch."

"What about California?"

"I've taken a leave. I can't go back until my mom is settled here."

His stare was unfathomable. "How long of a leave? Are you considering coming home for good, Elizabeth?" A note of hurt had crept into his tone.

Her breath caught in her throat as Elizabeth considered how to answer that. A few weeks ago, she wouldn't have hesitated. Now? She had no idea.

Before she could answer, Flynn stepped closer and put his arm around a puzzled Elizabeth. "Hate to be rude, but we're off to Bob's to get a late dinner. We'd invite you to come along, but you're obviously busy. Nice seeing you again, Sam." Flynn ushered Elizabeth through the stairwell door.

"Goodnight, Sam" Elizabeth yelled over her shoulder as the heavy door closed. She glared at Flynn as they descended the stairs.

*****

Sam stood there watching the door close behind Elizabeth. And Flynn. His fingers tightened on the bag of rapidly cooling fast food. Remembering why he had come, he headed around the corner to the nurse's station.

Katie was in a conversation with another nurse but looked up as he approached. She excused herself and headed in his direction. Sam raised the bag of food. "I brought you dinner."

Her lips curled in a smirk. "The first time you bring me dinner in months just happens to be the same night I pick up a shift on Diane Abbott's unit? Coincidence?" Her laughter rang through the hallway. "I think not."

"And who exactly texted me that info and their food request?"

"True. That was me. But you chose to come." Katie stared at him for a moment. "What? No rebuttal?"

Sam held up his hands in defeat. "What could I possibly say, Katie. I'm an idiot. I came here hoping to catch a glimpse of her. Pathetic I know. And I see her with that man's hands on her."

The petite redhead was suddenly paying very close attention. Katie's mouth curled in a frown. "Let me guess. *That man* wouldn't happen to be a cardiologist we both know, would it?"

Sam merely nodded his head. "And thanks for not giving me a head's up that Elizabeth is working here." His heart had leapt at the sight of her in navy scrubs and a lab coat. For one brief, glorious second, he allowed himself to believe she was moving home. For good. He really was a fool.

"Oh that. I actually just found out this evening when I came in to work."

"You still could have warned me." The rise in his normally deep voice gave away his surprise.

Katie tilted her head. Her voice softened. "It's only temporary, Sam. She's going to leave when her mom gets better. Her life is in Los Angeles, not Windsor Falls."

Suddenly the peace was disturbed by an overhead voice calling for the rapid response team. Katie thrust the bag back at Sam. "That's me. I gotta go. Go ahead and eat in the lounge. I'll be back when I can." She was already sprinting for the stairway door when she yelled the last part to Sam.

He moved out of the way as several staff flew past him. When it was clear, Sam went into the staff lounge. He microwaved his now soggy tacos before sitting at the table. His appetite was gone, but Sam ate anyway. It had been a long time since lunch. He took a few bites before his acid soaked stomach protested. The image of Elizabeth with her arm linked through Flynn's was not conducive to digestion. He balled up his dinner and tossed it into the trash with disgust.

Before she had noticed him there, she had been smiling at Flynn. Her real smile. The one that had been doing funny things to him since high school. Maybe he was a dreamer, but he wanted her to smile at *him* like that.

Sam had already spent his entire adult life wanting her. He had lost her once to another man because of his inability to express his feelings for her. The fact that the other man had been Connor was the only thing that made it bearable. But Flynn Reynolds was another thing altogether. He might have his eye on Elizabeth, but he was going to have to get through Sam first. While he had no idea how to approach her and overcome their past, he wasn't going to give Reynolds a clear playing field. He sent a brief text to Katie explaining that he had left.

As he walked down the stairs and out into the warm night, Sam felt lighter than he had in a long time. She might return to California. She might not share his feelings. But Sam wasn't going to be on the sidelines in his own life for one more moment.

Chapter Eleven

Elizabeth got into her mother's car and drove home. She tuned the radio to a local country station and rolled down the windows. The evening had cooled while she had dinner with Flynn. The air blew through her curls, making Elizabeth smile. She'd always loved that sensation; especially after a long, grueling day at work.

Flynn was good for her, Elizabeth decided. He was funny and outrageous. She needed that right now. So what if he did tend to push buttons? Like telling Sam that he was her date for Donovan's and Nora's anniversary party. Overall, he was fun and lighthearted and totally committed to his career; a quality Elizabeth could appreciate.

Elizabeth thought about her first day in the ED at Windsor Falls Regional Medical Center. While it may not have been the inner-city chaos she was used to, she certainly hadn't been bored. She was continually amazed at the growth of the facility. When she had been an OB/GYN nurse ten years ago, Windsor Falls General Hospital had been a small, community facility that served just their town. Now, it was a major, regional facility with a trauma center and the specialty services that used to mean travel to Raleigh or Charlotte.

The fact that this was the only hospital for more than twenty-five miles guaranteed a very busy ED. Just what Elizabeth liked. Variety, both in patients and their chief complaints, had drawn Elizabeth to emergency medicine. She treated the whole lifespan, from the infrequent emergency delivery right up to the oldest of geriatric patients. And everything in between. Starting a shift meant she could be pulling something questionable that a small boy had put up his nose or performing life-saving CPR. She just never knew. But no matter what she did, Elizabeth knew that she was helping someone. And that made her get out of bed every day.

All in all, it was a rewarding but highly demanding career. Elizabeth was acutely aware of the high burn out rate, having already lost colleagues to jobs with less stress in the few years she had been practicing. She didn't want to become a statistic, so Elizabeth took good care of herself, both physically and emotionally.

She rolled her shoulders, stretching the tense muscles there, and flexed her toes within her sneakers. Even an eight-hour shift took its toll. That's why her immediate plans held nothing more complicated than a hot bath, candles, and some Vivaldi playing softly in the background. But as she pulled into the driveway, she noticed a now familiar red pickup parked there. Sam was sitting on the top step of her mother's porch.

Steeling herself for whatever was about to happen, Elizabeth gathered up her white coat and purse and approached him warily. In the dim light, his handsome face was shadowed, but his stiff posture gave him away. This wasn't a social call. She hoped she was wrong. She simply wasn't in the mood for any more of his strange behavior.

"Hello, Sam. Again. Didn't I just see you at the hospital?" Without giving him time to even answer her flippant greeting, she unlocked the front door and went inside, leaving it ajar.

He followed her inside, pushing the front door shut behind him. Elizabeth had flopped down on the couch with her head thrown back and her eyes closed. Exhaustion evident in the lines of her face.

Sitting on the other end of the couch, Sam leaned down and picked up her feet off the floor, placing them in his lap. She had already taken the time to toe off her sneakers. Before she could protest, he removed her socks and began to rub her right foot. "I remember Connor doing this for you after a long shift. I guess being a doctor is just as tough on your feet as being a nurse." He fell silent, continuing to work his magic on her bruised sole.

Elizabeth uttered a sound of utter pleasure. The comfortable silence between them was very familiar. Maybe there was hope for them after all. "I'll only let you do that for a few more hours, Sam" she half joked. She was rewarded with a chuckle in response. He switched to the other foot and began to massage it. His strong, slightly roughened hands were working miracles on her sore feet. Elizabeth leaned further into the couch cushions as fatigue drained from her body.

But after a moment, tension began to fill the spaces between them. Elizabeth was acutely aware of Sam's hands on her skin. What had started as a gesture of comfort had evolved into something more. Something much sexier. A liquid heat spread from where he touched her and pooled low in her belly.

Elizabeth gazed at Sam from under mostly closed lids. She had never felt this attraction to him before. It was humming nicely along her nerve endings and yet odd and discomforting at the same time. This was not the Sam of her childhood. She wanted this Sam to never stop touching her. Maybe even move those magic hands higher.

"I can hear you thinking from over here, Elizabeth. What's going on in that head of yours?" Sam's hands had stopped, but he still held her feet. The muscles of his thighs were tensed under her heels.

Elizabeth pulled her feet off Sam's lap and sat up. She crossed her arms in front of her and avoided eye contact. She couldn't look at Sam. There was so much left unsaid between them. None of which was helped by the electricity that pulsed through her body whenever Sam touched her.

Slowly, as if to not startle her, he reached out and placed his hand along her jaw, turning her to face him again. He tenderly stroked her cheek. "I'm so afraid that you and I won't ever find our way back to what we once meant to each other, Elizabeth." His voice was strained.

Elizabeth nearly winced at the pain she saw in his warm brown eyes. She wanted more than anything to erase that. She reached out and lightly traced her fingers over the face that was so familiar and yet not. "Oh Sam, I've made such a mess of it. You're the last person I ever wanted to hurt." Regret echoed through the silent room.

"Tell me about your life, Elizabeth. Tell me, so that I can know you again."

"I don't know if I can make you understand what I went through when I lost them Sam. It all happened so fast. I went from being a wife who was newly and ecstatically pregnant to a widow to having a miscarriage, all in the span of a few days. I can honestly tell you, Sam, that when I came home from the hospital that second time, I wanted to die too. I thought that I would. If I just lie there, not eating or drinking, my grief would kill me." Sadness flashed through her eyes. "It didn't of course, but for a little while, I wished for that. I couldn't talk to anyone. I was just waiting to join them." She closed her eyes tightly against the memory, but hot tears still streamed out from under her lashes. Sam reached out and gently brushed them away. He took her clenched hands in his, giving her support.

"When that didn't happen, I knew I had to find a way to go on. I had to do something. I was in a terrible place, Sam. A dark place. Everyone wanted to help me, despite their own pain. But I couldn't be reached. I was drowning, but no one could save me. This was something I had to do on my own. I just couldn't stay here, in this place where everything reminded me of Connor. So, I left."

"Where did you go? How did you end up in California?"

She gave him a watery smile. "I just wandered for a while, staying a day here and a day there. I stopped when I reached the ocean. I stayed in Los Angeles because it was everything Windsor Falls wasn't. Large and impersonal. In LA I was just another face. Not a grieving young widow to be pitied and wrapped in cotton."

"That's not what people were trying to do here, Elizabeth. They all just felt lost after Connor died. They wanted to help. I wanted to help."

"I know you did, Sam. Y'all had great intentions and my best interest at heart. But that didn't make it any easier. Or less suffocating. I had been half of 'Connor and Elizabeth' for years. I needed to find who I was. On my own."

Sam had leaned in closer while she was talking. His hand lay next to hers on the couch. Near but not quite touching. She could feel the heat from his body. She inhaled deeply to gain some balance, but all she could smell was the cotton of his shirt and the scent of his skin. It was all male. All Sam.

"Coffee?" Elizabeth darted to her feet, almost stumbling in her haste. She rushed from the room as though the hounds of hell were chasing her. Escaping into the kitchen, she blindly chose a flavor and put it in the Keurig. Not that either of them needed coffee at this late hour, but Elizabeth desperately needed something to do with her hands. She hit brew and stared sightlessly into the darkness beyond the kitchen window.

Her insides were shaking. What was wrong with her? Why was she acting this way? After all, this was Sam. Sam who had always been her friend. Sam who she had known since she was seven.

But Sam was also a man. A very handsome one at that, with broad shoulders that stretched the material of his t-shirt. He had a lean build with long, athletic looking legs. Elizabeth wondered idly if he was still running. She loved his short but thick brown hair and the way a lock of it always seemed to fall over his forehead. It made her want to brush it back. Or just run her fingers all through it.

Ugh. She was truly losing her mind. One minute, she's was pouring out her heart to Sam, and now she's thinking about running her hands through his hair? Really? She needed to get a grip.

She attacked the few, dirty dishes in the sink with more vigor than needed. Anything to keep her head on straight. It was unsettling, to say the least, thinking of Sam in those terms. Elizabeth wondered if he was involved with Katie. It might help to explain Katie's less than pleasant behavior. But it was hard to picture the two of them together. In fact, she had a difficult time picturing Sam with any woman. For so long, it had been the three of them. Although he had dated in high school, and she had mercilessly teased him about his taste in girlfriends, Elizabeth couldn't remember anyone lasting more than a few weeks. He always seemed to lose interest in them quickly.

Lost in thought, she didn't hear Sam enter the kitchen. He slipped behind her and wrapped his arms around her slender waist, pulling her back to rest against him. Elizabeth stiffened at first, in surprise, but then her muscles gradually relaxed as she melted into him. He let out his pent-up breath in a long sigh that ruffled the hair on the top of her head. They stood there for what seemed an eternity, not talking. She was keenly aware of every point where her body touched his. His arm was wrapped around her stomach, just brushing the undersides of her breasts. Her nipples stood on end, aching to be touched. She leaned her head back into the crook of his neck and sighed.

Sam turned her slowly in his arms, as if giving her time to read his intent and to put a stop to this. If she wished. She didn't. Sam lowered his head and gently brushed his lips against hers. They were warm and firm, and she trembled ever so slightly in his arms. She didn't resist so much as remain passive. He turned up the persuasion a notch by kissing her once again, only this time increasing the pressure of his mouth on hers. He nibbled lightly at the edges of her lips, while burying his hands in her curly, dark hair. Almost on their own, they found their way to the sensitive spot at the nape of her neck. His fingers traced soft circles there.

When she opened her mouth to take a breath, Sam traced his tongue along the outline of her lips. Elizabeth moaned then, allowing him deeper access into her mouth. He shamelessly plundered its warm darkness, teasing her tongue with his own. The heat building between them was enough to make her surrender. She pressed her body into his more closely, not wanting any space between them.

Elizabeth groaned deep in her throat and could feel his body harden in response. Sam moved his hands from her hair and slid them down her sides, coming to a rest on her curved bottom. Lifting her ever so slightly, Elizabeth could feel just how much he wanted her as his erection prodded her belly.

She couldn't remember how they had gotten to this point, but she didn't care. She rubbed her sensitive nipples against his chest. Even with their layers of clothing, her nipples were taut. Elizabeth ran her hands under the edge of his cotton t-shirt, desperate to feel the skin there. Her fingers seemed to have a mind of their own, as they grasped the edge to bare more of his flesh.

Sam broke the kiss and released her, stepping back a few paces. Staggering a bit, Elizabeth reached behind her to grab the counter for support. She was having a hard time understanding that Sam was the man who had just kissed her so thoroughly and deliciously. But when she opened her eyes, he was standing there, right in front of her. Living proof. She had been initially surprised, but then pleasure replaced her shock. If he had been rough or demanding, she would have easily resisted. But there had been such a depth of both passion and tenderness in that kiss. She was more than a little disappointed when he ended it so abruptly.

Sam cleared his throat. "I'm not going to apologize for that. I'd be lying if I said I was sorry, Elizabeth. We've meant too much to each other to start lying now."

Elizabeth drew in a shaky breath and answered in kind. "And I would be lying if I said that I didn't enjoy that, Sam. You know that I did." Her nipples, which were still standing at attention, more than gave her away. "But I will say that I'm confused. I'm just getting used to being here with you again, and there's so much still unsaid between us. I don't want to screw this up…"

He stepped forward and enfolded her in his arms. She felt his warm breath tickling her hair. "I know, Elizabeth, I know. That's why I backed off. The last thing I want to do is frighten you away. Maybe my timing was off, but I'm not sorry that I kissed you. Someday soon, we're going to have that conversation. For now, you have enough to deal with. I'll let you get some sleep." He lightly kissed her forehead and walked away.

Elizabeth stood where she was until she heard his truck pull away. She turned to the coffee maker, pulled out the mug, and dumped it in the sink. Sleep was going to be elusive enough. Caffeine was the last thing she needed.

Walking up the stairs, Elizabeth glanced around at the faded paint on the walls. She continued into her bedroom, stripping off her clothes before she walked into the adjoining bathroom. After brushing her teeth and washing her face quickly, Elizabeth pulled an old t-shirt over her head and slipped into bed with just the soft whisking of the ceiling fan for company. She had no idea what had just happened, but she knew one thing for sure. Her image of Sam was changed forever. In all the years she had known him, she never really thought of Sam as a man; a sexy man at that. But as she lay there in the dark, with sleep a million miles away, she thought about it. A lot.

Sam had been a part of her life the entire time she lived in Windsor Falls. But from that very first kiss with Connor, there hadn't been any room in her life for another man. While first loves sometimes burn out quickly, theirs had not. Theirs had only been snuffed out by a cruel twist of fate.

She had been honest when she told Sam that she had thought about him often through the years. But her thoughts of him were often troubled ones. She had missed him terribly. After losing Connor, she had needed Sam even more than she normally did. But it had simply been too painful, and so she had pushed him away. Just like she had pushed away everyone else who tried to help her.

Elizabeth fluffed her pillow and settled in to hopefully sleep until morning. Her last thought was that of Sam and the way his hands had felt on her. She drifted off with a slight smile curling her lips.

*****

Miles away, away, Sam sat on his patio with a cold beer in his hands. He was not so at peace with himself. The chill of the bottle against his lips could not erase the memory of how her lips had felt against his. Or how her body had melted into his. Even now, his skin felt singed, as though contact with her had seared his flesh. He sighed and took another sip. There wasn't enough alcohol in the house to erase the memory of what had happened.

If he was being honest, though, he had no desire to erase it. The attraction between them was real. Finally! But if he had any chance at all with Elizabeth, he had to make her see him as something other than her friend. Sam hoped that he hadn't make things harder between them.

Everything he ever felt for Elizabeth led up to this. The few moments that he held her in his arms had been pure heaven. But now he just wanted her more. Sam needed to feel her body rest along the length of his. He wanted to see her eyes cloud over with passion as he claimed her. And he wanted to look deeply into those same eyes as she plunged over the cliff in an aching release. But more than anything, he wanted to wake up in the morning with her beside him.

Knowing there was nothing more he could do tonight, he got up and walked inside. Glancing around his mostly empty house, Sam realized that he still had a lot to do if he wanted to have that house warming party soon. Since he had already mentioned this in passing to Katie, who had told Maggie, there was no backing down.

Sam dumped the rest of his beer in the sink. Hard, physical work was a good thing. It would keep him busy and keep his mind off Elizabeth. Okay that was wishful thinking. At least it would give him a much-needed physical outlet for all his frustrations. She needed time to think about what had happened between them tonight. Sam took one last look around his kitchen before heading upstairs for a cold shower. He had the feeling it wouldn't be his last.

Chapter Twelve

Elizabeth buried her head under the pillow and groaned at the ringing of her phone. When it didn't stop, she gave up and glanced at the clock. Just after 8:00 AM. Really? Who calls at this ungodly hour on a Saturday, she thought crossly. "Hello?" she muttered groggily.

"Well hello, dear. Did I wake you? If so, what are you still doing in bed on such a fine morning?" Maggie Fitzgerald's cheerful voice boomed through the phone.

"Hello, Maggie. I didn't get home until later, and I worked a lot this past week. I was hoping to sleep in today." Elizabeth crossed her fingers, knowing that she had just told at least a partial lie. She hadn't gotten a lot of sleep last night. That was true. But it didn't have anything to do with work. It had everything to do with Sam, her confused feelings for him, and that kiss they had shared earlier in the week. Possibly not in that order either. "Is something wrong, Maggie?"

"Of course not honey. I called to see about your plans for today. Please don't tell me you're working again."

"No, I'm actually off until next week, which is a good thing. I have a lot to do around here. And I'll be stopping by to spend some time with my Mom later today. She's being transferred to rehab soon. As early as tomorrow. Did you need something?"

"That's wonderful news! Please tell Diane that I've been thinking about her and will be by to see her soon. As for today, all I need is your company. Sam is showing his puppy, Griffin, for the first time today, and I promised him I'd be his cheering section. Nora's coming as well, but you know what they say. 'The more the merrier!' You might as well say yes, because we'll be at your house in 30 minutes. Bye dear."

Elizabeth shook her head and gave up on the idea of sleeping in late. She knew Maggie well enough to know there wasn't any point in calling back to beg off. Seeing Sam again would be nice but complicated. It had only been a few short days since they shared that amazing kiss. Since he had touched her. Since they had practically melted into each other. But she had been busy working in the ED and spending time with her mom. And, yes, avoiding him.

After the world's quickest shower, dressing and throwing down some food, Elizabeth was sliding her feet into a pair of flip flops. She looked at the microwave clock just as a horn blew impatiently outside. Grabbing her purse and sunglasses, she ran out to greet them.

Nora screamed as she jumped out of the car. The two women hugged, jumping up and down, both talking a mile a minute. Elizabeth didn't know how she had gone so long without these people. Without her family. Nora was the older sister she never had.

Maggie rolled down her window and yelled to the two women. "As touching as this is, we have to hurry. I told Sam we'd be there on time." Elizabeth and Nora finally let go of each other and got into the car. Maggie immediately jumped back into conversation with Nora about the anniversary party next week. Elizabeth was more than happy to sit back, listening to the two women as she enjoyed the beautiful day.

Nora turned and smiled at her former sister-in-law. "Sorry to be monopolizing the conversation, Elizabeth. There are just so many last-minute details for the party."

"No worries, Nora. I'm sure you're swamped. I can't believe it's next week. Is there anything I can do to help?"

"That's sweet of you to offer, but we're fine. Just wrapping up some final things. So, have you ever been to a dog show before? They're really fun, and Sam does quite well."

"I haven't gone to one ever, just seen one on TV."

Maggie smiled in the rear-view mirror at Elizabeth. "I've actually become quite fond of the sport. I try to go as often as I can when Sam is showing locally. What you are referring to is called conformation showing, and it's very different than what Sam does. In that type of show, the dogs are judged on how they look and how they move. Sam explained it to me once. Basically, they're looking for the perfect example of a breed. Sam shows in the performance events, like obedience, agility and herding."

A few minutes later, they arrived at a local park. One thing Elizabeth had always loved about Windsor Falls was the chance to be outdoors, enjoying nature. Los Angeles was such a big city, and getting anywhere took forever. Elizabeth had never really grown to love it as she had hoped. But here there were mountains and lakes, parks and sporting events. All within minutes. Windsor Falls was known for its multitude of outdoor activities, from a simple walk enjoying the fall foliage to a challenging climb in the mountains and everything in between.

The two women in the front were putting on sun screen, and Nora held it up to Elizabeth. "No thanks. I already put some on."

Maggie nodded in approval. "With your fair skin, you can never be too careful. You must go through a lot of that stuff out in California.

"Not as much as you would think. I tend to work a lot."

"You can't work all the time, Elizabeth." Nora wagged her eyebrows. "There must be someone you spend your time with. Tell us everything."

Maggie swatted her daughter in law affectionately. "Nora! You can't go asking her for such personal details of her life. Of course, I'm an old lady, so I can. Everyone knows old ladies are busy bodies. Is there someone special, Elizabeth?"

All three women laughed. Amid protests that Maggie wasn't an old woman, Elizabeth escaped to the trunk to remove some chairs, avoiding the question. The last thing she wanted was to discuss her dating life, what there was of it, with Connor's mother and sister in law. Elizabeth was thankful she had dodged that bullet. At least for now. Once Maggie Fitzgerald got a bee in her bonnet about something, there was no stopping her.

The three women continued across the parking lot with Maggie in the lead. She apparently knew where to go. They had only gone a short way when Maggie turned to Nora and announced in a loud voice that Elizabeth was bringing 'that handsome new doctor' from over at the hospital to the anniversary party. How she knew this already was a mystery. But Windsor Falls was a small town, and gossip was a participation sport.

"Before you go matchmaking, Maggie, Flynn is coming as my friend. He's been great with my Mom, and he's fairly new in town, so I thought it would be a nice to chance for him to meet some people." She was sputtering by the time she finished.

The two older women stopped and Maggie turned to Elizabeth. "Honey, that's fine that your plus one is just a friend. Just like it would have been fine if he was something more." She lowered her voice and placed a gentle hand on Elizabeth's arm. "We all know how much you loved Connor. But he's been gone a long time. No one here would think any worse of you for moving on with your life."

Elizabeth looked from one woman to the other without finding a trace of censure. "Flynn is just my friend. But that's good to know."

Nora moved in towards Elizabeth and hugged her fiercely. "It's so good to have you back."

They were interrupted by a deep voice. "There's no crying on this beautiful day." Elizabeth didn't have to look to know who it was. Her skin hummed with electricity.

"Hi, Sam." She was thankful for the sunglasses she was wearing. Talking with Sam was suddenly much harder. Before she could even look into his handsome face, she was surprised by the placement of a very cold and wet nose on her bare thigh. Unable to contain her delight, she crouched down and peered into the soulful, brown eyes of an Australian Shepherd puppy. She rubbed his speckled ears, earning more kisses from his pink tongue.

"Griffin, you're such a ladies' man." Sam joked. "Hello Elizabeth. I take it Maggie roped you into coming with them today."

"She didn't exactly have to twist my arm, Sam. I've always loved dogs and was happy to come and lend moral support. But from what Maggie says, you certainly won't need it."

Sam laughed deeply. "You know that Maggie can exaggerate at times. I have enjoyed showing Cooper and Lily over the past two years. But this is Griffin's debut, so I'm not making any promises." He smiled at her and then looked at her companions as well. "Anyway, it's great to have you all here today. That means a lot to me. I should finish warming him up before our turn in the ring. Excuse me for a minute." Sam walked away, Griffin seemingly glued to his side.

Elizabeth enjoyed the show as he left. Glancing downward, she admired his well-shaped butt. The khaki cargo shorts allowed for a great view of his tanned, muscular legs. He was still running.

At the sound of near-by chuckling, Elizabeth dragged her gaze back to the other two women. She realized belatedly that she had been gawking at Sam in full view of them. Thankful once again for the sunglasses that concealed her expression, Elizabeth fervently hoped the red creeping into her cheeks could be blamed on the hot sun. The last thing she needed right now was for Maggie or Nora to gain any hint of her growing attraction for Sam. These feeling were too new and raw for public discussion.

"Our Sam has really grown into quite the handsome man, hasn't he Nora?" The comment was not addressed directly to her, but Elizabeth knew that Maggie really intended it for her. Nora smiled broadly, sharing a laugh with the older woman.

Striving to move the conversation to safer ground, Elizabeth asked Maggie about the sleek Border Collie who was currently being shown in the ring. The black and white dog moved as one with his handler.

"Mind you, I'm far from being an expert, but I have learned a thing or two from Sam. There's a set of exercises that each handler and dog must perform. The guy in the ring with the clipboard is the judge. He calls out what the handler is to do and then scores them as they go along. This is a Novice class, and it's the lowest level of difficulty. In a formal show, each team of handler and dog tries to pass each exercise and gain at least 170 points out of 200 to qualify. When they've done that at three different shows, they earn a title of Companion Dog or CD. But today they're just practicing, so there's less pressure. Have I lost you yet?" Maggie laughed at her own joke.

Elizabeth smiled and assured Maggie she was still with her. "Good! It's more pressure than I would want, but I do love to watch Sam. If you look closely, you can see the wonderful communication between dog and handler."

Elizabeth unfolded the chair she had carried from Maggie's car and sat down outside the ring to do just that. A young girl, probably no more than eight, was now entering the ring with a small, long haired dog that looked like a miniature version of a Collie. She knew the dog was a Shetland Sheepdog because the wife of a colleague in LA had several of them.

As she continued to watch, the little girl walked right up to the judge and shook his hand. She then walked her dog over to the starting position. At his commands, she started off in a confusing pattern, alternating both speed and direction at the judge's orders. Elizabeth was fascinated at the way the dog watched her young mistress so intently. Despite the crowd, it seemed as though they were the only two in the world.

Her amazement grew as the pair moved on to other exercises. When the judge signaled that they were done, the crowd roared its approval around Elizabeth. It warmed her heart to see the little girl blush with pride as she kneeled to hug her dog. The little dog seemed pleased with itself as it alternately barked happily and licked its owner's face.

"That's a tough act to follow." Elizabeth turned to see Sam standing next to her with Griffin at his side. "Wish me luck, everyone!" Sam waved jauntily and entered the ring.

Elizabeth sat rooted to her chair as she watched Sam and Griffin approach the judge. She found herself holding her breath. She glanced at Maggie. Both she and Nora were perched at the edges of their chairs as well.

Sam and Griffin were a great pair to watch. The flashy red dog was eager to please his master as they began their pattern. But Elizabeth gasped in dismay as Griffin's inexperience began to show itself. Although he was doing what Sam asked of him, even she could see that he lacked the precision of the previous team. Still, Sam was smiling and seemed to be pleased with his dog.

For their last exercise, Sam left Griffin in a seated position and walked to the other side of the ring. At a signal from the judge, Sam called Griffin to him. The young dog ran exuberantly towards his master, tongue lolling out of his mouth. But instead sitting in front of Sam, Griffin ran around him and flopped down in the grass under a nearby table. The judge declared the exercise over and asked Sam to please retrieve his dog. Griffin was as happy as ever to see his owner and jumped up on Sam repeatedly.

After gaining control over the unruly puppy, Sam left the ring and approached the little girl. He leaned down and shook her hand, whispering something in her ear. She giggled as he did so and then joined her parents.

"What did you say to make her laugh like that?" Elizabeth asked Sam as he approached their chairs.

"I told her to not get too confident. Griffin and I will be ready for her next time." His smile made her heart flip in her chest. Her insides quivered. There was something different about Sam. Or maybe there was just something different about how she was seeing him. Whatever it was, Elizabeth wasn't sure if it was a good thing or bad. Shrugging off her confusion, she smiled back at him.

"Despite the ending, I thought you guys did great today, Sam. Especially for such a young dog."

Sam leaned in closer to Elizabeth. His whole face brightened with his smile. "Well, I know that Griffin needs a lot of work, but I was still very proud of him today. He's a baby at only six months old. He'll get better as he matures. All in all, not bad considering his start in life."

"What do you mean 'his start in life', Sam?"

Before he could answer, Maggie broke into the conversation. "Our Sam has become quite the animal rescuer. He's a real hero, Elizabeth."

Sam dug the toe of his sneaker into the ground. "Now, Maggie, there's no need for embellishment."

She laughed loudly and squeezed his shoulder. "You're absolutely right, Sam. The amazing work you do with dogs requires no embellishment at all."

Thoroughly intrigued, Elizabeth turned back to Sam. "Are you involved in rescue, Sam?"

"I have been for the past few years. All three of my dogs are from rescue groups. I feel strongly about rescuing rather than buying dogs. To that end, I don't buy from pet stores that sell dogs or cats either."

"Wow! That's awesome, Sam." She squatted down and rubbed Griffin's silky ears. A wistful expression came across her face. "I miss being around dogs. Maggie, your family always had at least two at any given time."

"Oh my, yes. The kids were forever bringing home strays 'just for a few days.' Funny how they usually ending up staying. Connor was the biggest culprit of the bunch."

There was a moment of awkward silence. "His strays weren't always canine either" responded Sam in a soft tone.

Elizabeth looked into his eyes. "No, Sam, they certainly weren't." It was an old joke between the three friends. Both Sam and Elizabeth were only children, both with parents who worked too much. They were forever at Connor's house as kids.

Sam put an arm around Maggie's shoulder. "You were always kind enough to put up with us all those years."

Maggie's face reddened with pleasure. "Sam Bishop you are as dear to me as my own children. You and Elizabeth were never strays, as you well know." She hugged him fiercely. "I couldn't be more proud of you two if you were my own flesh and blood."

"Sam, are you and Griffin done?" As Elizabeth spoke the words, a woman walked to the edge of the ring and started to call numbers.

"Nope" he answered with his lopsided grin. "Now the fun begins. See you in a little bit."

The three women took their seats again. Elizabeth had no idea what to expect and watched as six sets of dogs and handlers reentered the ring. Sam and Griffin had been the last to go and therefore were at the end of the line.

"What's happening, Maggie?"

Nora laughed. "Watch out for your hands, Elizabeth."

Elizabeth barely had time to glance down when Maggie grabbed her right hand and sighed. "This is the part I hate. No matter how many times I watch this, it never gets any easier. How can Sam be so calm? How can he just stand there waiting? I don't think that I breather the whole time." She turned back in her chair to watch as the judge addressed the teams. Maggie still held onto Elizabeth with a death grip.

Sam was standing next to the small girl and her Sheltie. Elizabeth watched as the handlers each removed their arm bands and their dog's leashes. Sam turned and placed his behind Griffin, with the numbered arm band facing up.

Next, the judge walked into the center of the ring and gave a few last-minute instructions. After a moment, he walked to the side of the ring and turned to face the contestants. With a signal from him, each handler gave their dog a command to stay and walked across the ring, turning to face their respective canines when they reached the opposite side. Sam was standing just a few feet from them. Once again Elizabeth had a nice view of his rear. The thought crossed her mind to look away, but she didn't. What was the harm??

Nora leaned across Maggie and whispered to Elizabeth. "This is when Mom actually stops breathing. It's kind of funny to watch." She winked at the older woman and patted her sympathetically on the arm.

Maggie made a shushing noise but didn't comment. She was focused intently on Griffin as though mentally willing him to stay seated. She did however grip Elizabeth's hand more tightly.

A murmur arose from the crowd. A Beagle had risen from the middle of the line and was headed towards her handler. After a few steps, she stopped, seemingly rethinking her decision, and flopped down in the grass in the middle of the ring.

Just when Elizabeth thought she would pass out from lack of oxygen, the judge gave the command for handlers to return to their dogs. Each returned across the field to their respective dogs. The Beagle's handler had a shorter trip. At a final command from the judge, Sam reached down and gently rubbed Griffin's furry ears. Elizabeth exhaled loudly, finally remembering to breath.

Maggie clapped enthusiastically along with the crowd. She blew out a big breath and smiled at Elizabeth before looking back towards the ring. But there wasn't any time to relax as the handlers got ready for the next exerciser. She began to understand what Maggie had said earlier. This was torture.

On command from the judge, each handler told their dog to lie and then to stay and once again walked to the other side of the ring. Just before turning to face Griffin, Sam winked at her. She smiled to herself and prepared to wait.

"Did I mention it's for three minutes this time?" whispered Maggie.

"No, Maggie, you didn't." Elizabeth wiped the sweat that was forming on her brow. "Surely this time is easier. The dogs are lying down. What could go wrong?"

Her answer came just 45 seconds into it, when the Beagle once again broke her position. Just as she had previously, the cute dog walked towards her owner before lying back down in the grass. To everyone's amusement, this time she rolled over on her back with her legs in the air. There was soft laughter from the crowd and a distinct groan from the dog's handler.

When there was less than one minute to go, Elizabeth was perched on the edge of her chair, her breathing quick and shallow. Maggie wasn't the only one squeezing. She couldn't imagine how stressed Sam must be in the ring.

"How do they stand this?" she muttered quietly to herself. When she thought she couldn't stand it anymore, the handlers once again returned to their dogs. Sam turned and halted next to Griffin, and Elizabeth could see the pride and joy on his face. At the judge's final command, Sam released Griffin, bending over to hug the enthusiastic dog. In return, Griffin was washing Sam's face with eager licks from his long, pink tongue.

Without thinking, Elizabeth bolted from her chair and ran towards the entrance to the ring. She threw her arms around Sam's neck as he exited, almost knocking him over in her enthusiasm. "That was awesome, Sam, but how do you stand it? I was so nervous the whole time. I think I would have fainted if I had to be in that ring. But you looked so in control the entire time. Wow!"

"Coming from the woman who takes care of people with gunshot wounds and heart attacks for a living" Sam joked.

"I have control when I'm taking care of patients. I know what I'm doing. I've trained for it. This was torture."

"Well, I've trained for this, so I can be calm. The alphabet helps."

"The alphabet?" Elizabeth's brow wrinkled in confusion.

Sam laughed at her expression. "The three minutes is a bit much. So, I recite the alphabet in my head. Slowly. Several times. The key is to be relaxed and maintain eye contact with Griffin. That way he knows what to do."

Nora and Maggie approached them. Both made a fuss over Griffin. Sam smiled at the three women before him. "Even though he got disqualified for his earlier stunt, I'm so proud of him." He looked down at his dog and gave him a pat on the head.

As they talked, the same woman from earlier began to call out numbers again. At Elizabeth's look of confusion, Sam explained. "All the teams that passed go back in for awards. Because this is a match, no one gets anything towards their titles, but they do hand out ribbons."

In all, four of the original six teams reentered the ring. Griffin and the Beagle had both been disqualified. The judge turned to the gathered crowd and made some final remarks before handing out ribbons for first through third place. Just before handing out the first-place ribbon, he called the little girl and her Sheltie to the middle of the ring. "Now we all know this is just a practice match, but if it wasn't, I have it on good authority that this pair would be finishing their Companion Dog title today. While they don't qualify, they do get the first-place prize with an amazing score of 198! Let's give them a round of applause."

The crowd surged to their feet collectively and began to clap wildly. Elizabeth noticed with delight that the little girl's face was aglow with pride. "Sam, how did the judge happen to know that about her? Did you have anything to do with that?"

To confirm her suspicions, Sam turned away, hiding his face. He must have said something to the judge. That was just the kind of thing Sam would do. He was always looking out for others. It warmed her heart to think that some things had not changed after all.

"Sam, you really made her day. You always were such a thoughtful person." She grinned at him before bending down to pet a panting Griffin.

"OK, time to feed the heroes. Both of them." Elizabeth looked up at Maggie as she spoke. "Who wants hot dogs?" Suddenly, Maggie glanced at her watch and gasped in surprise. "Nora, we forgot all about our final appointment with the caterer." Turning to Elizabeth and Sam, she muttered a hasty apology. "I'm so sorry. We have to leave right now or we'll be late." Smiling a bit too brightly, she turned to Sam. "You don't mind giving Elizabeth a ride home, do you Sam?" With a quick round of hugs, the two women were gone.

To say she was speechless would have been an understatement. She had a sneaking suspicion the older woman was matchmaking. Elizabeth was sure that her face was bright red by now. "I'm so sorry, Sam. I have no idea what that was about. Neither of them mentioned anything about the caterer on the way here."

She stood up and shoved her hands in her back pockets. "It would seem I'm at your mercy for a ride home."

Sam took a step forward and plucked the sunglasses off her face. "Do I make you nervous, Elizabeth?" His voice was lowered for privacy, and the deepness of it did funny things to her stomach. Not to mention other parts.

She made herself meet his gaze. "No. Why do you ask?"

He gestured to where she had her hands tucked into the back pockets of her shorts. "You always have to do something with your hands when you are. It's a dead giveaway."

She instantly pulled her hands out of her pocket, but then wasn't sure what to do with them. Leaning down, she picked up her purse. "I'm fine, Sam. Just a little tired. It's been a busy week, and I had planned on sleeping in this morning." Sam's shoulders slumped, and Elizabeth immediately regretted her choice of words. She touched him on the arm. "I didn't mean it like that, Sam. I'm glad I got a chance to see you two in action."

Sam gathered Griffin's water and bowl and then straightened to his full height. "Well, Griffin and I are done for the day. Why don't we go get that hot dog? If you'd rather go back to my house, I could throw something on the grill."

"I'd love to, Sam, but I have a lot to do at home. I'm trying to get the house in order before my mom comes home. And I need to go see her in a little while also. Maybe we could just grab that hotdog here before we leave?" She may be a coward, but Elizabeth didn't think she was ready to be alone with him again after the other night. After that amazing, soul searing kiss. Just standing next to him now was giving her strange impulses. Like wanting to throw herself at him. She didn't trust herself.

Sam nodded in agreement. "That's fine. There's always food at these things." He turned, placing his hand in the small of her back to guide her. "The concession stands are over this way."

They stopped at a large oak tree near the food stand. Sam insisted on buying and left her there in the shade with Griffin. Elizabeth sat on the ground with her back resting against the tree. Griffin flopped down next to her and laid his silky head on her knee. She absently scratched between his ears as she thought about Sam and her feelings for him. Although they had gotten off to a rough start, things seemed smoother between them now. If you could forget about that kiss of course. But that wasn't happening. Ever.

In all the time she had known Sam, she had never thought about kissing him like that. Now it was all she could think about. She blamed it on her lack of a sex life, since it had certainly been a long time. And yet, she wasn't convinced that was it. She must have touched Sam thousands of times over the years, but she'd never felt the spark she was feeling now. Just standing next to him caused an awareness that skittered along her nerve endings.

She had to admit, however reluctantly, that she was physically attracted to him. He wasn't Connor, but Connor was gone. Had been for a long time. Connor was the first man she had ever loved. The only one really. And the first person she had slept with.

There had only been one man since. Jeremy Hendricks was a pediatric trauma surgeon at her hospital in Los Angeles. They met over a case several years ago. Jeremy was older and single by choice, completely committed to his career. They had an understanding. A 'friends with benefits' type of deal. She genuinely liked Jeremy, loved him really. She just wasn't in love with him. Her heart remained untouched since Connor's death. She was afraid it might always.

And then there was Sam. To think of him this way was both terrifying and exciting. They had been such good friends before she left Windsor Falls. She missed that and wanted it back. She certainly didn't want anything to mess it up. But there was no denying the sparks she felt when she was near him. Or how her girl parts sat up and took notice.

Best to let it go for now she thought. Elizabeth leaned back against the tree, sighing contentedly. She had more questions than answers, but she didn't care. The breeze was gentle on her skin, and for this moment, she didn't have a care in the world. She closed her eyes as the tension drained from her body. A smile played along her lips.

*****

Sam stood in line for their hot dogs and colas, impatient to be back with Elizabeth. While he waited, he was content to think about her. Having her back home was a blessing but not an easy one. He had never stopped loving her. Not telling Elizabeth how he felt was killing him. It was one thing when Connor was alive. He had loved Connor like a brother and would never have hurt him. His respect for Connor and their relationship had kept his feelings for Elizabeth safely beneath the surface. But Connor wasn't here anymore.

Need for Elizabeth, to touch her, to hold her, to bury himself in her was a physical a torture for Sam. She had fit perfectly in his arms the other night. He longed to have her wrapped in them again.

Sam glanced in her direction. She was reclining under the tree with her eyes closed and a very satisfied smile on her face. The fingers of her right hand were buried in Griffin's soft fur. The fact that he was jealous of his own dog made Sam cringe. He stared thoughtfully at her face. The face he had held in his memory for so long. Although he knew every inch by heart, his memory of her did not do her justice.

Sam was finally able to order. After paying, he grabbed their lunch and started back towards her. He shook his head to clear it. He had no clue where they were headed, if anywhere. Elizabeth was only here until her mother was better. She would surely return to her life in California. But she was here with him today. He would enjoy it while he could. The tragedy years earlier had taught him to never take anything for granted.

Sam walked over to where she sat, propped up against the tree. Her deep, even breathing told him she was asleep. Griffin waged his stump of a tail, eyeing the hot dogs hopefully.

"Your lunch is served, Madame", he announced softly so as not to startle her.

Her eyes popped open. Elizabeth stretched her arms over her head. The material of her thin shirt was stretched tightly over her chest, allowing Sam a wonderful view.

She smiled at Sam as she accepted the simple offering of a hot dog, Coke, and a bag of chips. "Just what I was hoping for. Nothing beats picnic food, especially when it's eaten outside in the sunshine on a gorgeous day like this."

"I was afraid that living in California would have converted you to eating rabbit food. You know, only salads and stuff."

Elizabeth laughed out loud, nearly spitting her cola out. "Now you know me better than that, Sam," she scolded him gently. "One thing I'm not shy about is my appetite. Life's too short. I've even been known to eat dessert first. Thankfully, I was blessed with an active metabolism. I'd hate to start counting calories at my age."

Sam gazed openly at her gently rounded figure. She looked like she had gained a few pounds since she had left home, but they looked good on her. She had never been a stick figure, for which he was eternally thankful. He may be old fashioned, but Sam always believed women should be more than skin and bones.

"I don't think calorie counting is in your future. You don't have anything to worry about." He took a large bite of his hot dog to hide his wolfish grin.

Elizabeth blushed lightly at his compliment. She pushed her sunglasses up into her hair and took a bite of her hot dog. While she chewed, Elizabeth fidgeted with her soda as though she was nervous.

Elizabeth stared at Sam and then gestured to his face. "You have a little something there, Sam."

Sam wiped the corner of his mouth with a paper napkin. "Did I get it?"

She cocked her head and bit her bottom lip. "Uh no, you missed it. Let me." She leaned into him and wiped a dab of ketchup from his face.

Before Elizabeth could wipe her hand on a napkin, Sam grabbed her wrist, stopping her. Slowly and deliberately, he sucked her finger into his mouth, removing the ketchup. He watched as her eyes dilated. Not wasting the opportunity, Sam leaned in and covered her mouth with his.

With her back already against the tree, there was nowhere for Elizabeth to go. Not that she seemed to want to escape. Her arms wound around his neck, and her chest was pressed against his. He wrapped his arms around her waist and slid his hands up under the edge of her shirt, splaying them against the smooth, hot skin of her back.

When her mouth opened under his, Sam took full advantage. He thrust his tongue and tangled it with hers. The small moan that escaped her merely drove the flames higher.

Elizabeth gasped and broke apart from Sam quickly. The both turned to see that Griffin had placed his cold, wet nose up against her neck, trailing his tongue in a sloppy kiss.

Sam sat back and groaned in frustration. "I told you he liked the ladies."

"Well, you don't have ketchup on your face anymore Sam."

A broad smile lit his face. "Good to know, Elizabeth. Anything else you want to tell me?"

Elizabeth squirmed a bit before answering. "That kiss was something else, Sam. But I think you already know that." She hesitated before continuing. "I guess I'm just surprised."

"It was, wasn't it? Something else that is." A slow sexy smile spread across his face. "But a good surprise, right? Like finding twenty dollars in your pocket."

Her eyes widened. So did her smile. "Now you're just fishing, Sam."

A deep chuckle rumbled in his chest. "Maybe you could just give me a hint then?"

Elizabeth sat very still and didn't answer for a few moments. Then she grabbed a fistful of his t-shirt and pulled him in closer. Leaning in, she placed her lips next to his ear and whispered. "It was more like finding a fifty, Sam."

Sam sat back and stared into her bright blue eyes. Something warm and wonderful spread in his chest. His heart beat a little faster. "Well okay then."

Elizabeth glanced at her phone and groaned. "I had no idea it was so late, Sam. I really should be going. I still have so much to do at home, and I have to go visit my Mom."

Standing up, she reached around to brush some grass off her shorts. Sam's admiring glance followed her movements. "I'm sorry I kept you so long, Elizabeth." He tilted his head and grinned at her. "Actually, I'm not sorry. I really enjoyed it." He picked up and carried their trash to the can. "I'll take you home now."

They walked in a companionable silence towards the parking area. Their hands, swinging at their sides, brushed occasionally. Sam felt an electric shock pulse up his arm each time.

As they neared his truck, Elizabeth leaned in and brushed some grass that was clinging to the back of his shirt. Her hand lingered a beat longer than necessary before she jerked it back.

"I like it when you touch me, Elizabeth." The words were barely audible.

Sam reached up and tucked a silky curl behind her ear. He traced his fingers along the line of her jaw and then down her neck, all the while maintaining eye contact with her. "I like to touch you too, Elizabeth. In case you hadn't noticed."

Reaching down, he removed Griffin's leash from her hand and loaded the tired puppy into his crate in the backseat. When he was secured, Sam opened the passenger door and held out his hand towards her. Elizabeth placed her hand in his and stepped up into the truck. He held her hand in his for a moment, never breaking eye contact. Finally, he turned it over and placed the lightest of kisses into her palm. With that, he closed her door and walked around to his side.

Elizabeth curled her hand closed over his kiss. Her skin still tingled everywhere he had touched her. She leaned her head back and closed her eyes, savoring the feeling. She might be confused, but it was a wonderful feeling.

Sam started his truck, lowering the windows and blasting the A/C to cool off the interior. They made casual conversation on the drive home, each lost in their own thoughts. When they reached her mother's home, she turned to him.

"Thanks Sam. I had a wonderful time today." Elizabeth gave a last pat to Griffin in the backseat before swinging gracefully down and out of the truck.

Sam followed suit, jumping down from his seat and coming around the front of his truck to where she stood. "I'm so glad you had a chance to see us in action today."

Elizabeth pushed her sunglasses to the top of her head and smiled up at him. "Me too, Sam. I was so proud of you guys. I'd love to go again next time if I'm still here."

He glanced around the yard. "Your Mom must have been sick for a long time to let the yard go like this. It always looked so beautiful when we were growing up."

Sadness shadowed Elizabeth's eyes. "I know, Sam. It breaks my heart. Tomorrow, I'm going to start reclaiming this place for her. I want the yard and house to sparkle by the time she comes home." She tilted her chin up and squared her shoulders. "I may not have been here when she needed me, but I'm here now."

Sam reached out and touched her face. "She's lucky to have you, Elizabeth. When will she be discharged? Do you know yet?"

"Not yet. If all goes well, she'll be transferred to the rehabilitation unit of the hospital in the next day or so. She'll probably need to be there a week or so, although I know for a fact she disagrees."

"Not the best patient, huh?"

"Not even close. You know my mom. Stubborn as a mule. She always said that she came from 'good German stock'. That just means she's independent to a fault. She should have asked for help long before now."

"So, you come by it naturally then?" he teased her.

A pretty blush lit Elizabeth's cheek bones. "Yes, Sam, I did. Thanks for pointing that out to me." She stuck her tongue out at him playfully

"I'll let you go. Thanks again for coming, Elizabeth. And for having lunch with me." He hugged her gently, dropping a brief but hot kiss on her lips before walking away. Smiling, he backed out of the driveway and headed home. He waved one last time.

Sam smiled all the way home. Unloading Griffin from the back seat, he walked into the garage and opened the door leading to the kitchen. Cooper and Lily came out to greet him, and all three dogs rushed out to the grass to do their business.

Sam touched his fingers to his lips. It warmed his soul to know that touching Elizabeth, kissing her, was exactly as he dreamt for all years. The reality was, in fact, so much better. His mind wandered. He thought about what it would be like to touch her everywhere, feel her beneath him as he entered her. Gaze into her clear, blue eyes as he did.

He swallowed heavily. She was only here temporarily. The thought was a knife to his heart. What was he doing getting involved with her when she was on borrowed time in Windsor Falls? But Sam had never developed any self-preservation tactics when it came to Elizabeth. Not at sixteen and apparently not now.

Accepting that, he made the decision to spend as much time with her as possible while she was here. When she left, and his heart was once again shattered, he would deal with it. He could no more deny himself than to stop breathing. A huge smile split his face as an idea formed.

Chapter Thirteen

"Now Mom, we've been over this a hundred times. Yes, you have to go to rehab before you can come home." Elizabeth sat on her hands to stop herself from pulling her own hair out by the roots. Her mother really was a terrible patient.

"I understand, Elizabeth. I'm not a child, you know. I just want to go home." Her mother's voice quivered, and Elizabeth felt immediate remorse for her frustration.

"I know you do, Mom. And that's the plan. But first, you must be able to function there without hurting yourself. If you went home right now and tried to walk up the stairs, you'd end up right back here. I know you don't want that."

Diane sighed heavily and lifted her hands in defeat. "You're right. You're right. Believe me, this is the last place I want to come back to. I'm just tired of being a patient. Of having people poke and prod me."

Elizabeth's face softened as she squeezed her mother's hands. "I get it, Mom. I really do."

"There they are. My two favorite ladies!"

Elizabeth looked up to see Flynn lounging in the doorway. "Oh good, you're here. Please explain to my mother, again, why rehab is so important."

"And here I thought you were just happy to see me, Elizabeth." He walked right past her and to the other side of the hospital bed. "Well at least I know my patient has good taste. How are you today, Mrs. Abbott?"

Elizabeth was amused by the sudden rosy glow to her mother's cheeks. Flynn certainly had a way with the ladies. Of all ages.

"Now, Dr. Reynolds I've told you more than once to call me Diane."

"Then you, my favorite patient, must call me Flynn. Tell me, Diane. Why hasn't your daughter agreed to marry me and have my babies?" He pouted so outrageously that the two women burst into laughter.

When she could breathe again, Elizabeth fixed him with a stern look. "You know very well you haven't asked me, Flynn. Besides, don't go giving my mother any more ideas. She's always trying to fix me up with someone."

"I want you to be happily settled with a husband and children. Is that so wrong, Elizabeth?"

"But I am happy, Mom. I love what I do. And I already went down that road once."

"Yes, honey, once. And a long time ago. Connor would want you to marry again. To have a full life. He wouldn't want you working sixty hour weeks and telling yourself you're happy."

Elizabeth squeezed her eyes closed tightly for a moment. "You're right Mom, he wouldn't." She glanced at Flynn who was looking more than a little green around the gills. "But maybe that's a conversation for another time."

Flynn cleared his throat loudly. "I agree. That's women's talk for another time. Preferably one that I'm not invited to. Let's talk about you, Diane. Good news! A bed has opened in the rehab unit. You're on your way."

"What? Now?" she sputtered.

Flynn stepped directly to Diane's side and held her gaze. "Yes, Diane, now. Not an hour from now. Not tomorrow. The last thing you need is time to sit here and think."

Elizabeth could have cheered, but she didn't want to upset her mom any further. Instead, she thanked Flynn for the news.

"I wanted to come in and tell you myself since I happened to be on the unit when they got the phone call. Someone from patient transport will be up shortly to collect you." He leaned down and hugged Diane, whispering in her ear. Whatever he said made her mother very happy. A huge smile brightened her face.

Flynn turned to her. "You I'll see around this place." He left the room, turning back at the door. "Oh, Elizabeth, I've been meaning to ask you. Is this party black tie?"

"I believe it's optional, Flynn. Just wear whatever you have. Men get off easily. I have to go find a dress and shoes still." Her expression dropped as if she was facing a firing squad.

"Thanks, Lizzie." With a jaunty wave, Flynn left the room.

Elizabeth turned back to find her mother staring at her with open curiosity. "Party? You're taking Flynn to the anniversary party? Interesting." She could practically see the wheels turning in her mother's mind.

"Before you having my shopping for another dress altogether, let me just tell you that he's going as my friend. I haven't seen most of the Fitzgeralds yet, and I thought he'd be good for moral support."

"If I had a man who looked like *that* taking me to a party, I wouldn't be thinking moral support. And you need a killer dress. And some spiky heels. Maybe silver and a bit daring." Diane winked to drive her point home.

"Mother!" exclaimed Elizabeth in a tone several levels higher than her usual one.

"Don't 'Mother' me, dear. That man is hot!" She smiled at her daughter's look of shock. "I may be too old for him, but I'm not dead."

Elizabeth rubbed her temples with both hands and muttered to her mom. "Please stay out of my love life. Flynn and I are friends. Just friends. And that's all we're meant to be."

Diane raised her hands and looked at her nails. "Oh, I know dear."

"What do you mean you know? How do you know?"

"There's no spark."

"Spark?" she choked out, practically incapable of speech at this point.

"Yes, dear, spark. There isn't any. What good is pursuing him if there's no spark?" Her tone suggested that Elizabeth might be a little slow. "Now Will and I had a spark. We practically burned down the city."

"Will?" The headache that had threatened was now out in full force. "My father. You never talk about him." Elizabeth's parents had married briefly when they discovered that Diane was pregnant with Elizabeth. But Will had been a journalist yearning for a bigger life. When he had been given the opportunity to be a foreign correspondent for The New York Times in their Middle Eastern desk, he took it. The ink on the divorce papers was barely dry before Diane moved her daughter to North Carolina.

"I loved Will more than you'll ever know, Elizabeth. And that started with a spark the very first time I saw him. Just because it didn't work doesn't mean it wasn't true."

"Do you ever regret any of it, Mom?" Elizabeth's throat was dry and tight as she waited for an answer.

Diane stared off into the distance with a dreamy look in her eyes. "No, Elizabeth, I don't. I knew what your father was and what he wanted when I met him. I was just foolish enough to think I could change him. But I don't regret it for one second." She took Elizabeth's hands in her own. "How could I regret ever having you? You're the most special thing in my life and the very best of both of us. No, I don't regret the choices I made."

She looked directly at Elizabeth before continuing. "And that's why I worry about you, dear. I don't want you to have regrets either, Elizabeth."

"I don't regret loving Connor either Mom. He was the best thing that ever happened to me."

"Yes he was, Elizabeth. Connor loved you with his whole heart. You could see it in the way he looked at you. But he's been gone a long time. You could have that again."

Elizabeth shook her head. "No, Mom, I can't."

"Oh honey, maybe not the same exact thing, but you can love again. You could find someone and settle down. Have a family. There's still time. But you have to take the risk."

Elizabeth sniffled loudly. "That's just it, Mom. I don't think I can risk having my heart shattered again. I almost didn't survive it the first time."

She laid her head on her mother's shoulder. Diane stroked her hair and spoke soothingly to her. "That's the choice you must make, Elizabeth. You've been playing it safe for years. Jeremy was a safe choice."

Elizabeth stiffened. "How do you know about Jeremy?"

Diane chuckled. "I could tell when I met him the first time that there was something between you too. But I could also tell your heart wasn't invested in it. I'm assuming that hasn't changed."

Elizabeth thought back to the time her mother met Jeremy. He had joined them for dinner on one of her mom's yearly trips out to California. "Jeremy and I are friends." She hesitated before deciding on full disclosure. "Ours is a purely physical relationship. I mean we're friends and colleagues but we also…" She moved her hands restlessly as her face flushed a dull red. Was she really having this conversation with her mother?

"You're friends with benefits." She smiled at the look of horror on her daughter's face. "I watch TV dear."

Elizabeth did not want to know just what her mother was watching. "Yes, that's what we are. Or were. It's, ah, been awhile."

"Probably because that's not really your style, Elizabeth. You're more the whole-hearted type. Even if it means getting hurt. There's nothing wrong with that dear. But it does mean you have to be willing to take that risk again. For the right person."

"Yes, Mom, that's exactly what that means. Which is why I haven't done it. Plus, honestly, I've never met anyone who can make me feel the way Connor did." That made her think about Sam and the way he had made her feel this morning. And earlier this week.

"Anyway, before the aide arrives to move you downstairs, I wanted to talk with you about something." Dread pitted her stomach and Elizabeth ran her hands nervously through her hair.

"Now you're scaring me. What is it, Elizabeth?"

"It's about the house, Mom. Have you ever thought of selling it? Maybe moving into something a little smaller?"

"No, I never did. At least not until I woke up in the hospital with a tube down my throat. That makes you think about a lot of things, honey. But you're right about the house. I need something smaller and on one floor. I was speaking to a nurse about it yesterday. Her father is a widower and sold his house after his wife died. He just bought one of those cute garden homes in that fifty -five and older development near town."

Happiness flitted across Elizabeth's face. She had been dreading this conversation. "That sounds perfect. When you're feeling better, you could walk into town for a cup of coffee or a bite to eat."

"Exactly. And I'd still have a small yard I could tend." Her eyes were briefly darkened before she continued. "I hate to think what's become of my lovely garden now. I haven't had the strength to do anything in it for quite a while."

Elizabeth patted her mother's hand. "I don't want you to worry about that now. I'll help you with it." She pointed to the doorway where a young woman waited with a wheelchair. "Looks like your ride's here, Mom."

Elizabeth spent the next few hours getting her Mom settled in. She was exhausted by the time she left the hospital. The thought of all she had to do at home was enough to make her want to cry. But her Mom had always been there for her, and she wasn't going to let her down now.

Elizabeth stopped in the grocery store on the way home for a quick something for dinner and to stock up on cleaning supplies. She bumped into two people she had gone to school with. They were married and had three kids. James owned his own auto repair shop, while Lisa ran a small boutique in town. Elizabeth remembered seeing it on Evergreen when she arrived in home. It was where Sam's father had his hardware store. Lisa promised she'd be in to find something for the party.

By the time she arrived home and ate her dinner, Elizabeth was exhausted. She walked around the house, surveying all that needed to be done. Now that her mother was talking of selling it, Elizabeth used a more critical eye. Beyond the thorough cleaning that was long over-due, the house needed some TLC. Painting would go a long way. But that was another problem for another day.

Whipping through her nightly routine of brushing her teeth and washing her face, Elizabeth was finally able to fall into bed. But as tired as she was, her mind was still racing. Thoughts of Sam crept in at the weirdest times. Even when she had been busy with her Mom today, she was remembering his kiss and the way his body felt under her hands.

The memory of that alone curled her toes under the light blanket. She reached up to turn off the lamp when her phone chimed, announcing an incoming text. Since it wasn't a phone call, she knew it wasn't the hospital about her mother, and she almost ignored it. But curiosity got the best of her, and she grabbed her phone. The number was unfamiliar. Intrigued, she opened the message.

"Just wanted to tell you again what a great time I had today. This is Sam by the way."

Elizabeth forgot to breathe for a second. Sam? Sam was texting her? How did he get her number? Just then another text sounded.

"In case you're wondering, I'm not a stalker. I called Maggie for your number."

Elizabeth laughed out loud at the joke. Interesting how he could almost read her thoughts.

"So, you're psychic now? That's exactly what I was wondering."

As soon as she sent it, she could see that he was typing a reply. She waited, very conscious of the fact that she was lying in bed wearing only panties and a cami. She hoped his psychic abilities didn't extend that far.

"Sadly no. Just seemed logical. What are you doing?"

She read his question and wondered how to respond. Taking a deep breath, she decided to have some fun.

"I'm in bed actually. It's been a long day. You?"

There was a long pause before Sam started typing again. She wondered what that meant. She didn't have to wait long as the chime sounded.

"Alone?"

Elizabeth giggled and looked around. Sure enough, there was Fred, her faithful old teddy bear, propped in the corner. She had almost forgotten about him.

"No. Fred's with me. Very faithful that one. You?"

Although she knew the answer, the thought of Sam being in bed with someone, possibly Katie, upset her. But Sam wasn't like that. If he was in bed with someone, he wouldn't be texting her. Elizabeth got out of bed and cracked a window for some fresh air. Her old room felt warm suddenly.

"Ah. Good old Fred. Can't believe I'm jealous of a stuffed animal. Did anyone ever replace his missing eye? And yes, I'm alone. The dogs sleep in the living room in their own beds."

"How do you remember Fred? And his missing eye?" Elizabeth held her breath as she awaited his answer. Anticipation raced along her nerve endings.

"I told you, Elizabeth. I remember everything,"

Emotion choked her. That he remembered didn't really surprise her. That was Sam. Oh how she had missed him.

"Oh. Well I have a long day tomorrow. Good night Sam. Sweet dreams."

She pulled the pillow out from under her head and flipped it, seeking the cooler side. Her skin felt overheated. Elizabeth kicked back the blanket to the bottom of the bed.

"Same to you, Elizabeth. But my dreams will be anything but sweet."

Elizabeth read his last response several times. Did that mean he would be dreaming about her? Frustrated with herself, she plugged her phone back in to charge and flopped onto her back. Funny how she had been so exhausted before. Now she was wide awake.

*****

Sam replaced his phone on the bedside table and rolled over onto his side. He punched his pillow several times for good measure. After a few minutes, he rolled onto his back. The moonlight spilled into his room, casting shadows. Sam was thrilled with his new house and the progress he was making. He loved living away from town. He worked hard, and when he came home at night, the peace and quiet was relaxing.

The house was large. Way bigger than Sam needed. But in the back of his mind, he always planned on having kids. The fact that Elizabeth was the only woman he wanted to have kids with did not escape him. That was unlikely. He sighed and rolled to his other side, kicking off the sheet as he went. When she returned to California, he was going to have to get on with his life.

Chapter Fourteen

Elizabeth was up early the next morning, dressed in her oldest workout clothes and eating her breakfast. She had slept well, minus the decidedly X-rated dream about Sam, and was ready to tackle the house. She was still deciding on whether to tackle the inside or outside first when the doorbell rang. She had chosen outside since it wasn't scorching yet when she pulled open the front door.

Sam stood there. Along with Connor's whole family. And a few other people she didn't know. She felt her mouth hang open, but she was powerless to close it.

"Sam? What?" Her voice was drowned out as everyone started talking at once. Before she knew it, Elizabeth was being passed around for hugs. The noise level grew until a startling whistle pierced the air. The crowd parted and there stood Maggie.

"Good Morning, my dear. We've come to help." Elizabeth looked on, still speechless, as others nodded. "Just tell us where you want us."

A bewildered Elizabeth forced herself to speak. "I don't know. There's a lot to be done." She swept her hands in a gestured that included the yard and house. "Take your pick. Outside or inside."

A slight woman who looked to be in her late fifties stepped forward. "Hi, Elizabeth. I'm Maria Adams. I manage the garden department at Sam's store."

Elizabeth smiled, glad to put a face to the name. "Oh, Sam told me about you. The Hydrangeas were a nice choice. Thank you."

A huge smile split the older woman's face. "You're welcome. Of course, Sam still hasn't mentioned why he needed to apologize." She threw a meaningful glance his way. "Anyway, I brought my son, Quinn, and his friend Jack." She pointed to two handsome men standing at the back of the crowd. They were the only other ones Elizabeth didn't know. "They're both firefighters in town. I brought them for their brawn. I think we'll tackle the yard." The two men nodded and followed Maria around the side of the house.

As she was trying to understand what was happening, Connor's father, Joe, stepped forward and enveloped her in his arms. Elizabeth sniffed back threatening tears and returned the hug as hard as she could. Joe was a man of few words but big actions. She was more of a father to her than Will had ever been. It was Joe who walked her down the aisle when she married his son.

"It's about time you came back, pretty girl" was all he said before passing her on to one of his sons. Her throat was thick with unshed tears and gratitude.

After a few more minutes of chaos, as she reunited with Connor's family, Maggie stepped up once again. "Since mine is an unruly lot, I've assigned chores." She stepped up to the storm door and taped up a piece of paper amid groans. But one look from her silenced the bunch. No one argued with Maggie Fitzgerald. "There you go now. Get busy. And I don't want to hear any complaining or swapping chores. That never ends well."

Like a well-oiled machine, the group dispersed as ordered, leaving Maggie, Elizabeth, and Sam. Elizabeth could hear various people chattering as they worked. Laughter filled the air.

Elizabeth searched the list, not finding her own name nor Sam's. "What about us, Maggie? What are our assignments?"

"Since you two were always my easiest, I left that up to you." Maggie was whistling an old Irish tune as she walked into the house.

"Wow, Sam. That was like being caught up in a tornado. Thank you."

"Well, you mentioned that you were going to be working on your mother's house. All I did was tell Maggie. The rest is history." He stopped talking as she threw herself at him.

Elizabeth hugged him long and hard. "Sam, I'm so touched. I was really getting a bit overwhelmed, wondering how I was going to get it all done."

Elizabeth kissed him on the lips, meaning it to be a gesture of thanks. But the heat overwhelmed them immediately. She needed more than the lightest touching of their lips. She groaned in the back of her throat before backing away. All of Connor's family were here, plus one of Sam's employees. This wasn't the time or place. Elizabeth took a few steps back and felt the loss of his touch immediately. "I didn't mean to do that, Sam."

Sam cocked his head and grinned. "You didn't mean to kiss me, Elizabeth? Or you didn't mean to kiss me with a potentially huge audience?"

She narrowed her eyes at him. "The latter, as you well know." She placed her hands on her hips and fixed Sam with her best controlling unruly drunks in her ED stare. It didn't work. He chuckled.

"Good to know. Next time you start something, I'd prefer a little privacy as well." He hummed as he left the porch and grabbed equipment from his truck, leaving a bemused Elizabeth in his wake.

She went inside and grabbed her phone and purse. Googling "bar-b-q", she was pleased to see that Bubba's Smoke House was still in business. Known for their tender meat and tangy sauce, Elizabeth had dreamed of it when she first moved away. No one in California could make Carolina bar-b-q.

She dialed and was pleased to find someone there early. Explaining what she needed, Elizabeth ordered delivery for just after noon and read off her credit card number. Satisfied that no one in the crowd would go hungry, she disconnected and walked into the kitchen. Nora, Maggie and her youngest daughter, Riley, were waiting for her.

Elizabeth cocked her head at a loud thump from outside.

"That's just Joe and the boys putting up some ladders. They're going to check the roof and gutters."

Elizabeth laughed at Maggie calling her sons 'boys'. Donovan and Brendan were older then she, early forties and late thirties respectively. Aidan, Riley's twin was the youngest but still thirty. Each of 'the boys' stood over six feet tall and weighed in at around 200 pounds.

"This is too much, Maggie. How can I ever repay you?"

"Repay me? Are you meaning to insult me, Elizabeth? You're family. This is what we do. Now let's get to it."

The morning passed quickly. Elizabeth had left the outside to the experts, concentrating on the downstairs. There were baseboards and walls to be washed, floors to be vacuumed and mopped. She took down all the curtains and threw them in the washer.

By the time lunch was delivered, she was exhausted. House work had never been her favorite, and she was happy to take a break. There was a reason she had a cleaning lady in Los Angeles. She tipped the young man generously after he carried everything around to the deck. The delicious smells of the meal brought people from all corners of the house and yard. Maggie ushered everyone in to wash up, threatening to inspect fingernails as she had done when they were younger.

There was general chaos as the crowd loaded their plates. Elizabeth stood at the end of the line handing out sodas. She thanked each person for their help as they passed. When everyone was settled, she grabbed a plate and walked to the other end of the table. Her mouth gaped when she surveyed the damage. There wasn't enough food left to even fill a quarter of her plate.

"I have what you need right here." Drawled a familiar voice from behind her. She practically drooled as Sam waved a plate under her nose. She wasn't sure which smelled better, Sam or the food. "All you have to do is sit and eat with me."

"All you had to do was ask." She snatched the plate and led the way to a large shade tree in the backyard. An old wooden bench sat at the base. She took a seat and Sam sat next to her. They ate in companionable silence for a while.

"So yesterday was interesting. I had a conversation about my sex life, what there is of it, with my Mom. Then she told me she wants to put this house on the market."

Sam started coughing, so she turned and slapped him on the back a few times. "Are you okay, Sam? Did something go down the wrong way?"

He held up a hand, coughed weakly a few more times, before looking at her. His eyes were watering and his face was red. "You discussed your sex life with your Mom?"

"Well, she's been trying to get me 'back out there' for about five years. That naturally led to the other discussion."

"Uh huh" Sam muttered.

"Almost every time I talk to her on the phone she brings it up. It's more intense when she visits me in California. Something about wanting grandchildren before she's too old to appreciate them."

"Are you, uh, dating anyone out there?"

"No, not really. At least not for a while now." She thought about Jeremey and the fun they had in the past. She cared about him. They cared about each other. But sex without commitment had lost its appeal for her. She really needed to have a conversation with him.

"The look on your face doesn't exactly match your answer, Elizabeth."

She blinked as though just remembering where she was. "It's complicated."

"How is it complicated? As in you're still seeing him complicated?"

Elizabeth turned and searched his face. This handsome face that was as familiar to her as Connor's had been. She had no idea what was happening between them, but she owed Sam the truth. She had never been one for games anyway.

"I'm not seeing anyone in California. I haven't been for a while. I called it 'complicated' because Jeremy and I were never together per se. We just had an arrangement. For whenever one of us felt the need, so to speak." She turned away and resisted fanning her hot cheeks. This was harder than telling her mother yesterday.

"So, Diane is planning on selling, huh? Where will she live?"

Elizabeth burst out laughing and could have hugged Sam out of pure relief. "She, uh, mentioned a new older adult development close to town."

"Oh, I know where she means. Friends of my parents bought in there. It's nice. All the units are one story with a small yard. That would be perfect for your mom."

"With her health, that's exactly what she needs. Something smaller without stairs." She looked around the yard and was suddenly filled with a yearning. "You guys did a great job out here this morning. I miss this."

"What do you miss, Elizabeth?"

She gestured with her arms spread wide. "All of this. Having a yard to tinker in. Having some space and fresh air." She turned and pointed to the mountains. "Having that view." California was beautiful, but Elizabeth missed having the Blue Ridge Mountains practically in her backyard.

"I thought you were happy in California."

"I was. I am. I don't know. How's that for an answer?" she laughed mirthlessly. "I was in school for so many years. And then I was busy trying to become a good doctor. Work was everything to me. But now that I'm done with all that, I still work all the time. I need something else." She turned and smiled at him. "I hadn't even noticed until I came back here. Funny how that works" she stated without a trace of humor in her voice.

"Then maybe that should tell you something Elizabeth." Sam got up and walked away, leaving an even more confused Elizabeth behind. She balled up her napkin and threw it on the ground.

"You sure told that napkin a thing or two. Feel better?"

Elizabeth looked up at Maggie. "Still practicing your Ninja stealth moves I see."

Maggie sat next to Elizabeth on the bench and wrapped an arm around her. "Old habits die hard. They were necessary when y'all were young. What's wrong, dear heart?"

Elizabeth just shook her head. "Nothing. Everything. I don't know." She laid her head on Maggie's shoulder. "So, you see my issue then."

"I see someone who isn't entirely happy with their life. What are you going to do about it? That's the question."

Elizabeth straightened up and turned, sitting sideways on the bench to face Maggie. "That's just it. I was perfectly happy until I came back here."

"Were you, Elizabeth? Were you really happy?"

Elizabeth picked up the napkin and started shredding it on her plate. "I was content. I had my career and my routine. It all made sense."

"You didn't answer my question, dear."

Elizabeth shook her head. "No, I probably wasn't happy. At least not overall. I was going through the days. Why did it take coming home to see that?"

"I find it interesting that you still consider North Carolina home. You've been in California for ten years. Shouldn't that be your home?"

There was a large pile of shredded napkin on her plate. Elizabeth set it aside and clasped her hands in her lap. "I was only six when we moved here from New York City, but from the first day it was home. California has never felt that way."

"That should probably tell you something."

Elizabeth's eyes widened. "That's what Sam just said."

"I always did think he was wise beyond his years." Maggie chuckled at her own joke.

"Of course you do, since he agreed with you."

"That's my point, Elizabeth. If two people who care about you said the same thing in under five minutes, they might be on to something." Maggie stood and dusted off her capris. "Time to get back to work. The boss is a real slave driver" she joked to Elizabeth.

Elizabeth stood and gathered her garbage. "I can't ever thank you guys enough for today. It would have taken me months to get this accomplished. Especially now that my Mom is talking about putting the house on the market. The house needs more work to be ready, but this is at least a great start."

"Joe said the roof is sound. The boys cleaned out the gutters. Two less things to worry about."

"That's terrific. The inside just needs some freshening up. Maybe some paint and updated light fixtures."

"Good thing you know a great construction company."

Elizabeth laughed. "Good thing indeed." Maggie's husband Joe had started Fitzgerald Construction when they first married. Thanks to his excellent craftsmanship and honest business practices, the company had grown over the years. His two eldest sons, Donovan and Brendan, and youngest daughter, Riley, had since joined the firm. "You guys have made it into a real family affair, haven't you?"

"We certainly have." agreed Maggie with a beaming smile. "Mind you, that's not always the easiest thing. Working with family. Those four don't agree on much. But at the end of the day, they do great work."

"Maybe Mom can get the family and friends discount" joked Elizabeth.

"Of course, honey. Now let's get these lazy folks moving." Maggie marched on ahead, rousing folks from their sunshine and bar-b-q induced somnolence.

Elizabeth looked around in awe at all that had been accomplished this morning. The flower beds were all weeded and replanted. The lawn and bushes had been cut and trimmed. She walked around the front of the house, and found the same was true there. She waved at Donovan as he pulled a power washer off the back of his truck. The house and deck were apparently next.

Walking back inside through the front door, Elizabeth thought about her life in California. She loved her work, but what about her actual life? She had friends, she mused. But were they really the type who would drop everything for a day of cleaning and yard work? Probably not. They were more work acquaintances.

She had good reasons for leaving Windsor Falls, but that was ten years ago. She had dealt with her losses, and it wasn't painful to be here now. Did those reasons even count anymore? Being home was certainly raising a lot of questions. And that didn't even include the whole Sam issue.

Elizabeth tackled the upstairs bathrooms next. The physical labor was just what she needed. Unfortunately, it gave her plenty of time to think. And that meant a certain hunky friend of hers. Reconciling the Sam of her childhood with the man who could make her melt with a single molten kiss was still a challenge. Just thinking about that made her lips tingle.

She had made her way down to the first-floor powder room, when a knock on the open bathroom door startled her. She whirled with a toilet scrubber in hand to find the very man standing in the doorway. "You really are psychic." she scolded. Figures she would be a sweaty mess and cleaning a toilet.

One dark eyebrow arched. "Psychic? Why this time?"

"I was just thinking about you, and you appear. Psychic."

He folded his arms across his muscled chest and lounged against the doorframe. "Were they at least good thoughts?"

She ducked her head not wishing to give anything away. "Never mind." she mumbled. She attacked the rim of the toilet with more vigor than needed. "Was there something you wanted?"

"Always. But I'm here to tell you people are wrapping up. I thought you might want to come out and say goodbye."

"Oh, of course. I guess I lost track of the time." She stripped off her rubber gloves, tossing them in the trash. When she turned to the sink to wash her hands, Sam crowded in behind her in the small bathroom. He pushed aside the damp curls at the nape of her neck and placed a hot, open mouthed kiss there.

Elizabeth melted as she turned off the water. Sam handed her a towel and then took advantage of the fact that her hands were occupied. Without a word, he backed her into the sink, pressing his body along hers. Her hands, still clutching the towel, were pinned between them. Leaning in and covering her mouth with his, Sam thoroughly kissed her. Elizabeth only had time to notice that their bodies lined up perfectly before Sam broke the kiss.

"Thought I'd give you something else to think about" he said before leaving the tiny room.

A full minute had passed before she realized she was still holding the hand towel. She replaced it on the bar and went out to say good bye, hoping they wouldn't notice her flushed cheeks.

It took another thirty minutes for the round of goodbyes, even though everyone would be together again in less than a week for the anniversary party. Elizabeth had forgotten what it was like to truly belong.

When they were gone at last, she took a quick shower and went to see her Mom. Thankfully, Diane was settling in okay at the rehab center. Elizabeth had grabbed some Chinese take-out on the way, and the two shared the meal and some small talk.

Elizabeth could see that the program was exhausting her mother, so she left early, promising to return before her shift tomorrow. She had agreed to pick up a couple of night shifts in the ED this week.

She was just getting into bed when her phone chirped. Without looking she knew it was Sam. He really had uncanny timing.

"How's Fred?" she read on the screen. A delighted laugh bubbled out of her as she turned off the light and sank back into the pillows. She debated briefly how to respond.

"He's fine. Still faithful. Should I invest in opaque curtains?" She hit send and waited.

"No need. It's that psychic connection of ours. At least you have Fred. I'm lonely."

"You have Cooper, Lily and Griffin. How could you be lonely?"

"They're not in my bed. We should have one of our famous sleep overs."

Elizabeth laughed as she remembered the 'camping' they did in Connor's backyard. All his siblings, plus Elizabeth and Sam would crowd into a tent built for half that number. Joe would make a small fire before bedtime, and they would roast marshmallows and tell ghost stories. Inevitably their number would dwindle by morning, either from bathroom runs into the house or fear of ghosts. Donovan had been rather blood thirsty with his tales.

"I'm too old and too spoiled to sleep on the ground anymore." she replied.

"Who said anything about the ground? I have a perfectly good, king-sized bed."

Her nipples tightened at the thought. Elizabeth grew restless in her lonely bed.

"You're pretty brave when you're twenty minutes away."

"I'd be even braver if you told me what you're wearing."

Elizabeth glanced down her heated body. She was similarly clad to last night in a pair of panties and a cami. But even that felt like too much. She twisted one thin strap as she thought about how to reply to his challenge.

"A long flannel nightgown."

She giggled as she thought about his expression when he read her response. Take that, she thought with glee.

"Are there at least buttons? I love buttons. They make you work for it. Like unwrapping a gift on Christmas morning."

She hadn't expected that. It really was getting warm in here, she thought, as she fanned herself. Well, two could play at that game.

"Not fair. You haven't told me what you're wearing."

"That's easy to remedy. Nothing." The text was followed by an emoji that winked. Her breathe caught at the mental image. Her hands shook a bit as she replied.

"Nothing, huh?"

"Does the sheet count? That's up to about my...waist."

Elizabeth hadn't seen Sam without a shirt since they were kids. She and Connor and Sam had often gone swimming in the many lakes and falls in the area, especially the magnificent one that the town was named for. But she had been pressed up against his body just a few hours ago. The rugged hardness of his chest had instantly made her nipples sit up and take notice. She could only imagine what it looked like. He was a teenager anymore.

"Are you still there?" Sam wrote.

"Yes." That was lame as replies went, but Elizabeth was having putting two words together. Thoughts of Sam and his naked body robber her of coherent thought.

"Am I embarrassing you, Elizabeth? That wasn't my intention."

"No, that wouldn't be the word I used."

"What word would you use then?" Once again, Sam had thrown down the gauntlet. Time to up her game.

"Hot. Bothered. Frustrated. Turned on. Oops, that's two words."

Let's see how funny he is now, she thought. She waited for what seemed like forever. He didn't reply. Elizabeth jumped a foot when her phone rang. She looked at the phone in her hand like she would a Cobra. Texting was one thing… By the third ring, she knew she had to answer and did so reluctantly. She tapped the green send button but didn't speak.

"So, I make you hot, do I?" came Sam's drawled greeting. He chuckled low and sexy. "Nice to know it's not one-sided."

"Sam, what are we doing?" she whispered into the phone. Lying in her darkened room made it feel sexier.

"If I have to tell you, Elizabeth, then we aren't doing it right."

"Ha-ha very funny, Sam. You know what I mean."

"I'm not sure that I do, Elizabeth."

She sighed heavily. Was she really going to have to spell this out for him? "This thing between us. This flirtation. Or whatever you want to call it. What are we doing? We're friends, Sam."

"Can't we be more than friends, Elizabeth? Do you really need to define it?"

She didn't know what to say, so she said nothing. Just laid there and listened to him breathe. This was Sam. Her relationship with him had never been complicated in the past. Why now? But even Elizabeth couldn't deny the chemistry between them. So where did that leave them?

"I know you're still there, Elizabeth. I can hear you thinking."

"I'm leaving, Sam."

"Right now?"

"Well of course not. But eventually."

"When?"

"I don't know. Are you trying to get rid of me already?" She tried for levity.

"No. I want you to stay. To come home, Elizabeth."

So much for levity she thought. "Sam…" She never got a chance to finish.

"Your life is in California. I know. Please don't say it again, Elizabeth. What I want to know is why."

"You know why Sam."

"I know why you left. I don't know why you're still there."

"I'm not sure what you want me to say, Sam."

"Just tell me the truth."

She didn't even hesitate. "I'm not actually wearing flannel."

There was a pause before Sam burst out laughing. She knew what Sam wanted to hear, but Elizabeth wasn't sure what the truth was anymore.

"You lied to me? I don't think you've ever lied to me, Elizabeth."

"I, uh." She swallowed heavily, unsure what to say. "It was more of a joke?"

"I think you should be punished."

"Really? What am I, five?"

"You've always been the most inherently honest person I know. Yet you lied. Makes me think you don't want me to know what you're wearing, Elizabeth."

"Fine. I'm wearing a pair of panties and a matching camisole. Light blue if you need to know details."

It was Sam's turn to swallow hard. "Silk?"

"Yes."

"Maybe I should come over. Just to verify."

"Not necessary."

"You could always send me a picture."

"Say good-night Sam."

"Good-night Sam."

She sighed deeply and pressed the phone closer to her ear. "You know what I mean. Good-night, Sam." Elizabeth disconnected.

Chapter Fifteen

Elizabeth glanced into the full-length mirror in her bedroom one last time. She fidgeted nervously with an earring and ran a hand over her curls. She was normally a very low maintenance kind of girl, but tonight was different. The anniversary party was tonight, and she wanted to look her best. She could think of several reasons for wanting that, but the truth was she wanted to look good for Sam.

She had not seen him since the cleaning day at her mom's house. She had spoken with him every night, though. They had continued their nightly ritual of flirty texts and calls that bordered on phone sex.

It had been a busy week. Her mother had come home just this morning, having made remarkable progress in rehab. A physical therapist would be coming out daily for a while to continue her exercises. Diane also had sessions with a nutritionist to learn how to eat more healthily and maintain a diet that would help her heart failure.

Elizabeth had worked two night shifts in the ED this week as well as continuing to work on her mother's home. Her helpers had done all the heavy lifting, but there were still details to attend to. Elizabeth had been going through the personal belongings she had stored in the house. She had to decide what to get rid of and what to take back to California.

That was another tricky subject. Her mother had asked her several times this week when she would be returning to her life there. As had her boss. Although he was understanding of the situation, he also had to get coverage for her if she was going to stay in North Carolina longer. She had a decision to make. Sam had not mentioned California again, and Elizabeth wasn't sure what that meant.

She thought about Sam every day. When she was supposed to be working. When she was making breakfast. The time of day didn't matter. He was always on her mind. He was making her crazy. She was making herself crazy. She had a decision to make, and he wasn't helping.

She heard the doorbell ring, shortly followed by her mother's voice. "Darling, your date's here."

"I'll be right down", she called through gritted teeth. Dabbing a light perfume behind her ears and on her wrists, Elizabeth took a final look in the mirror. She was thrilled with the dress she had bought in town. Running into Lisa at the grocery store had been a stroke of luck. She had ducked into her boutique one day in between chores and found Lisa, true to her word, had put aside a few dresses for her to choose from. The woman was a genius, Elizabeth reminisced. She had ended up buying the very first one she tried. The shopping trip had been a huge success. She also bought a purse and strappy sandals to match.

"Well now, that was certainly worth the wait" was quickly followed by a long, low whistle of appreciation as Elizabeth descended the stairs. Flynn stood in the foyer and watched her approach.

The long dress of sapphire silk hugged her body in all the right places and flowed with her when she moved. Thin straps left her long, graceful neck exposed. The long slit up one leg left more skin bared than she was comfortable with, but Elizabeth had been unable to resist the dress. Her only jewelry were diamond earrings that dangled and caught the light. They had been a wedding gift from Maggie and Joe. She was grateful for the extra pains she had taken with her appearance. She might be happy to spend her work week in scrubs, but occasionally, she enjoyed dressing up and feeling feminine.

She glanced at Flynn and murmured her thanks. He looked great in his obviously custom made formal wear. Female heads would be turning at the party.

"At the risk of further inflating your already overblown ego, you clean up well."

"As do you. Are you ready?" Elizabeth nodded. "Well then, my lady, your carriage awaits." Flynn walked towards her offering his arm.

Elizabeth held up one finger briefly and turned towards her mother. "You know where I'll be and how to reach me. Please call me if you need anything. Anything at all." She fixed her mother with a serious look.

Diane shooed her daughter towards the door. "I'm fine, don't worry. Besides, I've got a hot date with a book I've been dying to finish. Have a nice time, dear." She turned then and slowly made her way up the stairs.

Elizabeth watched her halting progress and hesitated about leaving her alone. As much as she wanted to attend the party, she was reluctant to leave her mother so soon after being hospitalized. She wished she had been able to talk her mother into letting her hire a home health nurse to stay with her for a few hours. But Diane was proud and wouldn't hear of it.

"Oh, no you don't" Flynn scolded. "Your mother is a big girl and will be fine for a few hours. Doctor's orders."

She knew he was right but couldn't resist sticking out her tongue at him. "You're not my doctor."

"That's because you refuse to play doctor with me, Elizabeth." He wagged his eyebrows suggestively at her. "Besides, you invited me to this party, and we're going. It's been a long week. We could both use a little fun."

He was right. They both worked hard. She just wasn't as confident about having fun tonight as he was. She was, in fact, very nervous about seeing Sam again.

She allowed Flynn to lead her out to his waiting car. "Wow, Flynn, nice car!" A gleaming black Mercedes sat in the driveway. He handed her into the low passenger seat and walked around to the driver's side. She ran her hands appreciatively over the leather interior. "This car is exactly what I would have pictured for you, Flynn." She secretly preferred Sam's truck, but kept that fact to herself. Flynn would be horrified.

When they arrived at the Fitzgerald home, a valet approached Flynn for his keys, freeing him to open her door. Elizabeth was not surprised to see the number of cars on the street. At least half of them would belong to immediate family.

Elizabeth placed her hand in the crook Flynn's elbow as they walked up the front sidewalk. He turned to her and stopped walking. "Let's get this straight before we go inside. You and I are just going to be friends, right?" When she started to say something, he held up one hand. "I'm not heartbroken, Elizabeth, so don't fret. I like you, and I think we will be great friends. I also think you're beautiful, especially when you put some effort into it. But there isn't any chemistry between us. I just wanted to clear the air before we make our grand entrance."

The laughter bubbled up and out of her as they reached the front door. "Oh, Flynn, you are an original. I'm almost sorry things are the way they are since you make me laugh so much." She reached up and kissed his cheek, smoothing away a trace of her lipstick.

Flynn gave her a hug before opening the door. Elizabeth was grateful for his presence at her side. This would not be an easy night. Now that she was here, her palms were damp. Katie would of course be here, and Elizabeth had grown weary of their acerbic exchanges. And then there was Sam. Not allowing her thoughts to go there, she steeled herself and walked further into the room with Flynn glued to her side.

Elizabeth had made the rounds and was now standing at the temporary bar with a glass of champagne in her hand, when the tiny hairs on the back of her neck stood up. Turning, she spotted Sam across the room. She noticed under lowered lashes that he looked very handsome tonight in a tuxedo that fit as though it were made just for him. The snowy white of his dress shirt did wonders for his tan. She took another large swallow of her champagne for courage. It may as well have been ginger ale for all she noticed.

Nora had been talking to her, but Elizabeth had no idea what the other woman had been saying since Sam walked into the room. What was wrong with her? She struggled keep up with the conversation, hoping Nora hadn't asked her a question. "I'm so happy for you and Donovan. 20 years! That's amazing!" She leaned in and hugged Nora tightly.

"Yes, it is. It's also a lot of work. But so worth it. Seriously, Elizabeth, are you sure you're OK with seeing Liam? I know you're tough, but it had to be difficult."

"It's OK, Nora, really. Liam is adorable, and I know how long you guys wanted a third child. Of course, it makes me a little sad to think about the baby I lost. He or she would have been the same age." She stopped and struggled to hold back tears. "I know that Connor and our baby are both looking out for me."

Nora sniffed loudly and then laughed weakly. "That's enough of that. It won't due for the two of us to be crying when we should be celebrating. Tell me about that handsome man who brought you here. He looks like he has a bit of the devil in him."

"Did I hear someone asking about me?" Flynn laughed as he materialized at Elizabeth's side. Leaning down to kiss her outstretched hand with a charismatic flair, he introduced himself to Nora. He settled back next to Elizabeth, placing a possessive arm around her waist. "Congratulations on your amazing accomplishment, Nora. Twenty years is a long time to put up with the same man."

"Not if he's the right man." she replied.

"Touché."

"Don't you believe in happily ever after, Flynn? Doesn't being here inspire you to find the right woman and settle down?" Elizabeth took another drink of her champagne and considered the man next to her. Brilliant, funny, and charming as he was, he certainly made a great catch for some lucky woman.

"You might be surprised to know how much I do believe in all of that, Elizabeth. That's why I am so choosy. When I marry, it will be forever. I'm in no hurry." He smiled into her surprised face.

An old ballad about true love came over the speakers, and Flynn led her out towards the patio where several couples were already dancing. They passed in front of Sam, who had been making his way over to the bar. She looked up and smiled uncertainly as she passed.

The two men barely acknowledged each other. Elizabeth didn't know whether to laugh or kick them both with her pointy sandals. Flynn moved a bit closer to her and tightened his arm around her waist. "Come along darling. You did promise me a dance. What could be better than holding you in the moonlight?"

She glanced briefly back at Sam as she was pulled towards the patio. His eyes were nearly black with emotion. Anger? Desire? She didn't know. She didn't want to leave him with the impression that there was something more than friendship between her and Flynn. But she also didn't want to discuss this with him in the middle of a party. She allowed Flynn to pull her out onto the patio.

Once out of Sam's hearing, she whirled on Flynn. "What was that little show about? You and I aren't lovers. Just what kind of game are you playing?" She stopped and blew out an angry breath.

Seemingly unfazed by her anger, Flynn gathered her in his arms and twirled her around the patio. "I was just making your boyfriend jealous. Having a bit of fun at his expense. Proving my earlier point. Take your choice, Elizabeth." Much to her amazement, Flynn laughed aloud. "Purely harmless, I assure you, although I do believe he'd like to blacken my eye about now."

"And you find that funny?"

"Actually, I do." He twirled her further away from the lights of the party so that they were on the darkened edge of the patio.

"I won't even bother to tell you again that Sam and I are just friends." Given the way Sam had just looked at her, the statement sounded a bit hollow, even to her. Flynn merely raised a curious eyebrow. "OK I don't really know what Sam and I are to each other anymore. But that doesn't give him the right to act as if I'm his personal property. Just because we kissed…" She pressed her lips together, horrified. She hadn't meant to let that fact slip.

"There was a kiss? And you didn't tell me? You're holding out on me, Elizabeth. And I thought we were friends." Flynn chuckled wickedly into her ear.

Not to be outdone, Elizabeth answered him in kind. "A lady" she said haughtily, "never kisses and tells." It was too much effort to hold in her laughter. If nothing else, Flynn was certainly good for her stress level.

"Not telling is a very bad sign you know. That means it's serious. You are going to break my heart after all."

"Ugh! That's enough out of you. When I want advice on my love life, what there is of it, I'll let you know. But don't hold your breath." The song ended then, and Elizabeth made her escape. She stalked back into the crowded house.

Sam, who had been waiting just inside of the French doors, stepped in front of her, effectively blocking her path. "My turn" he said as he took hold of her arm.

Elizabeth looked into his darkened eyes. The protest died on her lips. Instead she placed her hand in his, and he led her back out onto the patio, maneuvering them into a deserted corner.

Sam gathered her into his strong arms and began to move slowly to the music. This corner of the patio was softly lit, only by torches and moonlight. They swayed gently to the rhythm of a Frank Sinatra tune, her body perfectly molded to his. With the difference in their heights, her head came to just below his chin. She felt a shudder ripple through his body. She closed her eyes on the perfection of the moment.

Elizabeth sighed and rested her cheek against Sam's chest. Even through the layers of his clothing, she could hear his heartbeat. She breathed in the unique scent of him. He smelled faintly of alcohol and the spice of his after shave. He smelled of promise and fulfillment. She knew this was dangerous, but she no longer cared. Tonight was not about thinking. Tonight was about feeling.

Sam reached under her chin and tilted her face towards him. She saw the question in his desire-filled eyes and answered with a seductive smile. Stretching up on her toes to better reach him, she closed the small gap by placing her lips firmly against his.

This kiss was different from their others. There was no hesitation. The desire that had smoldered between them burst into flames, threatening to consume both.

She groaned wildly into his opened mouth, sending shivers through both of their bodies. Sam gathered her even closer, cupping her bottom in both hands. She was molded to him completely, and there was no doubt of his desire for her.

Their tongues met in a dance of passion as old as time. She couldn't think as the flame consumed her. Elizabeth fisted both hands in the hair at the nape of his neck. She loved the silky feel. She loved even more the groan that she had elicited. It was exciting to know she wasn't the only one so deeply affected. She thought about removing his tailored suit to touch him all over. It no longer mattered that he was her old friend. She burned too hotly for him to care anymore.

The song changed, but Elizabeth barely noticed. It was replaced with another, lovely standard. She drank from his lips greedily. Her hands slid down to his chest, pushing the jacket aside so that she could feel the muscles of his chest. Sam was doing his own exploring as he ran his hands across her back and up the sides of her breasts, briefly teasing her nipples through the silky material of the dress. Elizabeth watched his eyes dilate with desire as he realized she wasn't wearing anything under the dress. His erection grew hard against her belly.

They remained locked in this embrace for another moment until Sam released his hold on her and eased back a step. Even in the darkness, the confusion shone in her eyes.

"Sam? What's wrong?" She wasn't sure why he had stopped so suddenly. She only knew that she felt the loss of his touch.

He gathered her up in his arms, gently this time. "Honey, we really need to work on our timing. Even though it's dark out here, anyone could come along. Believe me, considering what I'd like to do to you right now, I certainly don't want an audience." He buried his face into her neck and breathed in deeply.

Realization dawned painfully on her. She had thought only of making love with him. Right here. Right now. She never even considered where they were. This wasn't like her at all. What was she doing? Elizabeth struggled for some composure.

She finally broke the awkward silence of the moment. "I've had enough dancing for one night Sam, but I do think we need to talk."

Sam shook his head in agreement and led her around the house into a side garden. They sat facing each other on a small, stone bench. Neither said a word.

"I have a problem" she began. "I came home on a moment's notice when my mom became so sick. I didn't plan this. I didn't have any time to prepare, and it hasn't been easy adjustment for me. She's doing so much better, and I've enjoyed my time working in the ED at Memorial. But I'm on borrowed time here, Sam. And to confuse me even more, you kissed me. And now I don't know what to think. There's still so much left unsaid between us, and I don't know…well I don't know anything. Does that make any sense, Sam?"

"What don't you know, Elizabeth? Where you belong? If you don't know by now, my telling you won't help. Is it that you don't want to be involved with anyone now? I can't help you with that. If you're attracted to me? Well, I think we pretty much proved that tonight. Or maybe it's whether I'm the right person for you. I'm not Connor, Elizabeth. I never was, and I never will be. Maybe that's the problem."

Sam grew quiet. "I know you're not Connor" she whispered to him. There had never been any doubt in her mind whom she was with.

Sam stood abruptly. "I'm sorry, Elizabeth. I can't do this. I can't sit around wearing my heart on my sleeve while I wait for you to make up your mind." He walked away into the darkness. It took every ounce of will power she possessed to not go after him and throw herself back into his arms.

Instead, Elizabeth sat as still as the stone of the bench. What had just happened? One minute, they're breathless with passion, and then he's gone? Where had all of that come from? She had never compared him to Connor. The two friends were as different as night and day. Hot tears were threatening, and she willed them away. Not tonight.

Elizabeth stood, smoothing out the lines of her dress, and walked back towards the house. She thought ruefully that she should probably find a bathroom and fix her lipstick before she saw anyone. She wasn't in the mood to explain. She also didn't feel like celebrating anymore. She hoped she could find Flynn quickly and make her escape.

Slipping into the powder room to repair her make-up and splash some cold water on her wrists bought her a few moments to get herself together. Elizabeth rejoined the party just in time to have a very angry Katie sweep by her. She stepped out of the way to avoid being knocked over as the other woman went into the powder room and slammed the door resoundingly. A very satisfied looking Flynn approached. He was sporting a wicked smile and a suspicious red mark on his left cheek.

"Well" he drawled laconically, "you can tell that's her natural hair color. All I did was make one little, innocent comment about her dress." He rubbed his cheek thoughtfully. "I suppose she left a mark, eh?"

Elizabeth was almost afraid to ask what he had done to deserve being slapped. Katie might be a bit high strung lately, but she had never been prone to violence. "Care to tell me what your comment was?"

He shrugged his wide shoulders. "I merely said that if she was comfortable wearing a dress like that in public, I'd be more than willing to take her home for the rest of the show in private." He gingerly touched the reddened area of his cheek. "I guess that was a no."

"You're lucky she only slapped you, Flynn!" Elizabeth burst out into a fit of laughter. "Need I remind you that she has several very large brothers, not to mention a father who could still wipe the floor with you?" He just grinned in response.

"Well, if you're finished wreaking havoc, I'd like to go home. I don't want to leave my Mom for too long."

Elizabeth gathered her purse, and they said their round of good byes. Flynn gave his ticket to the valet, and the two waited in silence in the balmy night. If he noticed that she was unnaturally quiet on the short ride, Flynn was kind enough to not mention it. Elizabeth was thankful for the reprieve.

They arrived at her mother's home shortly afterwards. Flynn, ever the gentleman, came around to open her door. "Well I certainly had a wonderful time tonight. Thanks again, Elizabeth, for inviting me." He leaned down and kissed her cheek.

She thanked him for the ride and moral support before entering the house and closing the door.

Elizabeth peered around the darkened living room, relieved to see her mother wasn't up still. She walked upstairs, taking off her shoes as she went and curling her cramped toes appreciatively into the thick carpeting. There was a reason she didn't wear heels often. She really wanted nothing more than to wash away all traces of the night. After carefully hanging up the dress, she removed her make-up and turned on the shower. Elizabeth stood under the soothing, hot water, allowing it blast away the troubles of the evening. Fifteen minutes later, dressed in pajama shorts and a tank top, Elizabeth was more than ready to crawl into bed.

But just as she reached for the light, she heard her mother call out to her. Elizabeth rushed into her room, thankful to see her propped up in bed with a closed book on her lap.

"I didn't expect to see you home so early, dear. Is everything OK?" her mother asked.

"I'm fine, Mom. Just tired."

Diane gently patted the bed next to her. "Come sit down for a minute and tell me what's wrong. You look upset."

Elizabeth sank down onto the bed. Weariness was etched into the lines of her face. "It's Sam, actually. He's different since I've been back. It's hard to reconcile the Sam from my childhood with who he is today. And I know I've hurt him. I'm just not sure how to make things right again. Like they used to be." She buried her face in her hands.

Diane hesitated and then pulled Elizabeth's hands away from her face. Looking directly into her eyes, she asked, "Is that really what you want? To go back to what you had? Because I'm not sure that's possible. That was a long time ago, Elizabeth, and a lot has changed since then. You and Sam are both different people now. You can't come back here after so long and expect everything to be the same as it was. Life doesn't work that way."

Elizabeth sighed heavily and twisted her hands in her lap. "That's just it, Mom. I don't know what I want. Sam seems so different to me these days, and I'm not sure what to think about that. And then there's everything still unfinished between us. I have to fix that. I just don't want to make it worse than it already is."

"Sam's a good man, honey. A really good man. He was lost for a long time after you left. But he's pulled his life together. It's good to see him doing well now."

Elizabeth shook her head. "I don't understand, Mom. You were always so tough on Sam. He and Connor were my very best friends, Mom, and you were always standoffish at best. Now you're defending him."

The older woman shook her head and took Elizabeth's hands in hers. "I always liked Sam. I just didn't want to see him get hurt, so I tried to not encourage him." At her daughter's confused look, she continued. "The three of you were inseparable, almost from the very first moment we moved here. But that couldn't last forever. I always knew that Connor was meant for you. That you were meant for each other. And Sam would be hurt by that."

"You knew that Connor and I were meant for each other? Even before I did?"

"Yes. And I didn't want to see Sam hurt by it, so I tried to discourage your friendship. But that was wrong of me."

"Not nearly as wrong as how I treated him before I left. He deserved so much better from me. But I couldn't see past my own grief." She broke off on a sob and buried her face in her mother's lap.

Diane stroked her wet hair, pushing it back from her face. "If he's that good of a friend, then he already understands, dear. You were so young, and your whole life was ripped apart. No one should ever have to go through that. But look at you now. I'm so very proud of you! Talk to Sam. But keep in mind that just because things may never be the same as they were doesn't mean they won't be better."

Elizabeth sat up, mopping the tears off her face. "Since we're baring souls, Mom, tell me why you hid the truth from me for so long. Why didn't you tell me you were sick? I was too wrapped up in my own life far away to hear what you weren't saying. I'm a doctor, for goodness sake, and I couldn't even help my own mother. You could have died."

Diane grasped her daughter by both shoulders. "I almost died because of my own foolish pride, Elizabeth, not because of anything you did or didn't do. I could have told you. There were any number of people here in town I could have told. But I didn't because I was scared."

She paused and took a deep breath before continuing. "It all started slowly. I would feel more tired than usual. I got winded more easily. And I started noticing some swelling in my hands and feet. Then I started having real trouble catching my breath. I knew something was wrong, but I was afraid of dying. Ironically, that's what almost happened."

"Oh, Mom, if I had only been here…"

Diane held up a hand. "No, Elizabeth, don't do that to yourself. You were where you needed to be. I knew you'd come if I told you, and I didn't want that. I wanted you to come home because that's what you wanted. On your own terms. And you did come when I needed you, so there's nothing to feel guilty about."

"Well, I'm here now, Mom, for as long as you need me."

"And what about California?" asked her mother.

Elizabeth shrugged. "I don't know. I came home to be with you when you were sick, telling myself I'd go back once you were on your feet."

"And now? I'm doing better, honey. Out of the woods, so to speak. What's your plan?"

"If only I knew." She blew out a long breath.

Diane yawned mightily. "Obviously, I'm not back to full strength yet. I need to sleep. You'll make the right decision about California." She kissed her daughter then set her back and looked Elizabeth in the eyes. "You'll do what's right for you."

"But how will I know what that is?"

"You just will. Good-night, honey."

Elizabeth hugged her mom and wished her a good night, before heading back to her own room. She crawled into her bed and flopped on her back, kicking the covers to the floor. That's where they'd end up anyway. Sleep had proven difficult at best recently. She thought about Sam and about what they had shared over the years.

The three of them had really been the best of friends. But there was always a piece of himself that Sam held back. From her. Even from Connor. She only noticed it from time to time when they were young, but it happened more frequently as they grew older. There were times, when he didn't know she was watching, that a seriousness would shadow his features. He would smile at her when he realized she was looking, but it didn't always reach his eyes. There were other times when it seemed as though he wanted to say something to her, but then the moment would pass. He was always more complicated than Connor.

Things between them were even more convoluted now. She traced the outline of her lips, remembering the sizzle of his lips on hers. How good her body felt against his. They had been playing with fire since she came home, but the timing had never been right.

Elizabeth bolted out of bed. She knew what she needed to do. And she needed to do it now. She needed to see him. To talk with him. Now, before any more time could pass. Before any more confusion could build. She needed to fix things between them. He couldn't have possibly meant it when he said he didn't want to try anymore? Could he?

A sense of panic threatened to overwhelm her. She paused briefly at her mother's room to make sure she was okay. The older woman had turned out the light and was snoring softly. Feeling confident that her mother would be okay alone, Elizabeth paused only long enough to grab her keys before dashing out the door. She was more than five miles from home when she realized she wasn't even wearing any shoes.

Chapter Sixteen

Sam was also having a restless night. He had been wide awake since leaving the party hours ago, tossing and turning for a while before giving up completely on the pretense of sleep. Now he was lying on his back, staring at the ceiling. Images of Elizabeth ran though his head.

What an idiot he had been tonight. He hadn't meant to rush her, but the clock was ticking. Every day Diane got a little better. And while he was truly thankful for that, it also meant a day closer to Elizabeth leaving. Again. He wished he could take her somewhere alone and freeze time. There was so much he needed to tell her.

But all he had managed to do tonight was to embarrass her and send wildly mixed signals. How was he ever going to fix this situation? How could he ever make her understand the depth of his feelings for her? He didn't have any great answers, but Sam knew he better find them. Quickly.

A pair of headlights turned into his driveway, surprising Sam. No one ever came out this way, especially this late. And he didn't live in a place where people came to by accident. He grabbed an old pair of running shorts hanging off the back of a chair and put them on hurriedly. His heart was beating erratically, as though it might burst out of his chest. He crossed to the bedroom window and looked out into the darkness.

A summer storm had just started, and lightening split the sky. In its bright illumination, he could see the familiar outline of Diane's car. This was better than any fantasy. She had come to him. He didn't know why, and he didn't care. He ran through his house to the front door, throwing it open. The thunder that followed closely shook the house. Rain was now coming down in sheets.

Elizabeth stood in the driveway, hesitant and soaking wet. She appeared frozen, if not by the suddenly, violent weather, then by her own indecision. Her eyes were wide, and she twisted her keys in her hands. As he looked closer, Sam could see she was shaking. He met her half way as she walked to the porch, coming to a halt in front of her. The rain slashed down mercilessly, but neither seemed to notice.

"I'm so sorry, Sam. For so many things. I don't even know where to begin. I just…"She broke off then. Her breathing was shallow and rapid. Her chest was heaving.

He knew that there were so many things that they needed to talk about, but for the life of him, Sam couldn't think of a single one. He reached out and brushed her soaking hair behind one ear. Her clothing, what there was of it, was plastered to her body in the rain, and he couldn't help but stare at her beautiful breasts. Her nipples were peaked and straining at the wet material of her tank top. He could easily tell that she wore nothing underneath.

Struggling to maintain control, Sam dragged his gaze upwards. His throat tightened, and his chest ached from the effort of breathing. She was so damned beautiful. "I'm the one who should be sorry. I had no right to start something we couldn't finish. I had no right to speak to you that way either." He grinned at Elizabeth; a slow, sexy grin, trying to ease the tension between them. "Is that the famous cami I've heard so much about?"

Without a word, Elizabeth reached out, tracing a fingernail down Sam's bare chest. A shudder tore through him just as another burst of lightening split the sky. Sam drew in a ragged breath as her finger reached the taut plane of his stomach. He grabbed her hand in his.

"Elizabeth, you'd better leave now if you're leaving tonight." Sam held his breathe as he waited for her answer. The tension was palpable.

She met his gaze in the darkness. "The only place I'm going is inside, with you Sam." The storm raging around them was nothing compared to that which raged between them.

Without another word, he leaned down and swung her up into his arms. Pivoting on his heel, he bounded across the porch and into the house. He paused only long enough to kick the door shut with his foot, before continuing through the living area and his bedroom and into his master bath.

Once inside, he placed her gently on her feet and reached for a large, thick bath towel. He reverently dried the rainwater from her face and arms. There wasn't one inch of either of them that wasn't soaked. His heart was pounding so fiercely he was afraid she could hear it in the quiet of the room. Sam hesitated once again, giving her a chance to change her mind. But all she did was smile tentatively at him.

Elizabeth took the towel from his hands and returned the favor, guiding it up his chest and across his broad shoulders. "Sam" she said in a whisper.

That was all he needed to assure him that she was here with him and only him tonight. There wouldn't be room for ghosts. Something inside of him broke free. He leaned down and placed his lips in the sensitive hollow where her neck and shoulder joined. She sighed with pleasure. Encouraged, he trailed his mouth up the delicate line of her neck to the soft underside of her jaw and finally around to her ear. He took the very tip of her earlobe into his mouth and bit down lightly. Needing to taste more of her, he trapped her face in his hands and pulled her in for a kiss, his mouth plundering hers.

Elizabeth stretched up on her toes. She brushed against the full weight of his arousal. He groaned into her mouth. Their tongues met in an erotic tangling, a foreshadowing of what was to come. Elizabeth trailed her fingers over the coiled muscles of his back. Her nails sent shivers down his spine.

With a groan, deep in his throat, Sam broke the kiss and swept the sodden top from her, desperate to have nothing between them. He cupped her breasts in his hands, using his thumbs to tease her already taut nipples. He watched in wonder as her breasts fit perfectly in his hands. Somewhere in the small part of his brain that was still functioning he knew that she had been made for him. Elizabeth moaned aloud and moved her hips against him in silent invitation.

Sam backed her slowly out of the bathroom until her legs hit the side of his bed. He lowered her gently to the mattress and kneeled on the floor. Elizabeth raised her hips off the bed, allowing him access to the last barrier of her clothing. But Sam had other ideas. As much as he felt like he may explode at any moment, he wanted this night to last forever.

Instead, he planted a series of wet, hot kisses down her body. His tongue flickered out to trace the circle of her navel. He was rewarded with the plaintive noises she was a making in the back of her throat. Again, she pleaded with her body, lifting her hips off the bed. This time, he didn't disappoint her.

Placing both hands in the waistband of her loosely fitting shorts, he eased them and her panties down her legs in one smooth motion and tossed them aside. Sam picked up her foot and kissed the sole, nibbling down to her toes. Elizabeth grabbed fistfuls of sheet in response, twisting restlessly on the bed. He slowly made his way up her leg, nipping on the sensitive skin at the backs of her knees. She moaned loudly on the bed. Becoming bolder still, Sam ran his tongue up the inside of one thigh, pausing only at the junction of her legs. He was transfixed by the sight.

The lush, curly hair was already slick with anticipation. The sight alone almost sent him over the edge. His groin tightened. Sam gritted his teeth. There would be plenty of time for that later. This was just for her. He reached up under her body and pulled her to the very edge of the bed. With one last hot look at her, he lowered his head and darted his tongue into her moist core.

Elizabeth moved restlessly on the bed, clenching and unclenching her hands in his hair. She tossed her head back and forth, fighting for control. "Please, Sam. Don't stop."

Sam had no intention of stopping. He continued his onslaught, thrusting his tongue deeper and quicker. Her hips picked up on the rhythm that he created. Over and over, his tongue darted in and out, lapping at the tiny, overly sensitive bud of flesh. Seeking to send her hurtling over the edge, he inserted two fingers inside of her and moved them in and out as he sucked on her heated flesh. He knew the moment she came. Her muscles tightened and she cried out his name over and over in release.

Sam moved up onto the bed and enfolded her into his strong arms. He held her while sobs wracked her body. Placing his lips against her dampened hair, Sam whispered to her as she struggled for control. When the tears subsided, he wiped the remaining ones from her lovely face. He knew she was embarrassed by the outpouring of emotion when she hid her face in the crook of his neck.

"It's okay," he whispered to her over and over. "I'm right here with you. He gazed down at her with adoration in his eyes.

"I feel so stupid, Sam. I have no idea what that was about." She sighed and stretched out along his body. Sam gathered her in close. He continued to softly stroke her short curls.

"We don't have to do anything else, Elizabeth. It's enough to just hold you in my arms." What he didn't say was that this was a dream many years in the making. He instinctively knew she wasn't ready to hear that yet.

She shook her head against his dampened flesh. "I need you inside of me."

Sam's toes curled in anticipation at her words. He hissed in a breath as Elizabeth slid her palms over his chest, tangling her fingers in the light smattering of hair there. She followed it downward to where it disappeared into his shorts. Sam quit breathing altogether as she played with the waistband.

"It's your turn, Sam." She slid her hand under the soft cotton and wrapped her hand gently, yet firmly, around his erection. He was growing harder by the second and fighting for control once again. After years of anticipation, he didn't want to embarrass himself by exploding in her hand.

Sam wrapped his hand around hers, stilling it. Placing his lips against hers, he whispered hotly, "No, Elizabeth, it's our turn."

That was the only warning Sam gave her before flipping her over on her back and looked deeply into her eyes. The muscles of his abdomen tightened. He reached over to the bedside table and grabbed a condom. Urgently, Sam ripped it open and started to put it on.

Elizabeth stilled his hands with her own. "Let me" she said. Reaching up, she took the condom from his hand and placed it snugly over the bulging head of his penis. With deliberate movements, she rolled the latex down the length of his shaft. Ever so slowly.

Sam was just about done in by that. He leaned down and gave her one hard, thorough kiss before he knelt in between her open legs. He placed one finger inside of her, pleased to find she was still wet and ready. Moving slowly to ensure he didn't hurt her, Sam gently pushed into her. Elizabeth took his whole length, sighing happily.

Sam held perfectly still, keeping most of his weight off her. "Are you okay? I'm not hurting you, am I?" He was anxious to know how she was feeling. He wanted everything to be perfect for her.

She shook her head mutely, answering him by raising her legs and wrapping them around his hips, squeezing him even as she did so from within. That was enough to shatter what little control he had left. Sam began to withdraw and thrust back into her, harder and quicker as he went. She ran her nails up and down his back begging him for release. With one last thrust, he sent them both spiraling over the edge of sanity. Elizabeth cried out his name once again as he collapsed upon her and buried his face in the damp, heated skin of her neck.

Slowly, their breathing returned to normal. Sam reluctantly withdrew from her and rolled over onto his back, taking her with him. He cradled her in his arms, with her head on his chest. The ceiling fan helped to cool their slick, overheated bodies. Neither could speak. Sam sent a silent prayer of thanksgiving for the incredible sense of peace that overcame him. He grudgingly got out of bed and went into the bathroom to clean himself up, returning before she could even protest. Sam eased back into bed, gathering her closely in his arms once again. He reached down and pulled up a sheet to cover them. They stayed that way for some time, whispering to each other in the darkness.

Sam knew the exact moment she surrendered to sleep. He felt the muscles in her body relax. He was not so willing. He held her while she slept, watching her, afraid she might disappear. He had never truly believed this moment would happen. Never believed he deserved to be this happy.

Eventually the doubts began to creep back in. Nothing had changed between them. Nothing had been resolved. These thoughts kept him awake long after her breathing had evened out. They still had not talked about the day Connor had died. Even though she denied it, he believed the specter of Connor still hung between them. It was a very long time before Sam finally fell asleep.

*****

Elizabeth was awake with the dawn. Some habits die hard. She lay there for a moment, enjoying the warmth of Sam's body, listening to him breathe. This was the thing she missed most, living alone over the past ten years. Waking up with another person. Even in his sleep, Sam's arm was thrown possessively over her bare stomach. The memories of their love making last night left her tingling still. She felt a stiffness in certain, long unused muscles. She smiled as she remembered reaching for him in the middle of the night. Or maybe Sam had reached for her. Either way, the result was wonderfully the same. Reluctantly, she gently extracted herself from his embrace. Pausing to gaze down into his face, she was touched by the vulnerability she saw there.

Elizabeth crept into the bathroom to dress. Sam had thoughtfully hung her clothes over the towel bar to dry sometime in the middle of the night. She snagged a t-shirt of his along the way to cover her skimpy top in the bright light of day. She knew this was a cowardly thing to do, leaving without waking him, but she had an early shift, and she was going to need a long, hot shower, not to mention appropriate clothing, before she was ready. Elizabeth moved into the kitchen to find her car keys. She thought about leaving a note and pulled open a few drawers in search of paper and a pen.

Rooting through a drawer, she was surprised to see a much younger version of herself staring back. She smiled at the memory of that long-ago day. The picture had been taken in the summer after high school graduation. They were having a going away party for Sam, who was leaving in a few days for college in Virginia. She and Connor had been so surprised when Sam had chosen to go so far away for school.

In the photo, Elizabeth was wearing a pair of denim cut offs and a bikini top. Her hair, which had been much longer then, was pulled back in a casual pony tail. She was wearing a baseball cap from Connor's high school team. Waves of nostalgia rolled over her. Things had been so simple then.

Elizabeth thought about that person in the photograph. If she had only known what the future held, would she be so carefree? The older and wiser version of herself had seen too many things, both in her personal and professional life, to ever be that innocent again. But even knowing what would happen, she wouldn't trade her time with Connor for anything. Loving him like she had, even for too brief a time, was worth the pain his death had brought. Even so, her heart squeezed.

She closed the drawer and gave up on her search for pen and paper. What would she say in a note anyway? She slipped out of Sam's house quietly and drove home lost in thought.

*****

At the sound of her car pulling out of the driveway, Sam sighed loudly and rolled over onto his back. He had known the very instant she left his bed. He also knew from the tension in her body that she needed time to adjust to what had happened between them. He reached over and picked up her pillow, pulling it to his face. It was still warm and bore a trace of her scent. Sam inhaled deeply. He had hoped to get up in a leisurely fashion, maybe share some breakfast and a shower with her. But he understood her need to leave.

Sam threw back the covers and quickly got dressed for his morning run. He had been running since his early teenage years, for the school track and baseball teams. Now Sam for the physical and mental benefits. Besides the obvious health benefits, Sam enjoyed the way it cleared his head. He preferred the land around his new home to any gym.

Sam stretched carefully before setting out. The only sounds other than his shoes slapping the road were the wind sifting through the trees and occasional rustle from the forest flanking the road. He loved the peace and solitude of this road. Although there were neighbors here and there, the lots were large and private. He rarely met another human on his trip.

Another advantage of running in the mountains was the amazing cardio he got. His driveway was just over a quarter mile but mercifully flat. The road beyond it not so much. By the third mile, Sam's lungs were burning with effort.

As he often did, Sam thought about the day Connor died. Although the passing years had taken the knife's edge off his pain, he still missed his friend. Sam tortured himself with endless 'what ifs'. What if he had taken a different street? What if they had left the house one minute later? Or sooner? Sam knew intellectually that the other driver, whose blood alcohol level had been three times the legal limit, was responsible. But what he felt in his heart was another matter. Sometimes when he closed his eyes, Sam could still see Connor's vacant stare as they lay trapped in the car. Or the lost expression on Elizabeth's face as she stood by the open grave.

Sam snapped himself out of that train of thought. He knew it was self-destructive. Sam felt closest to Connor when he ran, so he thought instead about the hundreds of miles he'd logged with Connor over the years. They had both been serious athletes in high school, running cross country in the fall and playing baseball in the spring. Sam had been the more disciplined of the two, while Connor made up for it with raw, natural talent.

It was the one area of their lives they didn't share with Elizabeth. She had never been much of an athlete. But he had to give her credit. She never missed a single meet or game throughout their four years of high school. No matter how many fans were in attendance, Sam unerringly picked her out of the crowd. He had a sixth sense where she was concerned.

Elizabeth being back in Windsor Falls was amazing. Having her in his bed last night defied description. Although he had been fantasizing about this for longer than he cared to remember, the reality was so much better. His pulse kicked even higher as he remembered the feel of her skin under his hands. The taste of her.

But having her leave without saying good-bye seemed like an omen to Sam. And not a good one. Soon, she would be leaving for good. Making love with her would make this departure so much worse. And he had barely survived last time. Disgusted with his train of thought, Sam kicked it into high gear for the last mile home. He pushed himself physically in the hopes that he would be too tired to think. But even as he reached the limits of endurance, thoughts of her kept him company.

Chapter Seventeen

Elizabeth signed a final set of discharge instructions with a weary sigh. The past twelve hours had been grueling but rewarding. She patted the adorable six-year-old on the head and squeezed his nervous mother's hand reassuringly. Little boys would be little boys. This one had thought wearing shoes outside was unnecessary. An old board with a nail poking through had taught him otherwise. Luckily, all that was required was a few stiches and a stern lecture.

Elizabeth decided to run up to the ICU before leaving the hospital. Her day shift had started with the successful resuscitation of a young father of two. He had been brought in by paramedics in full cardiac arrest after a near drowning incident. The unfortunate man had made the poor decision to swim alone in the family pool. Most likely banging his head on the side, his frightened wife had found him floating face down. Luckily, she had had the presence of mind to call 9-1-1 right away and to administer CPR while she waited for medics to arrive. The man's age and overall good health, combined with a rapid response time by EMS all added up to a happy ending. She felt compelled to check in on him before going home, despite the long day she had just worked.

Elizabeth stood outside his ICU room, watching his pretty wife hold his hand as tears streamed down her face. They were talking softly. She started to turn away, when the young woman spotted her.

"Doctor, please, can we speak with you for a moment?" Elizabeth stepped into the patient's room as his wife rushed around the side of the bed and enveloped her in a hug. "I don't even remember your name, but I had to thank you." She broke off as sobs wracked her body.

Elizabeth introduced herself to both her patient and his wife. "Mr. Thompson, you certainly look better than the last time I saw you. How are you feeling?" Her patient was on his way to a full recovery but being held for observation in the critical care unit.

"Please, call me Dan." he said as he reached out to shake Elizabeth's hand. "I can't begin to thank you doctor. That was a close call."

"Not to mention an incredibly stupid chance you took." his wife added. She smiled tremulously at Elizabeth. "I'm Carrie by the way. But he's right about one thing. We can't ever thank you enough for saving him."

Striving to lighten the moment, she offered up, "Well I guess there's no reason for my standard lecture on the dangers of swimming alone. But seriously, Carrie, I couldn't have done my job without what you did. Getting him help right away and starting CPR made all the difference. Dan, I'd say you owe her some very nice flowers at the very least." She grinned at him and noticed he was staring into his wife's eyes.

"That's the least of what I'll be doing for her, don't worry."

Elizabeth said her goodbyes and walked out into the hallway. She couldn't help but make comparisons between this situation and her own. She felt the old, familiar ache in her chest when she thought about what had happened to Connor. But it was no longer the searing pain it once was. At the time, she would have given anything for a chance to save Connor, but she had long since come to terms with that loss. She was just pleased that this young wife had been spared.

She turned a corner and came face to face with Katie. Elizabeth mentally prepared herself for another battle. But it never came.

"I heard about what you did for them. That was terrific. Can we talk for a minute?"

Elizabeth nodded and followed her old friend into the staff lounge. She hoped that this was finally going to put an end to their differences. She and Katie had once been so close, and she desperately hoped they could regain that.

Katie began haltingly, as if unsure of herself; a rarity for the normally outspoken woman. "I know that I've been a bit tough on you since you came home." At Elizabeth's raised brow she laughed good-naturedly. "OK, I've been a miserable bitch. I was terrible to you, and you didn't deserve it. So, I'm sorry. But in my defense, I just didn't know how to deal with all of the emotions that seeing you again has dredged up."

Knowing how much apologizing had cost the other woman, Elizabeth felt grateful for this chance to finally express her own remorse. "I'm sorry too, Katie. I'm sorry that I hurt so many people when I left. It wasn't easy for me, being so far away and without any support, but it was the only way I knew how to do it. I just felt like I couldn't breathe here. Everything reminded me of what I had lost." Tears were now flowing freely down her face. Not for the first time recently, Elizabeth was glad she didn't regularly wear makeup.

"That's just it, Elizabeth. We lost Connor too. He was my brother, and I loved him. We were all hurting so badly, and then we lost you as well. It seemed like one day you were just gone. You can't imagine how this affected everyone, especially Sam. It was agonizing to watch. You guys were a trio and he lost the two of you in a matter of weeks." Elizabeth's heart constricted at the thought. "He just withdrew deeper and deeper into himself, until we thought we'd never get him back. Eventually he began to heal, but it was years before he finally understood that he did NOT kill Connor and your unborn child." Huge sobs racked Katie's slender frame, and she buried her face in her hands.

Elizabeth's stomach rolled at Katie's words. She blindly reached for a chair and sat heavily. The color drained from her face. "What are you talking about? Connor was killed by a drunk driver. A person who was so intoxicated that he never even tried to stop. Why would Sam blame himself for Connor's death?"

"Sam was driving the car, Elizabeth, and he had to watch his best friend die. You and I both know it's often the emotional injuries that cause the most damage. He has scars that none of us can see." Katie cocked her head and looked directly at Elizabeth. "He needs to know that you don't blame him. He needs to hear it from you"

"How can I make him understand that? I *never* blamed him for anything that happened. I blamed the other driver who was too drunk to be on the road. It was all a matter of very bad luck and timing. I never thought about what Sam was feeling. What he was going through afterwards. I was beyond thinking about anything except my own grief and losses. I was barely functioning."

"No one expected you to take care of anyone else, Elizabeth. We were all so worried about you. But we neglected to worry about Sam. We totally underestimated the grief he was feeling."

Katie stopped and took a deep breath before continuing. Normally a direct person, Elizabeth noticed that Katie was not looking at her. "Here's the thing, Elizabeth. Sam's been doing great these last few years. I feel like he's come back to us. So please don't hurt him again." When Elizabeth tried to protest, Katie held up a hand, cutting off whatever Elizabeth would have said. "No, let me finish. I know that he cares about you. I see the way he looks at you. I'm not sure if you're serious about staying or even ready for another relationship, but Sam isn't looking for a one night stand with you."

Elizabeth's face flamed at the reference. She hadn't spoken to Sam in days, not since she spent the night with him. In his bed.

"I would never hurt him. You have to know that, Katie."

"I know that you would never *mean* to hurt him, just as you hadn't meant to hurt him by leaving. But he was hurt just the same. Badly."

Elizabeth nodded her head in acknowledgement. "I have to go home now, and you have to get back to work. I'm glad that we had this conversation, Katie. I'm glad we got a chance to clear the air. I hope that we can be friends again. I've really missed you." She affectionately squeezed the other woman's hand before quietly leaving the lounge.

*****

Katie sat there for another moment and buried her face in her hands. She cried for herself and for Elizabeth. She cried for Connor. She cried for the little niece or nephew she would never know. She hoped that Sam and Elizabeth would find a way to come to terms with the past. If not, they couldn't have any future together.

She jerked her head up as the door to the lounge opened. Flynn walked in but stopped abruptly at the site of her. Hunching her shoulders, Katie turned her back to him and angrily rubbed her face, dashing away the last of the tears. "Not now, Dr. Reynolds, please. Any other time I can hold my own against you in a verbal battle. But not now."

Flynn wore a shocked expression as he approached Katie. He reached down and pulled her up from the chair. Gently he turned her to face him.

"Katherine, what's wrong?"

Shock registered on her face at the use of her proper name. "Nothing's wrong. I was just talking with Elizabeth, and it brought up a lot of memories. No big deal. Don't worry, I won't compromise your patient's care, if that's what you're worried about." Defiance began to shine in her eyes.

"Now that's the Katie we all know and love. What you need are good memories to replace the sad ones." Without warning, he leaned in and captured her mouth with his own. The flames that had been simmering for months between them instantly leapt to life. When she opened her mouth to protest, he took advantage and swept his tongue inside. Katie moaned in pleasure and just when she felt herself weakening, he broke off the kiss. With a wicked grin, he saluted her jauntily and left the room. The door closed behind him just as a coffee mug smashed against it.

*****

Elizabeth sat in the middle of her bed with her legs folded, staring at her cell phone. She picked it up and then set it back down for the twentieth time. She needed to call Sam. She wanted to call Sam. Too much time had already passed since that night. He hadn't called, but then neither had she.

She was startled as the phone suddenly rang beneath her hand. Her breath hitched when she saw his name appear on the screen. She clicked to answer. "Hello, Sam."

"Hello, Elizabeth." The deep timber of his voice sent shivers down her spine. "I've been thinking about you. How are you?"

"I'm fine, Sam. I meant to call, but I've been busy with work and my mom. How have you been?"

"Busy also, but I miss you."

The pure longing in his warmed her heart. "I've missed you too. When I didn't hear from you, I didn't know what to think."

"It's been a hectic week." There was silence and then. "That's just an excuse. I wasn't sure what to think when you left without saying goodbye, Elizabeth. I didn't want to pressure you."

She slid down into her bed and wrapped her fingers harder around the phone. "I'm sorry about that. Really. I had an early shift." She cleared her throat. "But the truth is that I wasn't sure how to handle the morning after."

There was a long pause. She could hear Sam breathing. The muscles of her stomach tightened as each second ticked by. "Do you regret what happened?" he asked quietly.

"Oh no, Sam. Never that. I'm sorry that you thought that for even a moment. My life is a mess right now, and I have no idea what I'm doing with it. But I do not regret sleeping with you."

His relief was palpable through the phone. "Well alright then. That's something. And I meant what I said, Elizabeth. I don't want to pressure you. I know you have a lot on your plate right now."

"I talked with my boss in California this week. Twice. He really needs to know when I'm coming back." She decided against saying 'if'. Things with Sam were confusing enough already.

"And what did you tell him?"

"It's really more what he told me. I need to let him know by the end of next week."

"I see. I guess you have a decision to make then."

She didn't respond right away. She did have a big decision to make. And Elizabeth wasn't sure what was stopping her. She loved being back home, but it wasn't easy. Elizabeth thought she had dealt with the loss of Connor and their baby. But coming home made her realize she hadn't. Her life in California was far less complicated. But it was also lonely, she was coming to realize. It all came down to what she was willing to risk.

"I'm sorry to bring up all the tough stuff, Elizabeth. How's this for lighter fare? What are you doing Saturday? As you saw, I have almost nothing in my house. I need to do some serious shopping, and like most men, I'd rather be shot." He chuckled. "I figured bringing a woman along is always a good idea. Not to be sexist, but you ladies have better taste."

Elizabeth laughed, completely caught off guard. "If you had ever seen my condominium in California, you'd be asking someone else. Let's just say it's decorated in a minimalist style."

"I'm willing to take my chances. Besides, I'd really like to spend the day with you." That last part was said so softly that Elizabeth had to strain to hear it. "You're not working, are you?"

"No, I'm off all week-end. I'd really like to spend some time with you too." There, she'd said it. "What time should I be ready?"

"Well, I have a whole house to fill, so let's make a day of it. How about 8am? Is that too early? I thought we could get some breakfast on the way."

"That's perfect!" They spent a few minutes talking hanging up.

Elizabeth turned off the light and slid under the covers. She was excited, and more than a little nervous, about spending a whole day with Sam. Hopefully they were getting back to how they used to be. With some changes. Her whole body lit up at the memory of those changes.

Chapter Eighteen

Early Saturday morning, Elizabeth finished applying a light coat of lip gloss and ran lightly down the porch stairs to where Sam was parked. She had left a note for her mother on the kitchen table, reminding her where she'd be. Diane had taken to sleeping in lately, and Elizabeth didn't want to wake her so early.

Sam was already out of his truck and walking around to open her door. "Just what I like, a woman who's on time." He offered her his hand as she stepped up into the truck. Lust pooled hot and heavy low in her belly at just this slight touch.

"Just what I like. A gentleman. Good morning, Sam."

"Good morning to you too, Elizabeth. You look pretty this morning."

Elizabeth looked down at her faded jean shorts, tank top and flip flops and laughed. "Not very picky, are you Sam?" she asked as she waved a hand at her clothes.

"You always look good no matter what you're wearing." His eyes roamed the length of her. "I hope you brought an appetite." He gave her that boyish grin of his that made his dimples flash.

Her heart skipped a few beats in response. "You know me, Sam. I'm always up for a good breakfast."

Elizabeth turned and looked out the window. The day was going to be a gorgeous one. Living in Los Angeles, she had missed the endless greens of the mountains. In a few short weeks, the leaves would begin their spectacular show as they burst into a riotous sea of reds, oranges, and yellows. She wondered if she would be here still to see it.

"Penny for your thoughts."

She turned from the window. "I'm not sure their worth even that, Sam. I was just taking in the natural beauty."

He looked directly at her before turning back to the road. "So was I" he said under his breath.

After a few miles, Sam pulled off the road into the parking lot of a small diner. Elizabeth chuckled as her stomach chose just that moment to grumble loudly. "I did warn you!"

They went inside and were told to sit anywhere. At this hour, the place was crowded, so they chose one of the few remaining booths. A waitress bustled over leaving them with menus after taking their drink orders.

Elizabeth took advantage of the fact that he was perusing the menu to watch him surreptitiously. Her eyes wandered over the features of his face. Why had she never noticed his strong, squared jaw or warm chocolate eyes fringed by ridiculously long lashes? She wondered how he was still single. He was handsome and charming, intelligent, and successful. Were the women of Windsor Falls blind? She realized she had been staring and looked away, her face flaming.

He leaned across to cup her chin in his hand. "You don't have to be embarrassed. I like it when you look at me. I don't want things to be awkward between us. Ever."

The waitress took their orders then, topping off their coffees and saving Elizabeth from having to respond. She was more than grateful for the brief reprieve. It gave her a moment to gather her thoughts. She took a deep breath for courage and said "Sam, we have to talk about the other night. I don't regret what happened. I wanted to say that first in case you thought that I did. That night was wonderful. Making love with you was magical."

"But? It feels like there was meant to be a 'but' in there."

Elizabeth realized she was speaking too rapidly. She had so much she wanted to say to him. She moved her hands restlessly between them. "I'm just surprised by this thing between us. The amazing chemistry. But I'm still only here temporarily. And we still have so much unfinished business. I just think we should deal with some of that before we get in over our heads. Do you understand what I'm trying to say?"

"I do understand. The last thing I want is to make your life harder."

"The truth is, Sam, that I've missed us. A lot. And I feel like I'm just getting you back. I'm not interested in doing anything that's going to endanger our friendship." Elizabeth winced inwardly at her own selection of words. Considering their last encounter, friendship probably wasn't the best word choice here.

"Believe me, Elizabeth, I would never do anything to risk that either." The waitress hurried back with their food then, and Sam took a few bites of his omelet. Elizabeth did the same. Both were quiet as they ate.

Sam drank some coffee and looked at her over the rim of his cup. "You told me you don't regret what happened, but that's not how it sounds now. We can't go back and undo that night, Elizabeth. I wouldn't even if we could."

Elizabeth reached across the table for his hand. "I'm not saying this right, Sam. I absolutely do not regret what happened. Not even for a second. But I am concerned about our friendship. I've already done enough damage to it. I don't want to make things worse. I want to be sure of what we're doing."

"Maybe you're right" Sam muttered. "Maybe we should just stick to being friends." He reached for the check and rose to pay it.

Being right wasn't what it was cracked up to be she thought as she watched him walk away. She hadn't really hoped that he would agree with her. Maggie always warned to be careful what you wished for.

*****

Sam thanked the woman behind the cash register and walked back to the booth to leave a tip. 'Friendship', huh? He jammed his wallet back into his pocket in frustration. One step forward and two back it would seem. How could she not know, after their night together, that he was interested in far more than friendship? A frown flitted across his face. *Maybe because you never told her* he thought to himself in disgust. He had thought about this in the wee hours of the morning, while sleep alluded him. He knew what he wanted from her, but Elizabeth didn't have a clue. But none of it mattered if she was intent on returning to California. His life was here. Maybe they were better off keeping things light between them.

He approached the booth as she was exiting it. Nothing was settled between them, but Sam was determined to salvage this day. "Well now that I've fed you, you have to earn your keep. We have a job to do. Remember, we can't quit until the whole place is furnished." He threw down some bills. "Ready?"

"Then you're doomed to never getting back home if you're relying on me. What's the big hurry? Rome wasn't built in a day as they say." Elizabeth walked ahead of him, opening her own door before he could. Sam merely got in on his side and pulled back onto the country road.

"Well, maybe not today" he admitted. "But it has to look decent soon. Katie is helping me plan a house warming party. And when I say 'helping me', I mean that she has taken over everything. If I'm not careful, all of Windsor Falls will be at my door."

"Do you and Katie spend a lot of time together? I don't remember you two being such good friends before." Her voice had lost its teasing note.

Sam was careful to hide his smile. A little bit of jealousy might help his cause. "Well, of course we've known each other since we were both kids, but we didn't really become good friends until a few years ago." The fact that it happened after Connor's death and during her absence went unsaid. "I like her. A lot. She's fun to be around. She's good for me too."

Sam watched her out of the corner of his eye as he drove. Elizabeth might not be saying anything, but her body language was a dead give-away. Between her crossed arms and refusal to look at him, Sam knew she was miffed. He decided to cut her a break.

"OK, since you didn't ask, I'll tell you all the gory details. Katie and I dated, sort of, a few years back. If you could even call it that. It was one dinner. There's no chemistry between us. But, she was exactly what I needed at the time. Actually, we needed each other. She had just come out of a relationship that hadn't ended well. She was devastated. And I was, well…" He broke off, unsure how to complete that sentence.

Elizabeth turned to look at him, laying her hand on his thigh in support. "You were what, Sam? If you want to tell me, I'd really like to know."

Sam didn't say anything for a few moments. It was hard to think let alone talk with her hot little hand touching him like that. He pulled the truck off the side of the road. Turning it off, he moved in his seat so that he faced her. "I was a mess for a long time, Elizabeth." Noticing the stricken look on her face, he held up his hand. "Please let me just get this out. I don't mean to hurt you by anything that I say, but if you really want to know what my life was like, it's not pretty."

"I was lost for a while there. Connor was gone, and then you, leaving a huge hole in my life. So, I filled it with work. At least I tried to. The store had been struggling for a long time, and I needed to fix that. To be honest, dealing with work was much easier than trying to fix my personal life." His eyes had darkened with the memory of that terrible time. Elizabeth reached out and squeezed his hand.

"Eventually, I was back on my feet, both financially and emotionally. But I didn't have much of a life. That's where Katie comes in. One day, out of the blue, she just showed up. She got right in my face, and asked me out for dinner. We both already knew that wasn't going anywhere. She's like the little sister I never had. But it was enough to snap me out of my funk. As it turns out, she really needed a friend as much as I did."

Sam halted at the questioning look in her eyes. "That's her story to tell. Anyway, we had that dinner. Then we went to a movie. After that it was Sunday lunch at her family's home. We ended up becoming good friends, and I found my way back to the Fitzgeralds. I owe her a lot."

"I'm glad you told me, Sam. I needed to know what life was like after I left here. I'm sorry it was so hard on everyone. On you. I couldn't see past my own pain. I couldn't think about Maggie and Joe losing their son and Connor's siblings losing their brother. I couldn't think about my mother losing her only grandchild. I couldn't think about you losing your best friend. All I could see was my own grief." She bowed her head with the weight of her grief.

Sam slid across the front seat, closing the gap between them. He gathered her in his arms and rubbed her back soothingly. He could practically feel the grief surrounding her. Gradually, Elizabeth relaxed against him. He breathed in the citrus scent of her shampoo and his resolve to keep it casual weakened.

"I'm such a mess" she muttered into his shoulder.

Sam hugged her before moving back behind the wheel. He started up the truck and drove several miles before she finally spoke. "I've been fine in California. But being back here has brought a lot of emotions to the surface. In a way, Sam, I was just like you. I threw myself into my medical training and then work. It was so much easier to focus on other people's problems."

He nodded but kept his eyes on the road. "Exactly."

"Being in a large, impersonal city made it even easier for me. I've been thinking about my life in California a lot since I've been home, Sam. I've really played it safe these past ten years. No entanglements. No messiness. No chance for more heartbreak. I have a few friends, but no one I've gotten really close to." She stopped as a huge smile lit up her face. "Well except for Charlie."

"Charlie?" Sam asked casually. At least he hoped he had come off casually. He really wasn't prepared to hear about some guy that made her smile like *that*. Finding out about Jeremy had almost killed him.

"Charlie is short for Charlotte. Dr. Charlotte Grace Avery. Charlie was the person I was closest with in residency. She was everything that I wasn't; fun-loving and extroverted. She's living in Chicago now, but we talk daily."

Sam gripped the wheel tightly to avoid throwing a celebratory fist in the air. "Chicago, huh? I guess you miss her."

"Charlie is so much more than a friend. She had been the exact 'therapy' that I needed. In the first weeks of our residency, over way too many drinks one night, I told Charlie the whole story of my life. She's the only person that I'd told in California up until then. It was the best thing I could have done. Just saying the words out loud to another human being helped me to heal."

"She sounds like an amazing friend. I'm so glad she was there for you."

"Thanks, Sam. She really was. I miss her a lot. We had so much fun together, when we weren't up all night cramming. I wish she hadn't moved to Chicago. She keeps trying to get me to move there with her, but I could never handle the cold."

Elizabeth went back to watching the passing scenery for a few moments before rewarding Sam with a brilliant smile that made his stomach flip. "This day is just perfect, Sam. The sun is shining, and I'm spending it with a handsome man. What else could I possibly want?"

He could think of a few things. Starting with them both naked. "You'd better be careful, Elizabeth. Say things like that, and I might just think you like me."

She looked at him from under lowered lashes. "I wouldn't think there were any doubts after the other night, Sam."

"Uh, I don't really need any furniture, right? I could just pull over right here for a while..." He leered at her, only half-jokingly.

"Oh, no you don't! I've seen your house, Sam. You NEED furniture. Let's go. Focus, Sam, focus."

"Oh, don't worry, I can definitely focus." He wiggled his eyebrows at her suggestively, and she playfully slapped his arm.

"Yes, I'm aware." Laughter gurgled up out of her throat.

They arrived at an old, beautiful barn that had been converted to a store for estate sales and antiques. "Here we are" announced Sam as he parked his truck off to the side.

They walked into the barn, side by side. Their hands were mere inches apart, and Sam was itching to hold hers. She turned to him then with happiness shining from her eyes. "How did you ever find this place, Sam? This is wonderful."

"Maggie has been bugging me about living in a cave, as she refers to my empty house. She suggested this place because they have a little bit of everything, and I need everything. But now that I'm here, I have no idea where to start…"

She grabbed his hand and pulled him further into the building. "I think you just have to start. This place is huge and a bit overwhelming. Let's just look around and see what appeals. Although I may not be very good at this stuff, I do think even I can do some damage here!"

Her joy was infectious, and Sam suddenly found himself happy to finally be tackling this. Of course, that had more than a little to do with the woman at his side. She was still holding his hand, but he wasn't going to point that out to her.

They roamed up and down makeshift aisles, perusing every vendor. The place was crowded with other treasure seekers. Sam used this as an excuse to stay close to Elizabeth.

They came upon a craftsman who was selling hand-made furniture. Sam shook hands with the man, who introduced himself as Gus, and asked some questions as Elizabeth ran her hands lovingly over the wood of a farmhouse table.

"Sam, come feel this." she squealed excitedly. "It's so smooth. This would be great in the kitchen."

"Your wife has excellent taste." Gus joked with Sam.

Sam's heart did a funny little tumble at his assumption. "She certainly does."

"The top is made from an old barn door. When I'm not creating these, I like to drive around in my truck to find old wood that I can use. The table may be new, but there's history in the wood."

Sam walked over to the table and watched as Elizabeth ran her hand lovingly over its surface. The curved legs were painted deep, forest green, reminding Sam of the trees that surrounded his house. There were six ladder-back chairs that matched.

She glanced up at him. Her appreciation for the fine craftsmanship shown on her face. "This reminds me so much of Maggie's. Only without all the damage we did to it over the years. You have to buy this, Sam. If you don't, I'll be forced to buy it for you."

Sam would do anything to keep her looking that happy. He turned to Gus. "We'll take it."

Gus's grin split his homely weathered face. "Always good to keep the little woman happy."

As Elizabeth was watching, he chose not to respond. Instead he handed his credit card to Gus and made arrangements for delivery during the week. After their business was concluded, Sam and Gus shook hands. When they were out of earshot of the older man, Elizabeth punched Sam lightly on the arm. "Little woman, huh? I notice you didn't bother to correct him."

Sam tried to remain casual as he answered her. "Gus is from a different generation. I wasn't going to try to correct him. Besides you are little and a woman. So, technically, he was right."

Elizabeth tried to pull herself up straighter to appear taller, but she dissolved in laughter, defeating her purpose. "Okay, Sam, I'll give you that one."

She turned to admire a display of hand-woven rugs, exclaiming over an oval one that was shot through with hues of burgundy and dark green. "This is perfect for under your new table, Sam. I can just picture the dogs lying on it as you have dinner."

Something tightened painfully in his chest at the choice of her words. 'You' and not 'we.' She wasn't picturing herself there with him. He rubbed his chest absently and tried to slow down the feeling of dread that was building. Just because he had been thinking about a life with her for years didn't mean that she would be. In fairness, it had only been a few days since their status as 'old friends' had been blown out of the water. But the clock was ticking louder in his head each day as she got closer to leaving him once again.

Several hours later, Sam groaned kiddingly as he loaded the last of their finds into the back of his truck. Elizabeth had not been shy about telling him exactly what she liked and what she thought would look good in his house. She had found several more, colorful throw rugs for the hardwood floors. Sam had also found several larger pieces of furniture that he liked, including a lovely china cabinet for the dining room, not that he owned any china, and a Shaker style armoire for his bedroom. He had arranged to have these delivered to his house as well.

Elizabeth had busied herself looking for smaller items that, as she put it, make a house a home. There was some pottery in beautiful earth tones that was made by hand locally. She also found a lovely, antique copper light fixture for his kitchen. There were several other items that she pointed out that Sam had just agreed to without question. Just because she had put thought into where they would go in his house.

It had been easy, for a while, to believe that they were picking out items for *their* home, instead of his. Sam felt a little melancholy when reality returned. He wanted so much more from her. Possibly more than she was willing, or able, to give him. Maybe someday…

*****

After loading all his purchases into Sam's truck, they left the village and drove out to the Blue Ridge Parkway. Even though the day was still hot, Elizabeth lowered her window and leaned out to breathe in the mountain air. She pulled her head in and turned to Sam grinning.

"You can't get that scent in California" he said.

"True. I do however have the ocean close by."

"We do too" he replied somewhat defensively.

Elizabeth smirked. "If by close you mean five hours away."

Sam pulled into a scenic overlook. He turned off the truck and got out, leaving a confused Elizabeth in his wake. The day had started off fun and lighthearted, but Sam had grown quieter as it continued. He stood at the low retaining wall now with his shoulders hunched and hands jammed in his pockets.

Elizabeth got out and stood at his side, aching to soothe away the tension oozing from him. "Are you okay, Sam?"

He turned to her and nodded, smiling tightly. She wasn't convinced. He stepped over the small wall and down the steep, rocky path to a large flat rock bathed in late afternoon sunlight. She stood there watching him go.

When Sam reached the rock, he turned to face her holding out his hand. "I thought you were a mountain girl. Guess all that big city living has softened you." His words drifted up to her on the gentle breeze.

Never one to back down from a challenge, Elizabeth eyed her flip flops doubtfully but scurried over the wall. She scrambled down the trail, hoping to not break her neck, and managed to arrive next to Sam in one piece and only slightly winded. "City girl, my ass" she replied saucily to him before climbing up on the flat rock and stretching out.

Sam joined her, sitting close by but not quite touching her. Still, he was close enough for her to feel the warmth of his tanned skin and breathe in the subtle scent of him. They stayed that way in silence, enjoying the spectacular view. The majestic Blue Ridge Mountains stretched out in all directions as far as the eye could see.

Elizabeth felt more confused than ever. It was so wonderful to spend time with Sam again. She could honestly say this was the best day she'd had in ages. But he seemed to be avoiding any physical contact with her. She knew he was as powerfully attracted to her, as she was to him. The other night certainly proved that. Maybe he was being careful because of what she had said this morning. But that didn't stop the sparks that flew between them each time they had accidentally brush against each other.

She should just ask him. But she was reluctant. Things were so new and different between them right now. And how could she ask him to explain his feelings when she wasn't sure of her own? Needing to decide about California weighed heavily on her.

So instead of asking anything, she merely inched closer and laid her hand upon his thigh. She was happy to just be touching him. She thought she felt Sam stiffen momentarily before taking her hand in his. She sighed contentedly and snuggled in as close as she could get.

"Penny for your thoughts" she said softly. "It feels like you're a million miles away, Sam."

He smiled at her and squeezed her hand. "I'm right here. I was just thinking about the house and everything we bought today. I still have a long way to go, but we sure made a good dent. I'm just worried about being ready for the party. I don't want people thinking I live in a cave." He laughed self-consciously.

"There's nothing to worry about, Sam. Everyone who's coming is your friend. There's no one to impress. They just want to celebrate with you. Just relax. It'll be fine. You'll see."

"Thanks for all your help today, Elizabeth. Despite your initial protests, you have excellent taste." He pulled out his cell to look at the time. "Wow! It's almost dinner time. We didn't even stop for lunch. You must think I'm a terrible person."

"I was going to say no big deal, but I'm starving."

"Do you have time for dinner? I thought we could unload all of this at my house, and I'll throw something on the grill."

"Are you sure it's not too much trouble?"

"I'm sure. It's the least I can do. Besides, then you can help me find a home for all the stuff we bought today."

"OK then. Let's do it! I'm excited to see the rest of your house. I didn't exactly get the tour last time." Unless of course you counted his bedroom and bathroom she thought while a delicious thrill shivered down her spine.

Chapter Nineteen

When he pulled into his driveway, Sam turned to her before getting out. "I hope you're still here when I have the party. I'd love for you to come." More than you'll ever know, he thought silently. Pain stabbed his chest at the thought of her returning to California.

"I'd love to, Sam. If I'm still here." His heart leapt at the shadow that passed briefly over her eyes. The more time Elizabeth spent here in Windsor Falls, the less happy she seemed about returning to California. Maybe he could get Connor's family to work on her a bit.

"Would it be okay if I brought someone with me, Sam?"

Sam almost choked on the gum he was chewing. Never in a million years did he expect that question. He knew, without a doubt, who she wanted to bring. Dread filled his chest as he nodded, still trying to clear his throat.

"Great! Flynn really had a great time at the anniversary party, and I think I saw some male bonding between him and Connor's brothers. He's far away from his family, and I know he'll have a good time. Besides, I know you'll really like him, once you get to know him."

Sam doubted that. A lot. He could never envision a time when he would like the too smooth cardiologist. But he wasn't going to tell Elizabeth that. With a fake smile glued to his face he answered her. "Bring him. It's always good to have another for volleyball." How could she possibly believe he'd want Flynn at his house?

"Super! Thanks for understanding. I remember how hard it was to be the new person. Flynn is a great guy, Sam. He's wickedly funny and an excellent physician. I know he's the reason my Mom is alive today."

Hard to argue with that Sam thought bitterly. He got out of the truck and opened the garage doors. "I promised you dinner, and I know we both worked up an appetite. Why don't you head inside while I unload the truck? I'm just going to store everything in the garage for now."

"I'm happy to help. It'll take half the time if we both do it." She reached for the first item and started towards his garage. They worked in companionable silence until all the purchases had been tucked away.

As soon as Sam opened the door to the kitchen, they were greeted by three very exuberant Australian Shepherds. Elizabeth dropped to her knees in the front yard and was instantly surrounded by dogs, as Cooper, Lily, and Griffin all competed for her attention. The friendly dogs were alternatingly circling her and covering her face with kisses. Sam was amused at the sight of their stubby tails wagging.

He started towards the crowd to pull the boisterous dogs off her. But he stopped at the sound of her laughter. It was strong and clear, a harkening to the good old days when the three of them had laughed like that all the time. It was a sound that he had almost forgotten and certainly one he had not thought he would hear again. A warmth spread through his chest.

Elizabeth, covered in dog hair and slobber, grinned foolishly. "I'd almost forgotten how wonderful dogs are. I always had to get my fill of them at Connor's house when we were young. I wanted one so badly, but my Mom always said that she worked too many hours to have one."

"You don't have one in California?"

She shook her head sadly. "Turns out my mom was right. I work way too many hours at a stretch. And I live in a condo. My neighbors wouldn't be thrilled if a lonely dog barked all day and night."

"There's another reason to move back home. You could buy a house with a yard. Then you could have a dog." Of course, he already had the house, yard, and three dogs. He was more than willing to share.

She buried her face in Lilly's silky coat. Not to be outdone, Cooper stuck his nose up under her arm. Sam thought once again it was horrible to be jealous of his own dogs, but he would love to be the object of such spontaneous affection. From her. Elizabeth was unabashedly in love with his dogs.

Elizabeth stood up and brushed the dog hair off her. Sam whistled for all three dogs before moving into the house. "So, what can I do to help? Are you going to fire up that grill? I'm starving!"

"Wow, slave driver. Yes ma'am. Do you mind making a salad? There's some things in the refrigerator for one. I'm going to go throw some chicken on the grill."

Elizabeth moved to the sink and began to wash her hands. "Hey Sam, you didn't tell me you had a Jacuzzi" she said as she gazed out the window to his back patio. "Boy would that be nice after a long shift on my feet! I have a tub with jets in my condo but nothing like this. I'd never leave it if I had one of those!"

The thought of her in the hot, turbulent water nearly killed him. "I've only actually used it a few times since I had it installed. It's too hot during the day in the summer, but I love it at night. I can sit and look at the stars. It's so peaceful and relaxing after a hard day. You're right about that." He would never leave it either if she was in it with him.

"Well, Sam, since you worked me so hard all day, the least you can do is let me try it out after dinner. I even promise to wait an hour after eating so I don't drown." She joked about the dire warning they had all received relentlessly as kids.

Against his better judgment, Sam heard himself agreeing to her plan. How was he ever supposed to get through dinner if he was thinking about being in the hot tub with her afterwards?

"You go do your manly grilling thing, Sam. I'm going to work on that salad." She opened the fridge, studying the contents for a moment before making her selections. Sam grabbed the chicken and some bar-b-q sauce and then headed out to the grill.

Sam came back in to wash his hands after handling the raw chicken. He watched as Elizabeth was hard at work on their salad. Sam looked around, admiring the finished space that he and Aidan Fitzgerald had created. Although the room was still mostly empty, it held great promise. All the appliances were a gleaming stainless steel. The forty-two-inch pine cabinets and polished cobalt blue granite counter tops finished out the look. If he used his imagination a bit, Sam could see this room becoming the center of the house, just like it always had been at the Fitzgerald house.

Of course, Sam didn't want to live here alone. He glanced at Elizabeth who was still occupied with cutting vegetables. She looked so at home in his kitchen. In his house. If only, Sam thought.

Elizabeth turned and caught him staring. "Do you need something, Sam?"

Now there's a loaded question. "Just your opinion on drinks. I have some white wine or beer if you prefer."

"Sam, Sam, Sam" she called chidingly. "Once a beer girl, always a beer girl. Have anything local?"

As if he wasn't in love with her enough already. "As a matter of fact, I do. I have a few selections from Catawba Brewing. Would you prefer a Brown Bear or a Ted Light Lime? The former is a brown ale, and the latter is a lighter, summery one. I only keep it stocked for Katie. She was helping me paint last month."

"Now that she doesn't hate me anymore, I'm sure she won't mind if I try one."

"She told me that you two had talked. Cleared the air a bit. I'm so glad for both of you."

Sam reached into the fridge and grabbed one of each, popping off the tops and handing one to Elizabeth. They clinked bottles and sat at the counter to wait for the chicken to finish. He reached out to tuck a wayward curl behind her ear. His fingers were singed where they had touched her skin.

Her blue eyes darkened in response. "You felt that too" she stated breathlessly. A statement rather than a question.

Sam nodded, not trusting himself to speak. Why had he called a moratorium on touching her today? There must have been a good reason at some point.

She took a long swallow of her beer, red lips pursed around the top. Sam watched in fascination as her neck moved while she swallowed. He shifted in his seat to find a more comfortable position. But that wasn't going to happen as long as she had that bottle to her lips.

Sam grabbed his beer and headed for the sliding door. "Have to flip the chicken. Dinner should be ready in about twenty minutes if you want to grab the salad." He escaped to the relative cool of the July night.

Elizabeth followed behind, bringing the salad bowl and some plates and utensils. By the time he had finished at the grill, she had arranged a salad for each of them, along with several bottles of dressing she found in the fridge. "Still a ranch dressing fan, Sam?"

He sat opposite her. "I try to mix it up a bit" he joked and pointed to the various bottles she had set on the table. "But ranch is still my favorite." It warmed his heart that she remembered after all these years.

Elizabeth chose a blackberry vinaigrette. "This looks good. Local?"

"I think so. Maggie is always dropping by with 'care packages'. I think she's afraid that I'll starve without her help."

"That's sweet, Sam. Maggie always did love mothering us. You'd never know she had six kids of her own already, the way she fussed over you and me."

"Well, I'm not complaining. I eat Sunday dinner there almost every week and always bring home left overs. Keeps me from having to cook for one."

"I know what you mean. I pretty much live on take out and hospital food." She raised her hand and laughed. " If I lived here I could go to Sunday dinners as well. But then there'd be less left overs for you."

He looked deeply into her eyes before answering. "That's a sacrifice I'm willing to take." Before she could respond, he got up to grab the chicken off the grill.

The tantalizing aroma of bar-b-q sauce wafted upwards as Sam put the plate of chicken on the table. Elizabeth laughed when she saw how many he had cooked. "I'm not *that* hungry, Sam" she joked.

"Left overs, Elizabeth. Most nights I'm at the store until late. The last think I feel like doing is cooking when I get home. This I can pop in the microwave."

"Sounds like you need a wife" replied Elizabeth as she finished her salad. "Or at least a housekeeper."

Sam stared at her, his fork frozen half way to his mouth. "Are you volunteering, Elizabeth?"

She laughed lightly. "You'd starve if you had to depend on me, Sam. But what's wrong with the women around here? Seriously. How are you still single?"

"Just haven't met the right one." Sam crossed his fingers under the table at the blatant lie.

"I find that hard to believe, Sam. No one in Windsor Falls has turned out to be 'the one?'"

Sam leaned in and lowered his voice. "Well, there is one person who has stolen my heart." He was satisfied to see the pulse jump in her neck. "But Joe would kill me if I made a play for Maggie."

There was a brief pause before Elizabeth burst out laughing. The sound was light and silvery and danced along Sam's nerve endings. "You had me going there for a second."

"But seriously, I have long hours with the store, and I wouldn't even know where to meet someone these days."

"True. I have the same issue. And I'm a few years past the bar scene."

Sam shook his head. "Aidan, Brendan and I go out regularly for a beer or two and to play darts. I'm apparently their wing man. It works for them, but I'm not interested in meeting anyone in a bar."

"Wow, look at that" Elizabeth said as she pointed to the sunset. Deep reds and brilliant oranges streaked the sky. "Living on the side of the mountain has its advantages, Sam. The view is gorgeous."

Looking right at her, Sam murmured "Yes, it certainly is." She was still the most beautiful woman he had ever known, but her true beauty came from within. He wished they could stay right here forever.

"I imagine you can see a million stars out here at night." Elizabeth turned back to Sam and caught him looking at her. She made a funny face. "Do I have something stuck in my teeth? Why are you staring at me so intently, Sam?"

"Because you're here."

"Oh" she responded quietly, her breath hitching.

"I still can't believe you're really here, Elizabeth. In my house. At my table. There's no one else who shares my history the way you do. The way Connor did." There was so much more he wanted to say, but the night was lovely, and he didn't want to scare her off.

"Do you remember how you and I ended up going to the Junior Prom together? For some reason, I was thinking about that the other day. Those awful girls had me cornered, asking me why I wasn't going. Teasing me. And you came out of nowhere to rescue me. My white knight! You were always there when I needed you. I've really missed that."

Sam was instantly alert at the mention of that night, so long ago. He had wanted to ask Elizabeth for weeks, and those girls gave him the opportunity. He'd thought he was in Heaven. But that was also the night that Connor had finally woken up and seen Elizabeth for what she was becoming; a stunning girl on the brink of womanhood. That was the night that changed all their lives forever.

"I remember all right. I had the prettiest girl there on my arm. Who could forget that?" Sam struggled to sound casual.

Elizabeth laughed lightly. "Time really has colored your perception, Sam. I was so uncomfortable in that formal dress. I stepped on your poor feet because I couldn't dance in those shoes." She shook her head at the flood of awkward memories. "You sure were a good sport that night, Sam."

"True. It did take you a while to learn how to walk in those heels."

"I was such a tomboy back then, Sam. I still can't believe you were nice enough to take me. Especially when there so many girls who would have loved to be in my place."

"There wasn't anyone else I wanted to go with, Elizabeth." What Elizabeth still didn't know was that his feelings for her had begun to change long before that night. She didn't feel like just his *friend* anymore. Elizabeth had always seen herself as 'one of the guys', but Sam hadn't.

This change was not entirely welcome to Sam. But he couldn't help the way he felt. He would lay awake at night, long after he should be asleep, dreaming that she would feel the same way. But telling her was another matter altogether. Sam no longer felt comfortable around her, although he tried to not let it show. He wanted nothing more than to pull her into his arms and kiss her until they were both breathless. He was fairly certain she would have punched him. Worse, she might never trust him again. He hadn't been willing to risk that.

"I was honored to be your date, Elizabeth. Little did I know, though, that I'd be losing my best girl."

Even after all these years, he felt a flicker of regret. It never ceased to annoy him that Connor had reacted faster than he did. Who knew what might have happened? But in the end, things had gone the way they were supposed to go Sam supposed. Elizabeth and Connor had loved each other. There hadn't been another for either of them from that day until the day Connor died.

"You never lost me, Sam."

He had. She just didn't know. "Well at least you're back. For however long."

She reached across the table and grabbed his hand. "You're not going to lose me again. Even if I'm back in California. I promise not to be out of touch again."

He couldn't think about her going back to California. "I'm going to hold you to that."

"I believe you promised me a dip in the Jacuzzi." She released his hand and got up, heading across the patio. "I don't suppose you have an extra suit, do you?" When he didn't answer, she shrugged. "Oh well, it's not like it's the first time you've seen me in my underwear." She kicked off her flip flops and pulled her t-shirt over her head, revealing a navy-blue bra. The discarded clothing was soon joined by her shorts. Clad only in a matching set of underwear, Elizabeth leaned over to adjust the controls. Sam's breath caught in his throat at the site of her perfect ass. His breathing grew more rapid as she dipped the toes of one foot into the tub. Sighing, Elizabeth slid down into the water. "Why are you still all the way over there?"

It took him less than a heartbeat to make his decision. Screw common sense. Where had that ever gotten him anyway? Sam quickly ripped his shirt over his head and kicked off his shoes. Taking a moment to undo his belt, he pulled off his khaki shorts. He was left with only his boxers. Seeing Elizabeth in only her scant underwear was enough to render him fully sober. He felt her eyes upon him as he stepped into the hot tub. Sam settled across from her with his arms stretched out along the rim of the tub.

Feigning indifference to the scantily clad woman across from him, Sam sighed aloud. "Ah! I knew there was a reason I had this installed." His long legs reached across to her side, brushing her thigh. He rested his feet on the ledge next to her. "Hope you don't mind" he asked innocently. "All that driving today has made the muscles in my legs stiff."

Elizabeth was silent but watching Sam intently. He hoped that sliding his foot along the length of her smooth thigh would get her attention. He thought about his next move. This was a dangerous game he was playing. He had spent the day trying to ignore his attraction to her. Even though he had been dying to touch her. Everywhere.

He hesitated, and Elizabeth straightened up, bringing her breasts just above the water line. She stretched her arms over her head, arching her back. The night air, combined with her wet bra, brought her nipples to attention. Sam longed to put his hands, and then his mouth, on them.

"I know what you mean, Sam. All that heavy lifting has worn me out. The hot water feels so good." Her voice was low and sultry. Sam swallowed painfully. She arched her back once more, cracking her neck as if to prove her point. Her full breasts strained against the material of her bra. Elizabeth was so beautiful sitting there, bathed in moonlight. Her breasts were calling to him. He grew painfully hard just looking at her from across the hot tub.

As if she were silently accepting the gauntlet he tossed down a few moments ago, Elizabeth reached between her breasts and undid the clasp. She flexed her arms and the slight scrap of material floated free of her body. She smiled at Sam. It was a smile that held both a challenge and a promise.

Sam's resolve shattered. He lunged across the hot tub. Scooping her up in his arms with a low growl deep in his throat, he settled her on his lap. There was no way to hide his arousal. But he wouldn't have even if he could. Sam brushed away the damp hair clinging to her face and looked deeply into her eyes. Into her very soul. He gazed at her for what seemed an eternity before lowering his mouth to her breasts. He would not deny himself, or her, any longer.

Elizabeth moaned loudly as he sucked on first one breast, and then the other, with increasing intensity. The sound made heat pool in the very core of him. The temperature of the swirling water couldn't begin to match the heat Sam felt building between them. While he hungrily lathed her tightened nipple, Elizabeth blindly reached under the water to the seat of his desire. She slid her fingers up under the leg of his boxers, closing them around the hard shaft she found there. She slowly ran her fingers up and down him.

Sam broke off from kissing her breast. "You're killing me, Elizabeth. You know that, right?" he asked in a strangled voice. She merely smiled at him. She was a siren with wild curls and bare breasts. He gently disentangled her hand from him and stood up in the water, taking her with him. He set her down gently on the deck and climbed out after her. They barely made it the few feet to a chaise lounge. Sam lowered himself to the chair, pulling her down on top of him.

All traces of the game were gone now, as he peeled her wet panties off and tossed them to the patio. He lifted so Elizabeth could do the same for him. Without a word between them, Elizabeth positioned herself over his throbbing shaft and lowered slowly. The fit was perfect. For a long moment, he held himself perfectly still, savoring the feel of her perfectly sheathing him. But her desire was too close to the surface to stay that way for very long. Elizabeth moved up and down, allowing his engorged member to slide in and out of her with increasing speed.

Sam didn't even try to hold back. There would be time for finesse later. He ground his hips into hers, straining to fill her completely. He reached up and pulled her nipple into his mouth, sucking and teasing. Within seconds he felt himself tumbling into oblivion, content in the knowledge she was right along with him for the ride.

As their breathing slowly returned to normal, he shifted on the narrow lounger, rolling her with him. He smiled with satisfaction. She lay there with her eyes closed and a purely feminine smile on her beautiful face. "Don't get too comfortable, honey. I have more plans for you."

"You do, do you?" she said in return as she opened her eyes. Her desire for him was reflected in them.

Taking her hand in his, Sam rose from the chair and pulled her up with him. He was completely comfortable with his state of undress. He led her through the house and into his bedroom, gently laying her on his bed.

"That little scene in the Jacuzzi, combined with a whole day of restraint, was my undoing. I couldn't go slowly back there, Elizabeth. But I can now." He grinned wickedly at her as moonlight streamed through the windows. "By the time I'm done with you, there won't be an inch I haven't tasted." He backed up his words with his mouth as he bestowed a mind-blowing kiss upon her lips.

Elizabeth sighed into his mouth and opened her arms to him. He buried his face into the hollow of her neck, tracing his tongue along the sensitive skin there. She ran her hands along his back. Sam gently removed her hands from his body and placed them above her head. "This is all for you, Elizabeth. I want you to just lie there and enjoy." With that, he traced the fingers of one hand down along her jawline and over her throat. He continued, gently outlining her right breast. He ran his tongue around the already sensitive nipple, blowing lightly to tighten the flesh further. In reply, she wound her fingers in his hair, pulling his head closer in silent longing. He didn't disappoint.

Sam slid his hand in between her legs, pleased with the warm dampness he discovered. She might be ready for him again, but he had other plans for her first. Continuing to rake her nipple gently with his teeth, he slowly moved his fingers through the curls at the apex of her legs. Elizabeth writhed on the bed, unconsciously opening her legs to give him greater access.

Sam slid one finger into her damp heat, finding the sensitive bud of flesh at her very core. She cried out then, lifting her hips off the bed and grabbing the headboard with both hands. He raised his head from her breast to watch as Elizabeth closed her eyes. Knowing he had caused the play of emotion over her face meant everything to Sam.

"Please, Sam" Elizabeth whispered brokenly. Never one to deny her anything, Sam kicked his attention to her body up another notch. He inserted several fingers into her core, sliding them in and out with increasing speed. Her hips arched further off the bed, pushing against his hand in a desperate search for fulfillment.

That was all the invitation Sam needed. He reached into the bedside table and grabbed a condom. Tearing open the foil packet and sheathing himself in record time, Sam looked down at Elizabeth for a moment. Her bright blue eyes opened. "Please, Sam?" She reached between them and guided Sam home. At least that's how it felt to him.

He positioned himself over her and taking his weight on his arms on either side, he plunged himself fully into her again and again. Elizabeth scored his back with her nails as she cried out his name. She rode him hard, her back arched and her breasts thrust out. It was more than he could take. They were both spiraling out of control. Just then she cried out his name loudly one final time, and he was satisfied that she knew exactly whom she was with.

Later, as he held her in his arms, her head on his chest, Sam thought about their explosive lovemaking. It had never been like this with any other woman. He was sure it never would be. Sam had been involved with a few women over the years.

And while he had enjoyed these relationships, no one had come close to touching his heart the way she did. This thought both warmed him and terrified him.

He gently rolled to his side to see her face. Brushing back the dampened tendrils from her face, he looked deeply into her eyes. "Will I ever be able to get enough of you?" He tenderly kissed her forehead.

Taking a shaky breath, she answered him. "You make me happy, Sam." She placed a feathery kiss on his bare shoulder and snuggled down against him. Already, her breath was slowing and deepening. He felt her drifting.

Sam drew the summer weight comforter up around them. He looked down to where she had her hand lying over his heart. Even in sleep, she seemed reluctant to let go of him. He felt at peace for the first time in a very long time. Soon after, he drifted off to sleep himself.

Chapter Twenty

Elizabeth came awake all at once, surprised to see bright sunshine pouring into the room. She wasn't surprised to see Sam propped up against the headboard watching her. She felt a smile spread across her face.

"You do wake up rather quickly, don't you?" He reached down and played with a wild lock of her hair.

"It's all those years of training I had. You get used to waking instantly at the sound of your pager. You can't be half asleep when they roll in a trauma patient for you." She stretched fully, causing the sheet to slip to her slender waist. Not yet completely comfortable in front of Sam, she rolled to her stomach and stretched out next to him, trying to smooth out her wild hair as she went. "I must look a wreck" she mumbled into the mattress.

Sam wrapped the curl around his finger. "I've always loved your hair, Elizabeth. Especially when it seems to have a mind of its own."

"Well, as that's just about every day of my life, thanks." She reached behind her, trying to pull up the sheet without his notice.

"I've seen every inch of you. Tasted most as well. Unless you're cold, there's no need for that."

Elizabeth turned her head but didn't meet his gaze. "That was in moonlight. Daylight is less forgiving. I'm not twenty anymore."

Sam traced a finger along the line of her jaw before tipping her face up to his. "You were beautiful at fifteen. More so at twenty-four. Right now, you stop my heart. I can only imagine how you'll look at eighty." He leaned in and backed up his words with a long, heated kiss.

When he broke the kiss, Elizabeth looked deeply into his eyes. "Wow. Just wow." She inched over and laid her head on his chest, tracing a vague pattern across his abdomen with her finger.

"Can I ask you a question, Sam?" Her tone was serious.

Sam cleared his throat before responding. "Of course, Elizabeth."

"Why does this seem so natural to you, when I'm still trying to wrap my head around it?" She turned her face up to his as she waited for him to answer.

"I don't know, Elizabeth. Maybe because we've known each other for so long?"

"That's just it, Sam. We have known each other since we were seven. But not like this." She gestured to where their naked bodies touched. "You don't find this even the slightest bit unusual?"

"I was interested in baseball and bugs at seven."

She punched him lightly in the stomach. "You know what I mean, Sam."

"Not until you mentioned it actually. Are you regretting this, Elizabeth? I'd rather you be honest with me than try to spare my feelings."

She placed her warm lips against his and kissed him thoroughly before pulling back. "No, Sam. Not even for a moment. It's just a bit confusing. But then, my entire life is a bit confusing."

"Maybe it's getting clearer and you just don't realize it yet."

She smiled faintly. "Maybe."

Regret filled Elizabeth. She had broken the magic of waking beside Sam in his bed. Feeling another warm body next to hers, limbs entangled. This was something she hadn't done since Connor. As much as she liked Jeremy, and their arrangement, they never spent the night. Neither wished to blur the lines.

She reached for a folded t-shirt of Sam's that was lying on a chair. Pulling it over her head, she disappeared into the bathroom. Elizabeth splashed cold water on her face. She stared at her reflection in the mirror. She couldn't stop the grin that spread across her face. As confusing as the situation with Sam was, that was a satisfied person staring back at her. Elizabeth shook off her earlier trepidation. Life was good. Her mom was out of the woods and back home where she belonged. Elizabeth had begun to reconnect with old friends and fix the hurt she had caused.

And then there was Sam. She loved Sam. Always had. Now she was beginning to care for Sam in a way that was new to her. She had only loved one man. Connor. And Elizabeth knew in her heart that they would still be in love and married today had he not died. But he did. She had moved on with her life. And now she had a decision to make.

Was there really any good reason for returning permanently to Los Angeles? Sure, she had friends and a job that she loved. And there was Jeremy. But she had so much more here in Windsor Falls. She had family and history. True friends that she was just now getting back to. She could have a life here. Did she really want to leave? Again?

She returned to the bedroom, but Sam wasn't there. Hearing noises coming from the kitchen, she moved in that direction, still wearing nothing but his old shirt. She entered the kitchen to find Sam staring at the contents of his refrigerator. Walking up behind him and wrapping her arms around him, she breathed in the undeniably male scent of his skin.

"I would love to say that I could make you a big breakfast, but that's not happening with what I have in here." He turned, closing the door, and enveloped her in a bear hug. "Unless you want more bar-b-q chicken" he joked. "We could, of course, get dressed and go grab something. Or we could have toast and coffee."

"That's OK, Sam, I'll settle for coffee and toast. I have a lot to do today, and I really should check in on my Mom. Even though I spoke with her last night, I don't like to leave her for so long. I had such a big scare with her."

They sat at the kitchen island and had toast and coffee. Sam was here with her but not really. Once again, she regretted making that remark to him earlier.

There was a tension between them that hadn't been there before. "Is everything okay Sam?"

Sam looked at her across the rim of his mug. "Everything's fine. Why wouldn't it be?"

She thought she knew but didn't really want to, so she didn't ask. "No reason" she muttered half-heartedly before going back into Sam's bathroom to get dressed. He followed her in to get dressed as well. She looked longingly at his big, rumpled, unmade bed. The hours she had spent in it with Sam were seared into her brain. And on every inch of her flesh. Sighing, she left the room to retrieve her purse.

In the driveway, Sam grabbed her by the wrist and tugged lightly until she fell against him. Holding her face between his hands, he gave her one last scorching kiss, as if to remind her of everything they had shared. "About last night, Elizabeth. I've never done that before; made love without a condom." He ran an agitated hand through his hair. "I never wanted to put you in that position. I lost my head. Do we need to worry about that?"

"Not on my account we don't. I'm on the pill for my horrendously bad periods. And I'm clean as far as the other stuff goes." She was horrified to remember they had not even thought about protection out on the patio. How many times had she lectured her patients in the ED about the consequences of unprotected sex? That must have shown on her face, because Sam immediately reached out and touched her.

"I'm good too. I just had a complete physical for health insurance a few months back. It was comprehensive." His ears turned a dull red. "I haven't been with anyone since then."

"Then we're fine."

Sam dragged the toe of his shoe in the gravel of the driveway. "But if there was another issue, you'd tell me. Right?"

Her heart clenched at his question. He still didn't trust her. But could she really blame him? "Yes, Sam. I would tell you. But you really have nothing to worry about."

"Good."

Good that they didn't have anything to worry about? Or good that she would tell him if she was pregnant. Elizabeth thought about what he had been asking. Becoming pregnant with his child. He was worried she wouldn't tell him. Her uterus cramped at the memory of when she had been briefly pregnant. Elizabeth hadn't thought about if in a long time. She still wanted to have kids. Hoped to. She still wanted to fall in love again. She just wasn't sure when or how any of that would occur.

Sam drove her home. It was quiet in the truck with them both lost in their own thoughts. At her mother's house, Elizabeth reached for the door handle. "Thanks for everything. I had a great time."

She would have exited, but Sam grasped her wrist. Leaning in, he gave her what was meant to be the briefest of kisses. But the passion flared instantly between them, as it always seemed to do. Reluctantly, he broke the kiss and leaned back against his door, watching her.

"I have to go, Sam."

"I know. I just don't want you to."

Elizabeth's heart sped up a bit at his words. She didn't want to leave him either, but she had things to do. "Have a good day, Sam." she said as she exited his truck. She walked into her mother's house without looking back. She had to. Otherwise, she would be getting in and going back home with him.

*****

Sam sat there for a few moments, long after Elizabeth had closed the front door behind her. She hadn't even turned around for one last look. He had hoped she would be as shaken as he was from that last kiss. He had hoped she would turn around and come back. But she looked calm walking away. Finally, he placed the truck in reverse and backed out of the driveway. He missed her already, but he had more than enough to keep him busy all day.

Concentration was hard to come by at work. After going home to shower, Sam had headed in for a few hours. He always had a mountain of paperwork to do; advertising, bills, inventory, personnel. It was the least favorite part of his job. What he loved was wandering the store and talking with customers. Helping them to make the right decisions. He knew a lot of them, but as the store grew, he was seeing more and more new faces from surrounding towns.

He sat at his desk staring blindly at the inventory program. Blowing out a disgusted breath, Sam stood and paced his small office like a caged tiger. He didn't have to close his eyes to replay images from last night. He could feel her silky hair on his chest, her mouth on his overheated skin.

Unease snaked through him. He was still in love with her. Now more than ever. And she was still leaving him. Again. She may be merely returning to her life in California, but it felt exactly as though she was leaving him. He needed to tell her how he felt. What he was willing to offer her. His heart. His home. His everything. She needed to hear this before she decided to return to her life on the west coast.

But Sam needed to be sure that Connor's ghost had been laid to rest. He needed to know that she was with him, in the present, before he could tell her his feelings.

Feeling claustrophobic in the confines of his office, Sam roamed the store. He had only made it down a few aisles when a deep voice stopped him. "Hiding in plain sight, huh?"

Sam turned to see Aidan Fitzgerald. His heavy thoughts drifted away at the sight of his friend. "Not hiding. Just working as usual. What's going on?"

Aidan swung the basket in his hand. "Just picking up a few things for my house. Where have you been man? Missed you at the last game."

For the past few years, a group of them had been playing poker every couple of weeks. The group was loosely defined, with different people showing each time as their schedules allowed. All of Connor's brothers played, as well as Quinn Adams, a local firefighter and son of his garden center manager Maria. The last session had been just after Elizabeth returned to Windsor Falls.

"Yeah, sorry about that. I was busy."

"With a woman, I hope" suggested Aidan with a raised eyebrow.

Not sure how he would feel if he knew the woman in question was his former sister-in-law, Sam shook his head. "No, just busy with the house. When I'm not here, I'm there working on the interior. Almost done, thankfully."

"I happen to know a company you can hire for that sort of thing" Aidan joked. His family's business was construction of course. He was the youngest of the Fitzgerald siblings and an architect. After interning with a large firm in Charlotte, Aidan moved back home last year to open his own small one right here in Windsor Falls. Sam's house had been his very first project.

"Speaking of work, how's Fitzgerald Architects going?"

"Great actually. Better than I could have hoped. Having a family in the construction business doesn't hurt."

"Coming back here and starting your own firm took a lot of guts, Aidan. I'm really excited for you."

"Thanks, man. I got great experience in Charlotte, but it wasn't what I wanted. No skyscrapers for me. I'm psyched to be back home, and I love building houses and small businesses for families."

"That's great, Aidan, doing what you love."

"So, no woman, then? I figured you were too miserable to be getting any." Aidan laughed and slapped Sam on the back.

"I'm not miserable, and I wouldn't tell you if I was. Getting any that is."

Aidan spread his hands wide. "Okay, I was wrong. It happens; at least once a year."

"Not sure you've ever admitted that. What's the occasion?"

"Just maturity I guess. I am thirty now."

"That's right, the big 3-0. Maybe so, but you're still the baby of the Fitzgerald clan."

The casual remark caused just the reaction he had hoped for, as Aidan's face flushed a bright red. With his Irish complexion, Aidan had trouble keeping any secrets. It made poker that much more interesting.

"No one's every going to let me forget it either. Just because Riley had the luck of being born three minutes before me" he grumbled under his breath.

It was a long running joke in the Fitzgerald family, and Sam couldn't help busting the normally confident Aidan. "When is the next game? I could use some money for all the home projects I'm doing."

Aidan laughed, regaining his good nature. It was a well-known fact in Windsor Falls that their poker game was more about having some beers and bull shitting than actually winning any money. Sam had been invited to his first game not long after hiring Aidan to design his house. He'd been going regularly ever since. They were a great group of guys, and he enjoyed the time he spent with them.

"Speaking of home projects, are you about done yet? You know my Mom and sisters are itching to see the place. Gonna be ready for the party?"

"Does it matter if I am? They'll come anyway. I made the mistake of letting Katie plan things. I have no idea who she even invited. Apparently, the week of the event she's going to give me some grocery lists."

Aidan stared at Sam with horror on his handsome face. "Are you crazy? Have you met my sister? You'd better plan for the whole town coming."

Sam shook his head and groaned. "That's what I was afraid of. Sadly, that didn't dawn on me until after I agreed."

"Nothing you can do now. Don't worry. Your poker buddies will be there for moral support. I gotta go. Let me know what I can do for the party." He slapped Sam on the back before walking away. Over his shoulder he called, "Better yet, I'll just ask Katie."

He may be in over his head with this party thing, especially as it was the first he had ever thrown one. But Sam figured it was better than sitting around worrying about Elizabeth.

Chapter Twenty-One

Maggie had come by to pick up Diane for lunch, so Elizabeth went out onto the small back yard deck to take a seat on one of the rocking chairs. She rocked slowly, enjoying yet another pretty, summer day. It might be late August, but this was North Carolina, and fall was a way off yet. Sweat trickled down her back, but the shade of the old oak tree helped a bit. She sipped some tea and thought about the past few days. What was going on between her and Sam? Sure, the sex was mind-blowing. Nothing to doubt there. But while she hadn't expected a declaration of undying love, she also hadn't expected Sam to be quite so casual this morning. Had she misread his feelings for her? Or worse, had she read too much into their lovemaking? She gnawed her lower lip.

Elizabeth was sure this was more than a fling for both, but Sam was sending very confusing signals. He was so tender with her when they were making love, treating her in ways that spoke volumes. And he was certainly possessive and jealous in front of Flynn. Yet he had not said anything about his feelings for her. On the other hand, Elizabeth mused, Sam might be just as confused as she was. She hadn't spoken those words either. She cared about Sam. Loved him really, as she always had.

Her pulse quickened at the L word. She had loved Sam back then. In a platonic, best friend way. But what about now? She had certainly never thought of having sex with him before last week. Elizabeth got up and paced as if to outrun her thoughts.

He made her happy. He made her feel things she hadn't felt since Connor. She and Jeremy had their little arrangement, off and on, for over three years. And she genuinely liked him. But thoughts of him didn't tie her up in knots. Why was that?

There were still things to be said between them. There were issues from the past to be laid to rest. But talk was difficult when she went up in flames every time she was near him. She needed to know, for sure, that he had forgiven her for abandoning him. Elizabeth needed to hear him say the words. And mean them. This had to be about more than chemistry between them. They couldn't have any kind of future with the past still unsettled.

And she had a big decision to make. Soon. Her boss was very patient, but now there was a deadline. Next Sunday. Her mother was doing well enough at home for Elizabeth to return to her life in California. But was that really what she wanted?

She went back inside and tackled her few lunch dishes, straightening the kitchen as she went. Memories of the night they had shared sent a warm thrill throughout her body. Their chemistry was amazing, and even now her toes curled thinking about it. Did she really want to risk that by not dealing with the history between them? No. She did not. Today, she would finally put it all to rest. But there was one thing she had to do first.

Arriving at Saint Peter's cemetery, Elizabeth drove slowly along the winding path until she came to the right place. She got out of the car, carrying the flowers she had brought. Finding his grave, she laid them gently along the marker and sat in the grass. Elizabeth brushed her fingertips along its smooth surface, tracing Connor's name and dates of birth and death. Scrolled underneath was *Beloved Husband, Son, Brother, Friend*. She choked up a bit reading that. Connor had certainly been all those things; and so much more. She was pleased with the granite stone Maggie had chosen. Elizabeth had been too broken to do that.

Only his body was buried here. Connor's spirit had remained with her throughout the years. She thought of him often and was thankful that time had eased the rawness of her grief.

"I'm sorry that I haven't been back here since the day we buried you, Connor, but I know you understand. You and I both agreed that when one of us died, we wouldn't spend the rest of our life grieving the other at a graveside. It's just your body here, Connor. You're in a far better place. I've felt you with me all these years, watching over me."

Elizabeth leaned her head against the warm granite of the stone and took a deep breath before continuing. "I know that what I'm about to tell you won't come as any surprise to you. I've been running all these years. Away from anything that could hurt me again. Away from love. California has been wonderful for me, but I want to come home. I'm ready to be a whole person again."

Tears silently coursed down her face, but Elizabeth barely noticed. "It will always make me a little sad to think of you dying so young, Connor. We had just started our lives together and were so excited about having a baby. But there's nothing I can do to change what happened. You would want me to be happy again, just as I would have wanted that for you." She started to cry in earnest then; big cleansing tears.

"These feelings I have for Sam came as a big surprise to me. But who better than my other best friend? I hope that your family will understand, Connor. They know how much I loved you and our baby. But I've been alone a long time now, and I need more." The tears continued as she rested against Connor's headstone.

*****

This was how Sam found her. Walking over the crest of a hill, he saw her leaning over Connor's grave, sobbing. He was too far away to hear her words, but he didn't need to. He could read them in her body language. She was curled around the grave marker, her shoulders shaking with her grief. For all her brave words, she wasn't over the loss of her husband. If there hadn't been healing in over ten years, he doubted there ever would be.

Sam's heart ached at the site of her. A profound sadness settled over him, making him weary. She may have given her body to him, but her heart and soul belonged to another. Unfortunately, he wasn't willing to settle. Over the years, he had casual affairs with women who were willing and understood that was all he was offering. But this was Elizabeth, and that wasn't enough for him. He had loved her since he was fifteen. He wanted it all. He turned and left silently. She would never know that he was there as a witness to her grief.

Sam was home before he realized he had driven away. After thinking about her all day, all he had wanted was to find Elizabeth. He wanted to tell her how much he loved her. How he'd always loved her. He had gone in search of her with a song in his heart. Now there was nothing left to say. Sam's heart broke a little more as he realized that Elizabeth returning to California would be best for both.

*****

Elizabeth dried the few remaining tears with the hem of her t-shirt. The hot sun beat down on her head, reminding her how great it was to be alive. She felt renewed, cleansed. For the first time since losing Connor and their baby, she felt whole again. She would always love Connor, but it was time to close that chapter in her life. Funny that she had to come home to do so. She was ready to start a new one. Here in Windsor Falls. Hopefully with Sam.

She needed to find Sam and tell him everything. But doing so wasn't as easy as she had hoped. He wasn't at the store. She tried calling, but it went right to voice mail. She didn't want to say what she needed to say in a voice mail or text. So, she just left a general message to call her. Disappointed, she drove home.

Her mother was sipping sweet tea and reading the paper on the front porch swing when Elizabeth got home. Although each day brought small improvements, Elizabeth's heart clenched at the lines in her mother's face. She looked older since her illness. As a single parent, Diane had always seemed invincible. The truth was painful to see.

She leaned in and hugged her mother. The soft scent of lavender was achingly familiar. "It's so good to see you up and about Mom. All that time away, I could always picture you right here in this spot, doing exactly what you're doing now." A shudder ran through her body as Elizabeth thought about how close she had come to losing her mother. About all the wasted time.

Diane put down the newspaper and searched her daughter's face. "You've been crying. What's wrong?"

"Actually, it's what's right. I went to see Connor's grave. For the first time. I sat and chatted with him."

Diane smiled. "That was long overdue. Do you feel better now?"

"I do. I feel lighter. Happier. Settled." She laughed at herself. "Maybe all of the above."

"I'm glad, honey. So, what are your plans?"

"I'm coming home."

Diane looked her in the eye as if measuring something before nodding. "Yes, it's time, Elizabeth. I'm so happy." The two women hugged, laughing and crying at the same time, until both were breathless.

"I swear I've cried more since I've been back then the whole time I was away." She wiped the last tears from her face. "That's the first time I've said it out loud; 'I'm coming home.' You're the first person I told."

"What will Sam think?" Diane laughed at the look of shock on Elizabeth's face. "I'm old not dead dear. I knew where you were last night. And last week. How's that going?"

Elizabeth ran a distracted hand through her short curls. "I really don't know, Mom. It's Sam. The Sam from my childhood. It's still new and more than a little disconcerting." A warm smile spread across her face. "But wonderful. He's the first person since Connor that has touched my heart."

"Because he's the right one dear. And because you're letting him in. Jeremy seemed lovely, but I get the feeling you always held yourself back from him. Only giving him small pieces. Sam will ask for so much more. Are you ready for that?"

"I'm willing to try, Mom. I care about Sam so much. I've always loved him, but now I'm falling in love with him. Does that make any sense?"

"Of course it does, Elizabeth. Your relationship with Sam is changing. Just be honest with him. Tell him how you feel. Now that you're staying, you both have the luxury of time. Nothing needs decided right away. But you should tell him that you're staying."

"I've been trying to call him, but it goes right to voicemail." She ground her teeth. "I made the decision, and I want to tell him so badly. I want to tell him so many things. Where could he be?"

"Don't worry, you'll get ahold of him. Now, do you have time to tackle some more of memory lane?"

Elizabeth laughed. Diane was moving forward with selling her house, but she wasn't able to do most of the work of sorting through almost thirty years of stuff. "Sure, Mom, let's go tackle some more boxes."

After a late supper, Elizabeth decided to call it a night. She had an early shift in the morning and hadn't gotten a ton of sleep last night. The memory of why she lost sleep made her smile. A vague shiver of unease curled through her at not having reached Sam. Lying in bed physically exhausted but mentally wired was torturous for her. She wanted to move forward with her life. But how could she when Sam wouldn't even answer his phone?

After getting into bed, she grabbed her phone to send him another text. *"Either you're avoiding me or I'm a stalker. Either way, I need to talk with you. Soon. It's important."* She hit send and waited. Elizabeth got up and opened her window, allowing in a nice breeze. Although the days were still hot, the nights had cooled off nicely. Climbing back in bed, she checked her phone. No message. The she checked the ringer. Yep, still on. Disgusted, she turned off the light and went to sleep.

*****

Sam was in Aidan's kitchen grabbing a round of beers for the guys when he got the text alert. Before leaving the store today, Aidan had reminded Sam of the poker game tonight at his home. And though he certainly didn't feel like having fun, this was better than the alternative. The idea of sitting home alone and feeling sorry for himself held even less appeal. Before he looked at his phone, he knew it was from Elizabeth. It was the latest of several, not to mention a missed call or two, since he had seen her at the cemetery. Giving in, he took a long swig from his bottle and read her text. 'Important.' The normally delicious beer tasted of ashes, and he forced himself to swallow.

"Hey, hurry up" came from the direction of the table, and Sam shoved his phone back into his pocket. Grabbing his bottle, he rejoined the guys.

Aidan looked up when Sam entered the room. He motioned at Sam's lone bottle. "I thought you went for drinks."

Chagrined, Sam sank into an empty chair. "I was. Sorry." He continued to stare at the wall as he thought about her latest text. He didn't know how to lose her again. But if she wasn't over Connor, then going back to California was probably for the best.

Brendan, the second oldest of the Fitzgerald brothers, was seated to his right. "Hey man. What's the deal? You look like crap." At Sam's dark look, Brendan held up his hands in surrender. "Sorry, man, but it's the truth."

Sam looked at the other guys at the table. All of Connors brothers were there along with Quinn Adams. They were all giving him the same look. The 'what's with him' look. Brendan, who was a divorced, single dad, spoke. "This must be about a woman. I know that look."

Aidan, coming back from the kitchen with the forgotten beers, agreed. "Definitely. What happened, Sam? Another one of your many women trying to trap you?" There was a burst of male laughter around the table. It was a well-known fact that the only trouble Sam had with the ladies was convincing them he wasn't interested in anything long term.

Quinn spoke up. "I saw a lovely young woman hanging around you a few weeks ago at the store Sam. Looked like she was bringing you a pie. What happened to her?"

Before he could answer, Aidan cut in. "The same thing that always happens. Some poor girl thought she could change his mind, and Sam broke her heart."

"Kelly wasn't heart broken, just determined" Sam mumbled, more under his breath than anything. He looked up to find four pairs of eyes staring at him. "What? Are we really going to sit around and discuss our love lives? What's next? Pedicures? I thought we were here to play poker."

"Well, now that you mention it, Donovan could use some help with his feet." Aidan chuckled as his oldest brother swore a blue streak.

"You try wearing work boots all day every day, Aidan. We don't all have the luxury of a cushy job."

A general riot ensued as the men all took turns laughing at each other. Sam sat back and looked around in wonder and thanks. His love life might be a mess, and he was sure Elizabeth was about to hand his heart to him. Again. But he had great friends in this quirky town of theirs. He would be alright. Again.

The dust settled, and they restarted their poker game. Conversation turned to the various women they had dated. Except for Donovan, they were all single. Just when Sam could breathe a sigh of relief, Quinn asked about Elizabeth.

"So, what's the deal with Elizabeth? How long is she staying? I wouldn't mind asking her out if she's going to be here for a while."

All eyes were now on Quinn. Very carefully and through gritted teeth, Brendan answered. "You do know she's like our sister, right?"

Quinn, being a smart man, immediately picked up on the undertones. He held up both hands in surrender. "Whoa. Sorry. I forgot."

Brendan jaws loosened. A bit. "Didn't mean to snap your head off. It's just Elizabeth is special to us. And we just got her back." Quinn nodded in understanding.

Sam remembered to breathe, exhaling loudly. Tension rolled off him in waves. Quinn had been new with the fire department that pulled him and Connor out of the wreckage. He had stopped by the hospital later to check on Sam, and they had been friends ever since. He was a great guy, but he wasn't the one for Elizabeth. No one was. Not even him.

Donovan shuffled the cards and began to deal. Sam stood up suddenly. "Deal me out this hand." He walked into the kitchen and through the door to Aidan's deck. The stars were out, although not as brightly as at his house. He sat heavily in a lawn chair and waited for the feeling to pass. Sam didn't bother to open his eyes when he heard the kitchen slider open and close softly.

"You found me."

"You know that doesn't apply to you, right Sam? The thing about Elizabeth."

Sam's eyes snapped open. His heart pounded. Did Brendan know? He sat upright and stared at Brendan. "That would be great if she wasn't still in love with Connor. And heading back to California." He smiled weakly in the darkness. "But it means a lot."

"It should, Sam. You know how much we all love Elizabeth. And you're basically another brother." Brendan dropped into the chair next to Sam and lowered his voice. "And I know how much you love her. And for how long."

A roar filled Sam's head. His chest tightened. "How do you know that? I've never told anyone."

"That's not true, Sam. You told Connor. I was there."

Sam stiffened at the memory. "The night of Connor's bachelor party." Dread pooled in his belly. "I thought you were asleep."

Brendan turned to Sam. "I had just gotten up to go to the bathroom. I drank a lot of soda that night as the designated driver."

Sam leaned back in his chair and thought about that night. "We were very drunk that night. Connor and me. He was going on and on about how much he loved Elizabeth. Which he should have, since they were getting married in two weeks. But something snapped inside of me, and I told him that I loved her too."

He closed his eyes on the pain of the memory. "The funny thing is, he wasn't even angry. He just smiled and said 'I know.' We never talked about it again."

"He wasn't angry because he knew you were an honorable man. He knew you would never do anything to hurt them." Brendan paused and took a long pull of his beer. "More than anything in the world, I wish Connor was still with us. But all the wishing in the world can't make that happen. Elizabeth is still here, Sam. Not in California. If you love her like I think you do, then make this happen." Brendan tapped his bottle against the one Sam was holding before getting up and going back inside.

Chapter Twenty-Two

Elizabeth hadn't slept well, restless because she hadn't spoken with Sam. Told him her plans. She was embarrassed to remember how often she had checked her phone in the middle of the night. But it was all for nothing. Sam had not responded to her. She rolled her head on her tired shoulders and tried to focus on the electronic patient chart in front of her. Thankfully, the morning had been relatively slow so far. But that could change in a heartbeat, so she headed for the staff lounge to get some coffee.

As she walked in, she saw Eric doing the same. He smiled as he watched her walk in the room. "There's my favorite temporary doctor. Coming for some caffeine?"

"Absolutely, Eric. And about that. I need to talk to you."

"Oh? You look a bit serious. Do we need to go into my office?"

"No, unless you would prefer."

Eric pulled out a chair and motioned for her to sit. "How's your mom by the way?"

The first genuine smile of the day lit Elizabeth's face. All the way to her eyes. "She's doing great, thanks. I'm so pleased with her progress. But she needs help and California is so far away. That's actually what I wanted to talk about with you." She tapped the pen in her hand repeatedly against her coffee mug. "I was wondering if you're still looking for a full timer on staff."

Erik placed his mug on the table and raised a fist in the air. "Yes." he exclaimed loudly. He smoothed a hand over his white coat before continuing. "Sorry about that. I had sort of lost hope that you might stay. You are telling me that you're staying, right?"

Elizabeth laughed. "Yes, Erik, that was me asking you for a job."

"Well then by all means of course. I've been wanting to talk with you about this, but I didn't want you to feel pressured. I just heard from Jane, our doctor on maternity leave. It seems she's missing her own mom now that she is one, and they're moving back to Savannah. Your timing couldn't be better."

Elizabeth sat back and held her mug in her trembling hands. Wow. Just like that she had changed her whole life. She took a few deep breaths.

"Elizabeth, are you sure? You look a little shaky. Not that I'm trying to talk you out of this, mind you."

She straightened in her chair and exhaled deeply. "I'm sure, Erik. I just made the decision last night. I haven't had a chance to even speak with my boss in Los Angeles, so please don't say anything to anyone yet."

He rushed to reassure her. "I understand. I'll keep my celebration to myself. In all seriousness, Elizabeth, I am very pleased. I've heard nothing but the best about you from my staff. Even the nurses like you, and they're a tough crowd."

Elizabeth nodded. Doctors might get all the glory, but everyone knew that nurses ran the ED. "Thanks for understanding, Erik. I'm going to call him today. I'd better get back out there."

They both rose, and Erik extended his hand to her. "This is great, Elizabeth. I'll have HR get a contract to you. Of course, you'll have to apply for your NC license and permanent privileges. But that's just a formality."

Elizabeth grabbed her coffee mug and headed back out to the unit. She checked her phone once again. But there was nothing from Sam. Still. Her heart squeezed. She had finally decided, and Sam was the only person she wanted to share it with. His silence weighed heavily on her. One way or the other, she would get him to talk to her. A siren split the air, and Elizabeth put her phone back in her pocket. Sam was an issue for another time. Someone else needed her more.

*****

Sam unloaded bags of groceries from his truck. It had taken several trips, but now every available space on his kitchen counters was filled. Katie had been true to her word, helping him to get ready, even giving him a long grocery list that he had just finished. He wasn't sure what to do with half of the things he'd bought, but he trusted her.

Katie was a good friend, and Sam was thankful for the help. But now that the party was here, he wished it wasn't. It had been a long week, mostly spent avoiding Elizabeth. Not an easy feat in a small town. He was being a coward. He would have to deal with her. Most likely today. But Sam was dreading it. Elizabeth had broken his heart once, and he was sure it was about to happen again.

Sam picked up his cell phone from the counter and scrolled to his voice mails. There was one voice mail from Elizabeth from the other night. She had called several times in the past week, but this was the only message. He hit play and waited for the shaft of pain he would feel at hearing her voice, even over the phone.

"Hi, Sam. It's Elizabeth. Oh. You know that already. We, uh, really need to talk. Hopefully before your party. Please call me when you get this. I miss you." There was a moment of silence before the call ended. It seemed as though she had wanted to say something else but hadn't. Sam listened to the message once more before deleting it. He rubbed at an ache in his chest. Just hearing her voice was almost more than he could bear. He knew he should have called her back, but he didn't.

His gut churned as he thought about Elizabeth. He wondered for the thousandth time if she would even come today. And, worse, would she bring Flynn as she had said? Sam didn't know what to wish for. As much as he longed to see her, he dreaded it equally. He was hurting her by not returning her calls. But she was hurting him too. They needed to have a conversation, but he had absolutely no idea what that would look like. What could he say? Sorry you're still in love with your husband?

What he had witnessed that day in the cemetery drove home the fact that she was not over Connor. It told him, all too loudly, that there was no real place for him in her life. He wasn't willing to compete with a ghost or settle for a casual affair with her. Yet that was all it could ever be for them. She didn't have room in her heart for him. Sam was sickened at the thought.

*****

Elizabeth was just putting a lid on the bowl containing her mother's German Potato Salad when the doorbell rang. The recipe had been passed down for generations, and Diane had insisted on making it for Sam's party. Maggie would be picking Diane up later. This was her first real outing in public since her illness, and everyone had agreed that she should go later to rest ahead of time. Elizabeth was excited to see her mom up and around but worried about her overdoing things. Luckily, Maggie would keep a watchful eye on her old friend.

Wiping her hands on a towel, she rushed to answer the door. She opened it to a smiling Flynn. He was dressed casually in cargo shorts and a polo shirt, but he was devastatingly handsome nonetheless. Not for the first time, Elizabeth wondered why she couldn't be attracted to him. It would have been so much easier. Stretching up on her toes, she hugged him fiercely. It was good to have a friend during all the uncertainty. "Come on in. I'm almost ready." She led the way back to the kitchen.

"You look fetching Dr. Fitzgerald." His eyes roamed the length of her, and he nodded in approval. Dressed in navy shorts and a matching tank top, Elizabeth had gone for comfort over fashion as always. Small copper earrings were her only jewelry. "Flashing some skin to get Sam's attention I see. Nice touch."

Elizabeth flung an oven mitt at his head. Flynn easily caught it, laughing as he did. "For your information, it's going to be almost ninety degrees today. I dress for comfort, not to impress people." She wiggled her toes in her usual flip flops to drive home the point.

"Sure, you are." He cocked his head quizzically. "What's up with Sam?"

Elizabeth was thankful that she had her back turned to him as she placed the container of potato salad in a tote bag along with a large serving spoon. "Great question, Flynn. Wish I had an answer."

"I know something's up Elizabeth. You two could power this whole town with the electricity between you. You obviously care about him, and it seems the same is true for him. Sam's wanted to rip my head off every time he's seen me with you."

Elizabeth sat down abruptly in a chair at the kitchen table. Her eyes were downcast. Flynn pulled out the chair next to hers and took her hand in his. "Okay. Spill."

She blew out a long breath. "Things have gotten…complicated… between us. But I haven't spoken with him in over a week. He's avoiding me. That can't be good. Right?"

Flynn took his time before answering. "It's not great, but there's a million reasons why he might be doing this. You're not going to know unless you ask him."

She laughed bitterly. "You have no idea how many times to get ahold of him. No luck. Well, at least today he's a captive audience. He can't very well leave his own party."

"True." He glanced at his watch. "Speaking of which, shouldn't we be going soon?"

Elizabeth jumped up. "Yes. Yes, we should. Let's get this over with." Her heart was heavy at the thought of dreading this day. She had been so looking forward to it originally. How had her relationship with Sam gotten so muddled?

Flynn placed his hand on her arm. "We don't have to go. We could just stay here and eat ten pounds of your mother's potato salad."

The seriousness of his face let her know that he was only half joking. "Nice to know you'd take a bullet for me, Flynn. It's okay. This thing between Sam and me has to get straightened out one way or the other. It may as well be today." She covered his hand with her own. "But I appreciate having you in my corner."

He grinned in response. "Can't help it. That's what happens when you're the only son in a family of girls. It brings out the protective side."

Elizabeth said goodbye to her mother and grabbed her purse. Flynn carried the tote bag and held the door for her.

"Tell me more about your family, Flynn. Are they all in Atlanta still?"

"Most of them are, but my oldest sister, Beth, lives in Richmond with her husband Jerry and their three kids. I'm the youngest and only unmarried one, something my mom just can't let me forget."

"That sounds serious. And familiar. Has she started a campaign?"

"Why do you think I moved here?" At her startled look, Flynn laughed. "Okay, that's an exaggeration. I moved here because Sebastian, my partner, and I had a wonderful opportunity. But I wasn't kidding about my mother. She has been trying to fix me up for years. There's been an endless parade of her friends' daughters." He shuddered for effect. "That's a lot of first dates."

"Sounds exhausting. Poor baby." she teased.

"A little sympathy please."

"Don't you want to meet someone? Get married? Maybe have a few kids?"

Flynn opened her door and handed her into the car before going around to his side. When he was belted, he turned to Elizabeth. "More than you could probably imagine. My parents have been married for almost fifty years, and they're more in love every day. That's what I want. I just haven't met the right one yet, and I'm not willing to settle."

Elizabeth's eyes widened. "Wow, Flynn. I had no idea. So, the playboy façade is just that." She had heard the outrageous whispers at work but didn't pay any attention to them. When you had a doctor as gorgeous as Flynn who was single, there were bound to be rumors flying.

"Exactly. I've only been here a few months. Right now, Sebastian and I are busy building our practice and settling in. Miss Right is here somewhere." His eyes sparkled. "In fact, I may have already met her."

"Really? Who is this mystery woman who could bring down the might Flynn Reynolds" Elizabeth asked teasingly?

Flynn drove confidently with one hand on the wheel. "Too soon to reveal that, Elizabeth. Time will tell."

The rest of the drive to Sam's house passed in relative silence. Elizabeth was grateful for this. Her increasingly dry throat would have made conversation difficult. Not to mention the knot in her stomach. She watched out the windows as they made their way up into the Blue Ridge Mountains, where Sam had made his home.

At last, Flynn turned down the long driveway. He whistled appreciatively as the house came into view. "Wow. Your Sam has done well for himself." He pulled in behind a long line of cars and killed the motor. "It's not too late to bail, Elizabeth. Just say the word. We still have the potato salad."

She couldn't contain the laughter that bubbled up and out of her. "I'm so glad we're friends, Flynn. You're good for me."

He wagged his brows suggestively. "You have no idea just how good I can be."

"And I'm never going to find out. But thanks for offering." She opened the car door and got out, breathing in the fresh, pine-scented air. "Let's do this."

"Let's" Flynn agreed and tucked her hand through his arm, leading the way on the flagstone path around the side of Sam's house. There was already a huge crowd milling about as music played from hidden speakers. Groups of chairs were set up here and there. Several couples were in the far corner of the yard playing corn hole. By the amount of good natured ribbing, the game wasn't being taken seriously.

The delicious smell of roasting pig wafted on the gentle breeze. Elizabeth's stomach growled in anticipation. "You don't get bar-b-q like this in California. That's for sure."

Flynn halted their progress into the fray. "Speaking of California, don't you owe your boss an answer by tomorrow?"

"I did, but I already spoke with him this morning." Elizabeth murmured contentedly. No matter what happened with Sam, she was staying in Windsor Falls for good. That was reason enough to celebrate.

Flynn tapped his foot on the ground. "And? What did you tell him?"

Elizabeth smiled at his impatience. "Looks like you're stuck with me."

"Yes" Flynn yelled loudly as he swung her up in his arms. Unfortunately, the music changed at just that moment, leaving them in relative silence. Multiple pairs of eyes turned to them.

"Put me down" Elizabeth hissed. When Flynn released her, she grabbed him by the arm and pulled him into the house. "Only Eric Chambers and my mom know about this."

Flynn at least had the decency to look chagrined. "Oops. Sorry. I was just so excited by the fact that you're not leaving."

"No worries, Flynn. It's just that I haven't told Sam yet, and I need him to hear it from me."

Flynn mimed zipping his mouth and tossing away the key. "Got it. Sorry again." He placed the tote bag carrying the potato salad on the counter. "I'm going to grab a drink. Want anything?"

"No thanks. I'm going to put this in the fridge and head outside myself."

Elizabeth busied herself with making room in the fridge. The butterflies in her stomach had morphed into mice. All with sharp claws trying to get out. She placed a hand there, willing them to stop before straightening her shoulders and joining the party outdoors.

*****

Sam stood off to the side of the party, fists clenched at his sides as he watched an elated Flynn swing Elizabeth around. Everyone had seen it. He had no idea what prompted the show and he really didn't want to. He believed Elizabeth when she had told him, more than once, that she and Flynn were just friends. But Sam wondered if Flynn knew this.

The day had turned out to be beautiful, but Sam barely noticed. The last thing he needed today was to have a yard full of happy people. He had considered cancelling but knew that wasn't an option. Maggie would never have permitted that. And that was one person Sam wouldn't disappoint. And besides, Katie had shown up dreadfully early, way too cheerful and fueled by caffeine, to begin the last-minute preparations. Apparently, there was more to a party than grilling some burgers and hot dogs.

Sam took a pull of his drink as Elizabeth came out onto his patio. She was immediately surrounded by various members of the Fitzgerald clan. Seeing her laugh and hug people made his stomach churn. She might appear happy, but Sam knew the truth. Had seen it in the cemetery. This was so much harder than he could have imagined; seeing her here at his home and not touching her. His fingers curled at the memory of her smooth skin under them.

Katie had told him how well Diane was doing. Hopefully this meant that Elizabeth would be returning to California soon. He assumed that was what she was referring to in her message. He hoped. Because he wasn't sure he could keep his hands off her for much longer.

*****

When the first round of greetings ended, Elizabeth walked over to a cooler to grab something to drink. Even though it was late summer, the day was proving to be a scorcher. She hadn't spoken with Sam yet. Elizabeth wiped her clammy palms on her shorts. This was killing her. Better to just get it over with.

Flynn walked up beside her with a drink in his hand as well. "I take it by the look on your face that you haven't spoken with Sam yet."

She tried to feign ignorance. "What look? I'm just surprised by the number of people here. Sam's usually more of the small gathering type."

"I can see that."

Elizabeth turned to see what he meant. She spotted Sam right away. He was standing close to Katie, bending down to hear what she was saying. It was obviously amusing, as he had thrown back his head in laughter. She felt the jealousy slice through her. This had been a big mistake to come here. She turned back to Flynn and smiled a bit too brightly at him. He would never know how much she appreciated his presence besides her.

"So, I was right about him, wasn't I?" he inquired of her.

"Right about whom?" She had no intention of getting into a verbal battle with him here and now. Her nerves were already stretched too thin.

"OK, if that's the way you want to play it. But I was right when I said your childhood *buddy* had developed a larger interest in you. If looks could kill, I'd be a goner right where I stand." Flynn laughed loudly, apparently amused at his own brand of humor.

Elizabeth craned her neck to sneak another quick look at Sam. They made eye contact briefly, before he looked away. But not before she could see something troubling flit across his face. He turned his full attention back to Katie. Connor's sister was wearing a sleeveless blouse that she had knotted at her belly button, exposing a fair amount of tanned flesh. The bright aqua color was a brilliant foil for her flaming hair. Although she was short, her shorts and sandals did wonderful things for her shapely legs. There was more than one guy noticing Katie as Flynn mumbled something under his breath.

"What was that?"

Flynn turned back to Elizabeth. "Nothing that bears repeating. Are you sure those two are just friends. They seem a bit chummy."

Although Elizabeth wasn't sure of much anymore, she knew that Sam would not lie to her about his relationship with Katie. "I'm sure." She looked up at Flynn's face, but his eyes were covered by dark shades. "Why do you care? Is there something you're not telling me, Flynn?"

"What?" He looked back at the couple for a moment. "No. She and I are just sparring partners. She makes me crazy."

"Really?"

Flynn whipped off his shades and turned towards Elizabeth. "Okay maybe. I'm not sure. There's something about her. She drives me crazy at work, always challenging something I did with a patient. But then that's what makes her such a good nurse."

They both watched as Katie leaned up and kissed Sam on the cheek before turning away. She could feel the tension radiating off the normally laid back Flynn. Elizabeth poked him in the arm. "There's your chance to go talk to her away from work."

"Good idea, Elizabeth. Maybe I can stir up some trouble. Are you going to be okay?" When she nodded, he hugged her before heading off in search of his prey.

Now or never, Elizabeth thought. She looked around for Sam but didn't see him immediately. Needing to gather her courage, she ducked into the house. Elizabeth quickly found the powder room, and once inside, she locked the door and then turned to the sink. Splashing some cold water on her face, she hoped that would help her to focus. She just needed to get Sam to herself for a few minutes so that she could tell him her news. Maybe then things between them would be smoother.

Screwing up her courage, Elizabeth exited the bathroom and walked into the kitchen in search of something to do. What she found was Sam.

"Oh, I didn't know you were in here." She shoved her hands in her pockets and thought about backing out of the room. Although she had been trying to speak with him all week, suddenly that didn't seem like such a great idea. His face was devoid of any expression.

"No problem. I was just taking a break from the crowd. Can I get you anything?" Sam stood, seemingly nonchalantly, with a hip propped against the counter and his tanned, muscular arms folded across his chest. She noticed that the same lock of errant hair fell across his forehead. She clenched her hands in her pockets to avoid stepping forward and brushing it back into place.

Elizabeth started to say no but changed her mind. Her pulse beat wildly through her veins. Taking a deep breath and steeling herself, she took the plunge. "Yes, I do want something, Sam. I wanted to tell you that I'm staying. I took a full-time position in the ED and gave notice in California. That's what I've been trying to tell you all week." When he didn't say anything, or show any reaction, she hurried on. "I also want to know what's going on between us. Why haven't you returned my calls? Why are you avoiding me?" Elizabeth stopped then to take a breath, her cheeks flushed with emotion.

"I hope you're not staying here because of me. Because of what happened between us." Sam stayed where he was, seemingly unaffected by what she had said. "We had a little fun, but that's all it was. I'd rather not make more out of it than it is, Elizabeth."

A chill swept over Elizabeth. She stood as still as a statue, as if she had been frozen by his words. She heard what Sam had said, and yet she couldn't understand them. He didn't even look like her Sam; his face a cold mask. How could those nights spent locked in each other's arms not mean anything to him? She couldn't think of a single thing to say to him. She continued to stare as the color drained from her face.

The knuckles of her hand were white where she gripped the center island for support. Tears pooled in her eyes, yet she refused to shed them. With her heart shattering in her chest, Elizabeth turned and left the room. Her back was straight. She didn't make a sound. She wouldn't give him the satisfaction.

Elizabeth walked away calmly until she was out of his sight. Then she ran blindly through the house and out the front door. Too late, she remembered that she had no way to leave. Cursing silently, she walked around the side of another pickup with Fitzgerald Construction lettered on the door. Safely out of sight, she leaned against the truck with her face in her hands and finally let loose the threatening tears. She cried long and hard, the sobs wracking her body. It was awhile before she realized she wasn't alone.

She whirled around and found Brendan standing there. Without a word, he opened his arms, and she stepped into his embrace. The tears she thought were finished started all over again. Brendan braced his long legs and rocked her gently in his arms. Undone by his kindness, Elizabeth just stood there, lost in her pain and grief, with her face buried in his rock-hard chest.

Brendan was a good and decent man. Of all the Fitzgerald brothers, he had been the closest to the big brother Elizabeth had always craved. She remembered him joking at her wedding that she was finally, officially his sister.

When her tears finally slowed, and she took a deep, cleansing breath, Brendan released Elizabeth and set her back a few feet. He peered very seriously into her tear lined face. "What's wrong darling?" She tried to smile in reassurance, but she wasn't very successful. Instead she asked for a favor.

"Could you please drive me home, Brendan? I really don't want to bother Flynn." He would only ask too many questions. All she wanted to do was leave right now, before someone else saw her like this. She wanted to escape to the safety and solitude of her room. Brendan would take her home without an inquisition.

He smiled tenderly in return. "You know I could never refuse you anything. Go ahead and get in the truck. You're going to want the A/C." He tossed her the keys. "Just let me tell Ma that I'll be gone for a bit. She'll have to keep her eyes on the girls. I'll only be a minute." With that, he loped around the corner of the house.

*****

As Brendan spotted his mother, who was already with his daughters, he also noticed an unhappy looking Sam standing alone off to the side. Brendan genuinely liked him, but he knew instinctively that the other man was behind Elizabeth's tears. He didn't take his job as honorary big brother lightly. He made a beeline for Sam.

"What exactly did you do to her?" he asked without preamble. Brendan glared at his friend, waiting for a response. "Give me one good reason why I shouldn't pound you into the ground." The fierce expression on his face let Sam know he wasn't joking.

Sam stared at Brendan as if the other man was a total stranger. "This is between Elizabeth and me. I'd appreciate it if you'd stay out of it."

"It's my business when someone hurts my family, Sam. Even when that someone is you. Besides, finding her crying beside my truck also makes it my business. I don't know what's going on between you two or what just happened, but you better fix it." He poked a finger into Sam's chest to make his point. "I'm taking her home now. Please tell my mom that I'll be back. She needs to watch the girls while I'm gone." Brendan spun on his heel, not allowing Sam time to argue.

*****

Elizabeth was sitting in the passenger seat, looking sightlessly out the window. Although she had stopped crying, her eyes were reddened and still bore the traces of her sadness. Her mind, however, was still reeling. What had happened back there? She thought Sam would be happy that she was staying. Obviously, she had misread the situation. But this was Sam. He had never spoken to her so harshly.

She rubbed a hand over her face as Brendan returned. "Thank you for taking me home, Brendan."

"No worries, Elizabeth. Anything for you."

She was thankful for the silence as he put the truck in gear and drove away from Sam's house. However, her reprieve was brief. When they pulled into her mother's driveway, Brendan got out and came around for her. Taking Elizabeth by the hand, he led her to the front porch swing.

"You might as well tell me. You always do."

Elizabeth smiled at him, her true affection for him shining from her eyes. Brendan was right. She could always talk to him. He had always been there for her. She would never forget his kindness after Connor died. Even though he was mired in his own grief, Brendan had stood beside her at the grave, practically holding her up throughout the service. He just might be the one person she could talk to about Sam.

"It's complicated, Brendan." She paused then and he reached over to squeeze her hand, encouraging her to continue. "I need you to know that I loved your brother very much. Connor was my whole world." At his nod of agreement, she continued. "I never thought I would love anyone else like that again. For the longest time, I was lost in my pain and grief, merely putting one foot in front of the other."

"But since I've come home, I've developed feelings for Sam. I never expected this. I wasn't looking for it. It just happened. And I thought he shared those feelings, but as it turns out it was just a fling for him." She blushed as she realized what she had just inadvertently revealed to Brendan. She lowered her head to stare at the floor.

Brendan placed his hand under Elizabeth's chin and gently turned it up until she was looking at him. "I would never in a million years doubt what you felt for Connor. We all knew that you two loved each other with your whole hearts. But life goes on, Elizabeth. And you're human like the rest of us." Brendan reddened slightly at the tone of the conversation.

He cleared his throat before continuing. "You're both adults, and I care about you both. I consider Sam one of my closest friend. But I *love* you, Elizabeth. Just like I love Riley, Katie, and Nora. If he hurts you, I'm going to have to have a little chat with him." His grin was anything but friendly. "Did he actually say this was only a fling for him? Because knowing what I know, I'd find that difficult to believe."

Elizabeth tilted her head t that last part. Her face held a questioning look. "What are you talking about, Brendan?" He was not the first person to hint at the fact that Sam had feelings for her beyond their friendship.

Comprehension dawned on his handsome face. "You really don't know, do you? Wow! Sam has been in love with you since y'all were fifteen years old, Elizabeth. How could you not know?"

Elizabeth's whole body stiffened. "What? No." Could that be true? She shuddered at the thought. She had been so wrapped up in Connor that this never occurred to her.

"Maybe you were too blinded by your feelings for Connor to see anyone else. To be honest, I had a little crush of my own on you way back then."

Elizabeth would have laughed at the absurdity of that if not for the seriousness on his face. "Now, I know that's not true."

"Oh, it is Elizabeth. But that was a long time ago, and I survived it. I knew I never had a chance once you and Connor got together. I had always suspected that Sam had deeper feelings for you. It was the way he looked at you. The way he acted around you. But I knew for sure the night of Connor's bachelor party."

Her eyebrows disappeared into her hairline, but Brendan just shook his head. "Not my story to tell. But I will say this. That man loves you, despite whatever just happened."

Elizabeth stared at him in horror. "All those years? He's loved me all those years?"

Brendan dropped an arm around her shoulders and hugged her. "That's not your responsibility, Elizabeth. You can't be held accountable for his feelings for you. After all, people don't get to choose with whom they fall in love."

"I don't understand anything anymore, Brendan. If Sam has loved me for so long, why is he pushing me away? Why is he acting like this?" Her head was spinning. This was just too much to handle right now.

Brendan took her hands in his and waited until she looked at him. "Maybe he's doing this *because* he loves you so much, Elizabeth. It can't have been easy all those years, watching you and Connor. Maybe he's just trying to protect himself. I don't know. But what I do know is that you need to talk to him. You have to get this straightened out. If you don't, you may live to regret it."

She sniffed noisily. "Brendan, what would I do without you?"

"Luckily, you'll never have to find out. But no matter what happens, Elizabeth, I'm still your big brother. Just say the word, and he's toast." A sound escaped her, half sob, half laugh.

Brendan gave her one last hug. "Well, I'd better get back. Heaven knows what the girls are up to, even under Mom's watchful eye."

She hugged him back and watched as he left. Brendan was a single dad to six-year-old twin girls. His ex-wife, Gillian, had never wanted kids. A fact she conveniently forgot to tell Brendan when they married. Horrified to find she was pregnant, Gillian had wanted to abort the pregnancy. But Brendan had put his foot down. Weeks after Abby and Kerry were born, Brendan filed for divorce and came back to Windsor Falls with his infant daughters.

Elizabeth pushed the swing absently with her foot. She knew Brendan was right, even if the knowledge was painful. She did have to talk with Sam. But how could she ever do so with the way things were left between them? The Sam from this afternoon was a stranger to her. He had seemed so distant and unlike himself. How would she get past the walls he had erected? Well, her mother had always said that life wasn't easy. Elizabeth had to find a way. And soon.

Chapter Twenty-Three

Sam strode blindly to a far corner of the yard. It was the only place he could think of to be alone. Although he could still hear the sounds of the party, at least he could have some space. His heart ached with the memory of what he had just done to Elizabeth. Knowing it was for her own good in the end didn't make it hurt any less. He rubbed the heels of both hands in his eyes, trying in vain to erase the image of her stricken face. Being confronted by Brendan hadn't helped.

Sam laughed harshly at himself. He was more in love with her than ever. For years, he had longed to have Elizabeth back in his life. In his bed. But now that he knew the wonder of that, he had to let her go. She could never let him fully into her life, and Sam wasn't willing to settle. He sighed deeply and ran a hand through his hair. Knowing that she wasn't going to return to California only made things worse.

"Give me one good reason why I shouldn't kick your ass, Sam."

Sam whirled to find Flynn standing less than twenty feet from him. His entire body screamed fury, from his clenched fists to the flushed skin of his face.

"You may not think this is any of my business, but it is. What kind of a game are you playing with her?" His eyes glittered with barely controlled anger.

"If you're referring to Elizabeth, then you're right, I don't think this is any of your business. In fact, I know it isn't." He was really in no mood for this right now, not after the scene in the kitchen with Elizabeth. Sam had a hard enough time with Flynn even being in Elizabeth's life. He certainly wasn't going to discuss their relationship with Flynn.

Flynn bared his teeth in a poor excuse for a smile. "You don't strike me as a stupid man, so I'll give you the benefit of the doubt. Just this once. Elizabeth walked into the house earlier. She was fine. Then, you followed her inside shortly afterwards. The next thing I hear from Maggie is that Brendan has driven Elizabeth home. Suddenly, she's 'not feeling well'. We both know that's a lie. She was perfectly fine when she left my side ten minutes earlier. Care to explain?" His dark blue eyes were spitting fire.

Sam drew himself up to his full height and blew out a frustrated breath. "Actually, no." By all rights, Flynn should kick his ass for what he had done to Elizabeth. Even if he had done it to protect them both.

"Well, Elizabeth is my friend, something you're supposed to be as well. Yet she left here crying because of you. She's is a strong woman, more than capable of taking care of herself, but if this happens again I'm coming to find you." His eyes held more than a hint of malice as he turned away. Sam shook his head as Flynn stalked back towards the party.

Sam knew that both Brendan and Flynn had every right to be upset with him. After all, he wasn't finished cursing himself out for his hideous treatment of her. But knowing the depth of Flynn's feelings for Elizabeth didn't make any of this easier.

Although it was comforting to know that Elizabeth had people in her life who cared for her, did they have to be men? But why would this come as a surprise to him? She was a beautiful woman. Just because he was unwilling to settle for her guarded heart, that didn't mean others would be. Did he really think she would stay single forever?

Sam blew out a disgusted breath as he listened to the sound of people having a good time in his back yard. The day had soured for him completely, and he wished they would all leave. But with his luck, they would stay until dark. He sighed and made his way to the house. Maybe he could hide in there for a while.

As he approached the house, he saw Katie and Flynn standing off to the side, exchanging what looked like heated words. Although Flynn wasn't his favorite person in the world, Sam had to give him credit for bravery. Katie was visibly upset, and that woman had a temper on her. Even though Flynn may have almost a foot and more than sixty pounds on her, he'd still put his money on Katie. She certainly wasn't backing down, going toe to toe with Flynn and jabbing him in the chest with her tiny finger. Even from this distance, Sam could read her obvious body language. The doctor would be lucky to escape with his limbs still attached. If Sam's world wasn't crumbling, he might have found humor in the scene. But his heart was heavy. All he wanted was a beer and a silent house. At least he could get the first.

Sam grabbed a cold beer from the fridge and pulled the top off with more force than necessary. His jumbled thoughts turned, yet again, to Elizabeth. Had he done the right thing? Indecision plagued him now that some time had passed. He loaded the dishwasher for the third time today, wondering what she was doing. Had she really left here in tears? The thought pierced his heart. Sam had been thinking of her, trying to protect her, but he hadn't handled things well. While he meant to drive her away, he certainly could have found a kinder way to do so.

Sam turned towards the patio doors as he heard someone enter the kitchen. His heart sunk when he recognized Elizabeth's mother. "Can I get you anything, Mrs. Abbott?" He tried to keep a pleasant smile on his face, but it didn't reach his eyes. She was quite possibly the last person he wanted to speak to. She was probably aware that he had been the cause of Elizabeth's abrupt departure from the party. Sam squared his shoulders and braced himself for what was coming.

"Sam, I think we are long past the days of you calling me Mrs. Abbott. Don't you? I'm pretty sure you can call me Diane now." Her expression was open without a trace of contempt or anger.

Surprise flashed across his face. "OK then, I can do that, Mrs. Abbott, uh I mean Diane." The name felt foreign on his tongue.

"I know that you're a nice guy Sam, but right now I can see you're doing your best to hide your surprise. That's okay. I deserve it. I have some things to say to you, Sam, and they're long overdue." She stopped then as though searching for the right words.

"I've never been very nice to you, Sam, and that's completely on me. It certainly was never because of anything you did. I never meant to hurt you or make you uncomfortable. In truth, I was trying to protect you."

If Sam had been surprised before, he was certainly in shock now. He pulled out a kitchen chair for her, motioning for her to have a seat. He moved to nearest chair and sat facing her. Sam had never imagined having this conversation with her. "I never understood why you thought that I wasn't good enough for your daughter, but I guess that's a mother's prerogative."

Diane shook her head sadly. "Sam, to make you understand, I have to tell you about Elizabeth's father. Will was a dashing, older man, and I fell hard for him almost from the first moment we met. But I loved him much more than he ever loved me. He was an ambitious man who didn't want to settle down with a wife and family. He wanted so much more than that from life. And I knew that, Sam. Will couldn't change who he was. And neither could I. Despite all of this, I loved him fiercely, and I have never loved another man like that. That makes for a lonely life, Sam."

"Why are you telling me this, Diane?"

Elizabeth's mother smiled gently and patted Sam's hand. "I think you know, Sam. I knew how you felt about Elizabeth. I saw the change in your eyes when you looked at her. Especially when you thought no one was watching. But I also knew how much Elizabeth loved Connor. I didn't want you to be hurt the way that I had. As you grew older and your feelings for her didn't change, I could see more of myself in you. I thought that I could spare you the pain that I had felt. Is this making any sense to you, Sam?"

At his nod, she continued. "But it wasn't my place to try. You loved Elizabeth, and nothing I did was going to change that. I can see now that I was wrong, Sam. Can you ever forgive me?"

"Diane, there's nothing to forgive. I'm glad you told me this. But why now? Elizabeth is still in love with Connor, and she always will be. I tried to get through to her. I tried to show her that she could love again."

Diane smiled kindly at Sam. "I'm not saying that everything will work out exactly as you wish, but I do know my daughter. Yes, she loved Connor very much, and a part of her always will. That's to be expected. But she's not in love with a ghost or a memory, Sam. It's not Connor that has her lying awake at night, staring at the ceiling long after she should be sleeping. Maybe you should think about that, Sam." With that final piece of advice, Diane got up from the table and quietly left the room.

Sam remained seated at the table, shaken by her words. He clenched his hands together as hard as he could. He was terrified to believe her. More than anything in the world, he wanted Elizabeth to be happy. If she could find it in her heart to be happy with him, then he would never ask for another thing ever in his life. But as much as he longed to believe this, what he witnessed in the cemetery made it difficult. The memory of her raw grief left him feeling doubtful.

*****

Sitting in her old bedroom in her mother's house, Elizabeth stared at the pile of photographs spread out around her. She had found them in shoeboxes in the closet. Each one held images of Sam, Connor, and herself in various groupings. She sighed as she remembered those days. Things were so much easier then. In some ways, she wished she could return to the simplicity of her youth. But even as she had that thought, she knew it wasn't true. She liked her life now. She loved her job and the difference she was making in people's lives. It might not be easy or simple, but it was rewarding.

As she divided out the pictures by age, Elizabeth noticed a pattern emerging. As younger children, there were many shots of the three of them in a rough and tumble pile on the ground or with their arms wrapped around each other. And yet as they had gotten older, Sam was always a little set apart from her, never quite touching.

Now that she thought about it, as they had become young adults, it was hard to remember a time when Sam would ever voluntarily touch her. Even at her wedding, she practically had to drag him out on the floor to dance with her. He had remained stiff the whole time. She had just blamed it on the formal attire he was wearing.

Could Brendan really be right? Had Sam been in love with her all along? If it was true, and he really did love her, then why was he pushing her away? His words had been so cruel, that escape was her only thought. Elizabeth had not gotten the chance to tell him about her feelings. About the fact that she was falling in love with him.

Suddenly, she knew she couldn't waste another moment. She, more than anyone, knew just how fragile life could be. She had learned the hard way to not take anything for granted.

Elizabeth heard the front door opening as she stepped into her flip flops. Grabbing her keys and purse, she rushed out to greet her mother. "Hey Mom, did you have fun? I'm just on my way out for a bit."

"You're going to see Sam, aren't you honey?" She smiled at her daughter's look of surprise. "It's time, Elizabeth. I don't know what happened at the party to send you running, but that's not the Elizabeth I know. Go after what you want." Diane paused and stroked her daughter's hair. "Sam's a good man, honey. All I ever wanted was for you to be happy again, Elizabeth."

Elizabeth was touched by her mother's words. She was also relieved to know that her mother was supportive of her feelings for Sam. She may be all grown up and a doctor, but having your mother in your corner was something that you never outgrew. She hugged her mom tightly and ran out to the car.

Glancing at her watch, Elizabeth noticed it was still relatively early. She crossed her fingers that the party had broken up by now. She had some things she needed to say to Sam, and she would prefer to do it without an audience.

When she arrived at Sam's, Elizabeth turned off the car and sat, clenching her hands tightly on the wheel. Her heart was pounding. She was here for a reason. She had a purpose. But she was a wreck. The temptation to drive back home was high. But her mom was right. She had not been raised to be a coward. When she wanted something, she went after it. Like medical school. And even if the worst happened here, she would be fine. After all, she had already survived burying her new husband and losing their unborn child. She could do this.

Despite the pep talk, her knees wobbled as she exited her mother's car. Anxiety had formed a knot in her stomach. The knot was bathed in acid. She tampered down her nervousness and strengthened her resolve. This had to be settled between them. She was so happy to be moving back home, amongst friends and family. But she knew she would be so much happier if Sam was in her future.

Her resolve slipped a bit when Elizabeth spotted an SUV parked on the other side of Sam's truck. She took a deep breath and let it out slowly. Tossing aside any doubts, Elizabeth walked through the opened front door, letting the screen door slam behind her. Glancing around the open floor plan, it was evident that no one was in the house. With some trepidation, she moved through the kitchen and out onto the patio. She came to a screeching halt at the sight of Katie in Sam's arms. The other woman was weeping quietly. Dread filled her stomach. She tried to turn and leave before anyone spotted her, but she was too late.

"It's not what you think, Elizabeth." Katie said in a voice still thick with tears.

Her pride hurt, Elizabeth turned to leave, tossing over her shoulder, "It doesn't really matter anymore what I think. I made a mistake coming here tonight."

Katie broke away from Sam's embrace and walked towards her. She reached out and touched Elizabeth on her arm. "There's already been too much misunderstanding between us, Elizabeth. I don't want you to walk away thinking something that isn't true. Sam and I were just talking. He was being a good friend and trying to help me out with a problem I have. There's nothing between Sam and me other than friendship." She smiled warmly at Sam. "I should be so lucky…" Without another word, she scooped up her keys from the patio table and ran around the side of the house. A moment later, Elizabeth heard her car start and drive away.

She turned and stared at Sam. The brilliant words she had come up with in the car were long gone. As was her courage. She absently tucked her hair behind both ears.

"Is it that bad, Elizabeth?" Sam asked her gently. "You only do that when you're very nervous. I'm sorry that I make you feel that way."

"I have something to say, Sam, so you need to listen to me. I don't have any great way of saying what I need to, so I'm just going to start." She laughed nervously, overwhelmed with the monumental nature of the moment.

"What happened between us Sam? I just don't get it. I thought we were getting closer, and then suddenly you act like I don't matter to you at all. What did I do wrong, Sam?" She looked at him, pleading for him to make sense of this for her.

Sam was silent for so long that her stomach twisted even further. When he did speak, his voice was void of any emotion. "You didn't do anything wrong, Elizabeth. There's certainly nothing wrong with still being in love with your dead husband. Except of course, it prevents you from being in love with a living, breathing man. Someone who loves you more than life itself. I tried, Elizabeth, I really did. But I can't compete with a ghost. I can't be Connor, and I can't bring him back. And now I can't even be your friend anymore. It's simply too hard." He strode over to the very edge of the stone patio and turned his back to her.

Elizabeth was stunned at his words. She was confused, but at least she now had a glimmer of hope. "Is that really what you think, Sam? That I've been living in the past? You believe I see you as a substitute for Connor?" The more she thought about it, Elizabeth became angry.

She strode over to Sam, pulling on his arm until he turned to face her. "When we were making love, Sam, did I ever call you by anything other than your own name? Did I ever give you any reason to think that I wished you were Connor?"

Without giving him a chance to reply, she continued angrily. "No, Sam, I did not! It was you, Sam Bishop, that I made love with, not Connor." She had begun to shake as she stood there facing him. Her chest was heaving both with effort and emotion.

"But you never once said that you loved me, Elizabeth, did you? You never told me that you had forgiven me for Connor's death." He smiled sadly at that last part. "But that's okay, I could hardly expect forgiveness from you when I've never even forgiven myself. I'm very aware of how much better things would have been if I had died that day instead of Connor."

The full meaning of his words hit her like a hammer. Katie was right. The thought that Sam had blamed himself for all these years nearly crushed her. Tears began to run down her face. She didn't bother trying to stop them.

"All this time, Sam? You've blamed yourself for Connor's death for ten years? It was an *accident*, Sam. The drunk driver caused Connor's death. He chose to get in his car that day, even though he had been drinking. Even though his blood alcohol level was nearly three times the legal limit. It's his fault, and his alone, that Connor died that day. How could I have ever blamed you?"

She was crying uncontrollably now. "And the thought of you dying that day is too terrible to imagine, Sam. I would never have traded your life for Connor's, even if that had been possible. I was thankful that you had not been senselessly killed as well." She stopped talking for a moment and buried her face in her hands as she sobbed. When she could breathe again, Elizabeth looked at Sam. "But I never told you that Sam. Did I? No wonder you blamed yourself. I'm so very sorry."

Sam took Elizabeth into his arms and held her as she cried. His solid presence soothed her. Her sobbing slowed and then finally stopped. She hiccupped and then laughed self-consciously. "All I ever seem to do is cry on you, Sam."

Sam tightened his hold on her, burying his face in her neck. "I saw you that day in the cemetery, Elizabeth. I saw you crying at Connor's grave. It almost tore out my heart to see you in such pain. I knew then what I had always feared; that you were still in love with him. That you would never feel that way about anyone else. That you would never feel that way about me."

Elizabeth broke from his grasp and backed up a few feet. She smiled at him through her tears. She sought the words that would make him finally understand. "You're right about one thing, Sam. I don't feel about you as I did about Connor." At his stricken look, she reached up and gently stroked his cheek with her hand. "You're not Connor. I don't expect you to be. You're two very different people, Sam, so I wouldn't expect my feelings for you to be the same as they were for him. But that doesn't mean that I don't love you, Sam."

When she was sure she had his attention, Elizabeth continued. "Yes, Sam, I loved Connor very much. We were very happy together, and I believed we would have stayed so. But he died. Eventually, Sam, life goes on. It took me a long time to truly understand that. I wanted to die that day, but I didn't. I was meant to go on, even if it was unbelievably painful to do so in the beginning."

"Getting over Connor was the hardest thing I've ever done. I lost him and then our baby, all in the space of a few short days. Yet I was still here. You don't have the market on guilt, Sam. After a while, when I started to feel like a human being again, I was wracked with guilt. How could I be happy when they were dead? It took me years to understand that being alive, even enjoying life, didn't mean that I didn't miss him. It just meant that I had turned a corner. I was going to survive after all." Elizabeth stopped and took a long, shaky breath before continuing.

"After a long while, when it didn't hurt so much to think of him, I realized just how lucky I had been. I loved him with all my heart, and that love made me a better person. I was lucky to have had Connor in my life, even if it was only for a short while. And eventually, I knew I wanted that in my life again. But I just never met the right person in California, and I wasn't willing to settle."

"But I saw you that day in the cemetery, Elizabeth. I saw you sobbing at Connor's grave."

"Yes, you did, Sam. You saw, but you didn't hear. If you had, you would have heard me telling him about you, Sam. Yes, I was crying, but I hadn't been to his grave since we buried him. It was very emotional for me. But the tears were cleansing. Connor will always be a part of my life, just as he will always be a part of yours. But he's a part of my past. I was letting go of the past, Sam, once and for all. Something I thought I had already done. Only in letting go of the past can I look to the future, Sam. A future that I thought, hoped, you would be a big part of." She stared directly into his eyes, hoping he could see her love for him in hers.

In a flash, he was enfolding her in a hug that threatened to stop her breath. His kisses rained down on her hair and face, finally settling on her full lips. It was quite a while before either could talk.

Coming up for air, Sam took a step back and looked into her eyes. He held both of her hands in his. "I have loved you for so long, Elizabeth. I never thought you would come back to me. I never thought I deserved you."

"Sam, I need to apologize." She held up her hands at his protest. "Yes, Sam, I do. I'm so sorry for the way I treated you after Connor's death. It was just too much for me to bear, losing Connor and then our unborn child. But I should have never turned away from you, Sam. You were hurting also. You were grieving Connor just as I was."

Sam reached down and gently wiped away the remaining tears from her face. "I thought that you blamed me, Elizabeth. I'll never forget the look on your face in the emergency room that night." She could feel the shudder of his body. "You were so pale and so very frightened. I wanted nothing more than to tell you that Connor was fine. But I couldn't. I knew he was dead, Elizabeth. I should have been the one to tell you; to help you through it. But I was in shock and pain, and I couldn't find the words. Before I knew it, they had taken you away from me."

She smiled reassuringly at him, allowing Sam to continue. "In the days afterwards, you were always surrounded by Connor's family. I felt like I couldn't get near you, Elizabeth. And even if I could, I was terrified of what you would say to me."

"Oh, Sam." she wailed. "I was so horrible to you that last day. I just couldn't see past my own pain. I didn't think about you or what you had endured. By the time I was able to do so, too much time and too many miles had passed. I always wanted to talk to you, to fix things between us, but the more time passed, the harder it became."

Sam gently touched her wet face. "Elizabeth, I never blamed you for that. You were consumed by the pain of losing your husband and unborn child. We were both wrong. But that's all in the past. It doesn't matter anymore. Tell me that you love me, Elizabeth, even just a little."

"I can't do that, Sam." She stopped at his sharp intake of breath. "I can't tell you that I love you a little because I love you with my whole heart, Sam Bishop. I love that you have always been my best friend. I love that you cared about me enough to try and protect me, even if you were way off on that one. I love you, Sam, because being with you makes me happy and complete. And that's something that I haven't felt in a long time." She reached up to seal her words with a lingering kiss.

"I can't think of anything that I'd rather hear, Elizabeth." Just then he got a devilish look in his eye as he grinned that grin that was purely him. "Well, except that you'll marry me."

She blinked and burst into tears again. This time, they were happy tears.

"Say that you'll be my wife and live with me in this big house. Help me to make it a home."

"I will, Sam" she answered breathlessly. "I'm already home."

The End

Acknowledgments

They say that it takes a village to raise a child. Well, the same is true for publishing a book. Especially your first one. *Coming Home* has been a work in progress since 2002, when my husband and I were awaiting to adopt our first child from Russia. Our daughter is now a high school freshman. I wrote the very first version of *Coming Home* to save my sanity while we waited that summer. This final version is so much better.

Thank you to Romance Writers of America and my local chapter, Carolina Romance Writers, for providing me with a variety of lovely, creative friends. The women of CRW have been a constant source of knowledge and inspiration.

Jeni Burns, paranormal author extraordinaire, was the very first person I met at CRW. Her guidance has been invaluable. Her friendship, though long distance now, has been even more so.

I owe so much to the lovely ladies of the Wednesday Night Coffee Crew (even though I don't drink coffee.) April Alieda, Cate Dixon, Gracey Evans, Ness Harper, and Jane Balfrey: your support and camaraderie is more important to me than you could ever know.

Lauren Plude, my oh so patient and brilliant editor, thank you for seeing me through my 'rookie mistakes.' *Coming Home* is better for having met you. I'm looking forward to book two.

Rebecca Pau of The Final Wrap created this amazing cover. I sent the poor woman a completed work order with 'just something with blue and green on it' for my instructions. And out of that came this work of art.

Most of all, thanks to my family and friends for the constant encouragement and patience throughout this process. I love you all.

Want more of Kate & Flynn? Read an excerpt from the next Windsor Falls novel by Kimberley O'Malley, *Taking Chances*. Keep in mind this is a work in progress and is therefore subject to change. *Taking Chances* will be available soon.

Taking Chances

Katie Fitzgerald cursed under her breath as she ran across the gravel parking area in heels. Never a good idea. The idea had no more entered her head when there was a sickening snap. She stumbled sideways as the ridiculously high heel of her right shoe fell to the ground. Katie lost her balance and was about to join her heel in the dirt and gravel, as the items in her arms scattered everywhere. The string of inventive curses that followed colored the air around her.

Strong arms reached her just in time, picking her up as though she weighed no more than a feather and placing her safely back on her feet. "I thought nice, Southern ladies didn't know words like that" came an amused drawl from behind her.

Katie stood still and counted to ten in her head. *Do not look up* she ordered herself. It didn't matter if she did, though. She knew it was him. Just his voice alone was enough to send her female parts into a chorus of 'Hallelujah'. She was running late for the wedding rehearsal because she had worked last night. Without the benefit of sleep, she ran all day performing last minute wedding tasks. And now this. What else could possibly go wrong today?

Maybe finding Flynn Reynolds was indeed her rescuer, she thought morosely. Bending to pick up her broken heel, Katie spied a shiny pair of men's shoes next to her. Straightening slowly, her gaze tracked up charcoal gray dress pants that were the bottom half of what had to be a hand tailored suit. A snowy white dress shirt and bold red tie covered his broad chest. She didn't have to look any further to know it was him. Great.

Katie straightened up to her full height, which at just over five feet, wasn't saying much. She craned her neck back a bit to look directly at Flynn. His raven hair shone in the early evening sun. His piercing blues didn't miss a thing. There was easily a foot of height difference between them; just another of his faults as she saw it. Katie had gotten her mother's height in the sea of giants that was her family. The fourth of six kids and the oldest girl, Katie was by far the shortest. Her brothers were all over six feet, and even her younger sister, Riley, was five ten.

As usual, she made up for her lack of height with attitude. "Don't you dare laugh at me, Dr. Reynolds. I am so not in the mood."

He didn't have the grace to even try to remove the smile from his handsome face. "Did you hear me laughing, Katie? And what's with the 'Dr. Reynolds'? You don't even call me that at work."

Katie chose not to answer that. How could she? Letting him know that calling him by his title and surname put a wall between them that she needed for her own sanity would just give him the upper hand. No thanks.

"As interesting as this chat has been, Flynn, I'm already late." She took one step forward and almost stumbled again. Drat! Being this close to him always made her mind go blank. But how could she have forgotten about her stupid heel?

Flynn reached out and grabbed Katie's arm to steady her. Again. But the touch of his fingers was anything but. Her arm tingled where he touched her, and liquid heat gathered low in her belly. Wrenching her arm away, Katie turned back to face him. "I'm fine, thank you." With as much dignity as she could gather, Katie limped back to her car. Luckily, she always kept a spare pair of flip flops in the back. She might not be winning any fashion awards, but she needed a pair of shoes.

She glanced at the thin silver watch on her wrist. One minute until she was late. She turned and crashed into the solid wall that was Flynn. "Really? Are you trying to make me even later than I already am?" That was when she noticed the large, wildly colored bunch of ribbon in his hands.

"No. Trying to help actually. I think you dropped Elizabeth's bouquet."

Katie stared at him in amazement. "You know what that is?"

Flynn grinned down at her. "I have sisters, Katie. Let me help you. Please."

Knowing when she was beaten, she nodded. She shifted the large box she was holding to his arms, grabbing the 'bouquet' from his hand. "Thanks, Flynn. I just need to get inside before they start without me." She took off as fast as the gravel and her flip flops would allow. Muttering under her breath the whole way, Katie tried to ignore Flynn who was easily keeping pace with her. But the sight, and scent of him, made that almost impossible.

Flynn jogged ahead and held the door open for her as Katie sailed into the banquet hall where Elizabeth and Sam would be holding their wedding reception tomorrow. She had spent most of the day here, helping her family to decorate for the festivities. The lovely inn would be the site of both the wedding ceremony and reception tomorrow.

"You can just set that down over there" she directed Flynn, pointing to a table against the wall.

Flynn did so before turning back to her. "You seem a little stressed. Are you okay?"

"I will be. All I have to do is get through the rehearsal and dinner." Katie grimaced at the sound of that. "Let me rephrase. I'm excited about the wedding, but I'm exhausted. Once the rehearsal dinner is over, I'm going up to my room and sleeping for twelve hours straight."

Flynn leaned in closely. "That would explain the dark circles under your eyes."

The eyes in question widened. "Thanks for that. Like I wasn't aware already." She turned her back on him and rushed out the side door. The rest of the wedding party was already assembled on the terrace, and all eyes turned to her. Her face reddened as she remembered she was wearing flip flops with her dress. Oh well, nothing she could do about that now.